KEY WEST PROMISES

SEASIDE PALMS
BOOK ONE

ANNIE CABOT

CABOT PUBLISHING GROUP

Copyright © 2025 by ANNIE CABOT

All rights reserved.

No part of this book may be reproduced in any form or by any electronic or mechanical means, including information storage and retrieval systems, without written permission from the author, except for the use of brief quotations in a book review.

ISBN ebook, 978-1-966363-04-0

ISBN paperback, 978-1-966363-05-7

CHAPTER 1

Leah Lawrence had always been a morning person, but lately dawn felt less like a beginning and more like an accusation. The laptop screen glowed in front of her: $157.43. Their remaining balance. The electronic statement showed a parade of recent transactions—each one a testament to their dwindling grip on reality:

WITHDRAWAL—CUBAN COFFEE QUEEN—$14.75
WITHDRAWAL—SUNSET SAIL ENTERPRISES—$75.00
WITHDRAWAL—KEYS ELECTRIC FINAL NOTICE—$147.32

She clicked through their other accounts, each one telling the same story. Credit cards maxed out. Savings depleted. Their "emergency fund" reduced to loose change in a decorative rum bottle they'd bought during their first week in paradise. The money their sister Chelsea had given them the year before was gone, and Leah's guilt about that was more than she was able to carry.

A rooster crowed outside their yellow bungalow—one of the scrawnier ones that usually raided their forgotten herb garden. This particular bird, dubbed "Ernest" by Tess because he looked "literary," had outlasted their attempts at growing basil and mint for Tess's never-launched cocktail catering business. Now he strutted through the withered remains of their container garden, pecking at the expensive organic soil they'd bought in a fit of agricultural optimism.

Through her reading glasses, Leah watched early morning joggers pass by their rental, their expensive athletic wear and bouncy ponytails reminding her of the life she'd left behind in Boston. A year ago, she would have been one of them, power walking along the Charles River before heading to her sensible job with its sensible 401(k). She'd had a standing morning coffee date with other professionals—women who discussed investment strategies and retirement plans over perfectly foamed lattes.

Now here she sat in worn yoga pants and a faded t-shirt that proclaimed, "Life's Better in Flip Flops," trying to make sense of how she and her sister had managed to burn through their savings in pursuit of what Tess called their "island dreams." The shirt had been part of a bulk order—another of Tess's business ideas. "Tourist-wear with a personal touch!" The remaining boxes still cluttered their small, detached garage, along with other remnants of their abandoned enterprises.

Leah shook her head and was glad their other sisters, Chelsea and Gretchen, weren't here to see how bad things were.

"Any luck with the numbers?"

Her younger sister appeared in the kitchen doorway, honey-blonde curls wild from sleep, still wearing the flamingo pajamas she couldn't resist buying last month—even though their electric bill was due. At fifty, Tess radiated the same effervescent energy she'd had when they were kids and could talk Leah into anything. Like moving to Key West to "find themselves" at an age when most people were planning for grandchildren and retirement.

The smell of coffee filled their tiny kitchen—bargain brand now, not the special island roast they'd once justified as a "business expense" for Tess's coffee cart scheme. That particular dream had died around the same time they discovered that mobile food licenses required more than just a cute logo and matching aprons.

"Define luck," Leah said, closing the laptop. No point staring at numbers that wouldn't change. She watched Tess float around their kitchen, somehow making even impending poverty look like the beginning of an adventure. That was Tess's gift—finding silver linings in hurricane clouds. It was what had gotten them through their parents' divorce, through failed relationships (Tess's) and failed promotions (Leah's), and now, apparently, through financial ruin.

Their kitchen told the story of their year in paradise better than Leah could ever write in the novel she hadn't started. Mason jars filled with shells from Captiva beach walks they took when visiting Chelsea lined the windowsill, catching the morning light like broken promises. Coffee mugs from every bar on Duval Street crowded the open shelving—souvenirs of nights when they still believed their money would last forever. The ancient air conditioner wheezed asthmatically, fighting a losing battle against the Key West humidity that made everything feel slightly damp.

Their tiny kitchen opened into what Tess optimistically called their "great room," though there was nothing particularly great about its dimensions. The furniture told its own story of their declining fortunes—a wicker sofa they'd found at an estate sale ("It just needs some love, Leah!"), mismatched chairs from various thrift stores, and a coffee table that had once been a wooden cable spool ("Industrial chic is very in right now!").

Above the sofa, their "vision board" hung like an archaeological record of abandoned dreams. Photos and magazine cutouts created a collage of everything they'd planned: Tess teaching cooking classes on the beach, Leah writing her novel in quaint coffee shops, both of them hosting sunset cruises for tourists seeking "authentic island experiences." Beneath the board, a stack of business cards gathered dust, each representing a different failed venture:

"**Island Inspirations - Bespoke Beach Events**" (Three inquiries, zero bookings)

"**Keys to Success - Professional Life Coaching**" (Their one client had moved to Tampa)

"**Sunset Sisters - Making Paradise Perfect**" (The website had crashed and taken their hosting fee with it)

The Key West that greeted them a year earlier bore little resemblance to their dreams. The pristine beaches they'd imagined were nowhere to be found, and the fishing boats they'd hoped to charter sat in the marina, their rental fees far beyond reach. One by one, their plans crumbled like ashes, carried away on the salty breeze along with their hopes of building a life in this island paradise.

Tess opened their "pantry"—really just a set of decorative shelves they'd installed during their home improvement phase. The remains of their groceries looked like modern art—creative arrangements of whatever had been on sale, plus the endless supply of rice they'd panic-bought during the last hurricane warning.

"We still have cereal," Tess announced brightly, rattling a nearly empty box. "And, half a banana. Want to share?"

"We could always sell the paddleboard," Tess suggested, pulling out their chipped tourist wine glasses, the ones with "Key West: Paradise Found" written in fading letters. The glasses were part of a set of six; the others had met various ends during what Tess called their "entrepreneurial experiments," including one memorable attempt at hosting a wine-and-painting night at Fort Zachary Taylor State Park.

"The one you've used exactly twice?" Leah adjusted her reading glasses, a habit from her corporate days that surfaced whenever she was stressed. Her glasses, like her resume, needed updating, but both were victims of their dwindling resources. "Besides, it's eight in the morning."

"It's five o'clock somewhere!" Tess paused at Leah's expression. "Too soon for Jimmy Buffett quotes?"

The paddleboard in question leaned against their tiny porch railing, its cheerful tropical design already fading from the relentless Florida sun. They'd bought it during what Leah now thought of as their "active lifestyle" phase, right after the failure of their beach workout club but before Tess's brief career as a sunset yoga instructor. The only thing that had gotten a real workout was their credit card.

Through their glass louvered windows, Leah watched another tour group cycle past on their rented bikes, their matching helmets bobbing like tropical birds. The tour guide's voice drifted in, explaining the history of their street, embellishing facts with the kind of colorful stories tourists loved. Once upon a time, Leah and Tess had thought about starting their own tour company. They'd even printed brochures—now serving as coasters for their wine glasses.

"We need jobs," Leah said finally. "Real ones. Not selling those questionably scented candles at the tourist market."

"The candles weren't that bad," Tess protested, though they both knew better. Their garage still held boxes of unsold inventory, each candle a waxy reminder of their failed crafting phase.

"You named one 'Midnight at Margaritaville' and it smelled like tequila and regret." Leah remembered the craft fair vendor who'd suggested, kindly but firmly, that perhaps scented candles weren't their calling. "And let's not forget 'Paradise Breeze.'"

Tess's face broke into a mischievous grin. "You have to admit, 'Paradise Breeze' was inspirational. It's not my fault it smelled like someone microwaved coconut sunscreen."

Leah groaned, resting her forehead on the table. "We're two middle-aged women failing at the most basic part of paradise:

staying afloat. This isn't a rom-com. Nobody's going to swoop in with a boat and a business proposal to save us."

Tess grabbed her sister's shoulders, forcing her to sit upright. "You listen to me, Leah Marie Lawrence. We're not done yet. If the universe doesn't send us a rescue boat, we'll build our own dinghy and row our way to the finish line."

Leah stared at her. "That's...deeply unconvincing."

"But at least it's colorful," Tess countered. "And right now, colorful is all we've got.

"Speaking of colorful," Tess said, moving to the window where Ernest the rooster had graduated from pecking at their failed herb garden to strutting along their porch railing, "remember when we thought we could start that chicken-watching tour?"

"'Meet the Wild Chickens of Key West,'" Leah quoted from memory, another failed business card design floating through her mind. "'Where Every Fowl Has a Story.'"

"It wasn't our worst idea," Tess defended, though her smile suggested otherwise. "At least the startup costs were low. Just some laminated fact sheets and those vintage binoculars we found at that estate sale."

Leah remembered those binoculars. They'd spent forty dollars on them, only to discover they were better at creating double vision than magnifying anything. Like everything else in their Key West adventure, even their mistakes had style.

The morning sun crept higher, turning their yellow bungalow's walls into something almost golden. Their landlord had warned them the color would be "aggressive" in full sunlight, but like everything else about their move to the Keys, they'd romanticized it. "Like living inside a sunset," Tess had declared. Now it just reminded Leah of their bank account's warning notifications.

"We could start a blog," Tess suggested, pulling out their last clean coffee mugs—souvenirs from a seafood festival where they'd briefly considered starting a food truck specializing in "gourmet grilled cheese with island flair."

"About what? 'How to Fail at Island Life with Style'?" Leah pushed back from the table, her chair scraping against the uneven floor, another charming feature of their rental that had seemed quaint a year ago.

"More like 'How to Reinvent Yourself at Fifty—A Cautionary Tale,'" Tess mused. "Chapter One: Don't Spend Your Retirement Fund on a Coffee Cart Named 'Bean There, Done That.'"

Despite herself, Leah laughed. When The CoiffeeShop idea fell through, their first major investment was the coffee cart. It was still in their garage, its custom paint job featuring dancing coffee beans wearing sunglasses slowly peeling in the humidity. They'd spent three weeks developing the perfect logo, two days actually trying to serve coffee, and six months making payments on the equipment they'd financed at what now seemed like criminally high interest rates.

A group of tourists wandered past their house, phones raised to photograph Ernest, who chose that moment to display his literary credentials by attempting to crow and nearly falling off the railing. The tourists cooed in delight, and Tess's eyes lit up with that dangerous sparkle Leah knew too well.

"Don't even think about it," Leah warned.

"Think about what?"

"Whatever new business idea just popped into your head. We can't afford another 'opportunity.'"

"I was just thinking…" Tess began, but Leah cut her off.

"That's exactly what you said before we bought three hundred dollars' worth of seashells to make 'authentic island wind chimes.'"

"Those would have sold if we'd figured out how to stop them from tangling," Tess protested. "And if they hadn't sounded like someone dropping silverware during a hurricane."

The morning breeze carried the smell of someone else's success—fresh-baked Cuban bread from the bakery nearby. Another reminder of their dwindling options. They'd once planned to partner with that bakery for their coffee cart business, back when possibilities seemed as endless as the horizon over the Gulf.

"We need a plan," Leah said, more to herself than to Tess. "A real one. Not involving crafts, food service, or anything requiring a permit from the city council."

"You make it sound so limiting." Tess sighed, but there was understanding beneath her teasing tone. She moved to the vision board, studying their collection of failed dreams with unexpected thoughtfulness. "You know what our real problem was?"

"Besides saying 'yes' to every idea that popped into your head?"

"We tried to be something we're not," Tess said, unpinning one of their old business cards. "We tried to be 'island entrepreneurs' instead of just being ourselves."

The words hung in the humid morning air, heavier than their collection of unsold merchandise and lighter than their mounting bills. Leah looked at her sister—really looked at her—and saw past the flamingo pajamas and relentless optimism to the wisdom that occasionally surfaced between schemes.

"And who are we?" Leah asked softly, genuinely curious about the answer.

Before Tess could respond, Ernest let out another attempted crow, this one somehow managing to sound both triumphant and questioning. Like them, he seemed caught between who he was and who he was trying to be.

CHAPTER 2

The interior of Margarita Max's was exactly what Tess had imagined. The wooden beams were draped with string lights, their dim glow mingling with the neon signs advertising every tropical drink known to man. The bar itself stretched across one side of the room, covered in scuffs and dents that told stories of decades of spilled cocktails and overenthusiastic patrons.

Leah's first thought, however, wasn't about the charm of the place but about how sticky the floors were. Her sandals clung to the surface with each step, and she couldn't decide if the sensation was more unsettling or just depressing. The air inside was thick with the competing scents of lime, stale beer, and whatever tropical-scented cleaner they used to mop the floors, presumably between spring break seasons.

"This place has character," Tess said, beaming as she spun slowly to take it all in. Her enthusiasm seemed to brighten even the darkest corners of the bar, where ancient fishing nets and plastic lobsters created shadows on the walls.

"It has something," Leah muttered, glancing toward the bar where a middle-aged woman with a no-nonsense ponytail was wiping down glasses with the efficiency of someone who'd done it a million times. Her nametag read "Connie," though the letters were faded as if they'd been through as many Key West summers as the bar itself.

The walls were a testament to decades of island life, covered in photos of fishing tournaments, hurricane parties, and tourists who'd probably long since forgotten their nights at Margarita Max's. A dusty paddleboard hung from the ceiling, its surface decorated with the bar's logo, a cartoon parrot wearing sunglasses and holding a cocktail glass in its wing.

"Excuse me," Tess said, her tone chipper as she approached the bar. "We heard you're hiring?"

Connie looked up, her sharp blue eyes scanning the sisters with the precision of a drill sergeant sizing up new recruits. The towel in her hands never stopped moving, as if cleaning glasses was as natural as breathing. "You ever worked in a bar before?"

"Well, no," Leah started, but Tess cut her off with a confident laugh. The kind of laugh that had preceded many of their more questionable business ventures.

"Not professionally," Tess said. "But we've spent plenty of time on the other side of the bar, and I'd say that makes us pretty qualified. Plus, we're quick learners." She gestured to the row of bottles behind the counter. "I bet I could name every type of rum you've got back there."

Leah resisted the urge to groan. Tess's charm had gotten them into plenty of situations, but she wasn't convinced it would get them out of this one. Still, she had to admit her sister's ability to turn every situation into an opportunity was almost impressive. Even if that opportunity involved sticky floors and drunk tourists.

Connie arched an eyebrow, setting down the glass she'd been polishing with a soft clink. "You good with drunk tourists? Broken glasses? Karaoke?" Her voice suggested these were merely the tip of a very large, very sticky iceberg.

"Absolutely," Tess said without missing a beat. She leaned against the bar with the confidence of someone who'd never had to clean one. "And Leah here is great with numbers. She'd make an excellent cashier. She used to manage million-dollar accounts in Boston."

Leah gave a tight smile, wondering how her MBA had led her to this moment. "I'm also good at cleaning sticky floors." She demonstrated by lifting her sandal with an audible peeling sound.

Connie's lips twitched, almost a smile. A Jimmy Buffett song played softly in the background, as if providing the soundtrack to their descent into island unemployment.

"Fair enough. You're hired. Part-time for now. Show up tomorrow night at six, dressed in black. Comfortable shoes. And don't show up hungover."

"That's it?" Leah asked, blinking in surprise. In Boston, hiring processes had involved multiple interviews, background checks, and at least one personality assessment.

"This is Margarita Max's," Connie said, returning to her glass polishing. "The bar's low. No pun intended." She handed each of them a napkin with scrawled instructions, her handwriting as efficient as her movements. "Be on time. And remember, tomorrow is Trivia Tuesday. It'll be crazy in here."

As they stepped back into the blinding Key West sunshine, Tess clapped her hands together, the napkin fluttering in her grip. "See? That was easy. And we didn't even have to beg. Although I was prepared to if necessary. I had a whole speech planned about our extensive experience in customer service."

Leah shielded her eyes with one hand, staring at the napkin in the other. The instructions were simple: wear black, bring a positive attitude, don't be late. Nothing about the complex drink recipes she'd need to learn or how to handle rowdy bachelor parties. "I can't decide if this is a good thing or a sign that we've hit rock bottom. Did you happen to notice that we have no idea how much we're going to get paid for this adventure?"

"It's not rock bottom," Tess said, looping her arm through Leah's as they navigated the crowded sidewalk. A group of tourists on rented bikes swerved around them, their helmet straps flapping in the breeze. "And I assume it's more about the tips than anything else. Look at it as a stepping stone. We'll be slinging margaritas and charming tourists in no time. Think of the interesting people we'll meet."

Leah raised an eyebrow. "Interesting how? Like someone who owns a yacht and needs a crew? Or someone who leaves a $500 tip because they accidentally paid with the wrong card?"

"Either works," Tess said with a grin. "Though I was thinking more along the lines of a mysterious stranger with a business proposition. Or maybe a wealthy widow looking to invest in local talent."

"Your definition of 'local talent' concerns me," Leah said, but she was smiling. Something about Tess's relentless optimism was infectious, even in the face of their current situation.

They walked in silence for a moment, the heat of the sidewalk radiating through their sandals. Just around the corner, a group of cruise ship passengers shuffled past from Mallory Square, their lanyards swinging in perfect synchronization.

Tess and Leah walked several blocks before Leah pointed toward a large house on the corner. A simple sign out front read "Paradise Harbor House," offering no explanation of its purpose. A woman sat on the porch, radiating a quiet authority that lingered in Leah's mind. There was something about her.

"What do you think that place is?" Leah asked, breaking the silence. A pelican swooped overhead.

Tess glanced at her, adjusting her sunglasses. "What place?"

"The house with the blue sign, Paradise Harbor House."

Tess shrugged, her attention caught by a window display of

handmade jewelry. "Probably a bed and breakfast or something. Everything here is either a bed and breakfast or a bar."

Leah frowned, her curiosity piqued. "I don't think it's a bed and breakfast." She remembered the neat rows of chairs on the porch, the professional signage, the way the woman had studied her clipboard with such focus.

"Why not?"

"Because the woman on the porch looked…serious. Like she was running something important. Not like someone recommending breakfast spots to tourists."

Tess waved a hand dismissively, her bracelets jingling. "Maybe she was just bossing around the cleaning staff. Don't overthink it. We've got bigger things to worry about, like what we're going to wear tomorrow night."

But Leah couldn't shake the feeling that there was more to Paradise Harbor House than Tess's casual explanation. And for the first time in weeks, she felt a spark of curiosity that had nothing to do with bills or finances.

Leah sat at the tiny kitchen table, her laptop open to a half-finished spreadsheet of their expenses. Tess was curled up on the sofa with a glass of wine, scrolling through Instagram. The kitchen was quiet except for the faint hum of the air conditioner.

Through the windows, Leah could hear the distant sounds of Duval Street coming alive for the night. Music drifted in from multiple directions. Soon, they'd be part of that nightly ritual, serving drinks to people living out their vacation fantasies while trying to keep their own dreams afloat.

"What are you looking at?" Leah asked, not looking up from the screen where numbers refused to add up to anything promising.

"Just ideas," Tess said, the sofa creaking as she shifted position.

"You know, fun stuff we could do to spice up our social media. Maybe drum up some side income. Our follower count isn't terrible."

"Spice it up how?"

"Oh, you know," Tess said vaguely, her voice taking on that dreamy quality that usually preceded an expensive idea. "Something trendy. Maybe we make videos of us trying weird Key West foods or giving margarita tutorials. We could start a series called 'Sunset Sisters' Tips and Sips.'"

Leah gave her a sidelong glance. "You want to be influencers now?" She thought of their previous attempts at social media stardom, including the disastrous "Keys to Fashion" blog that had resulted in maxed-out credit cards and a closet full of tropical print dresses they'd never worn.

"Why not? Everyone else is doing it. And we've got personality. Plus, now that we'll be working at Margarita Max's, we'll have insider content. People love behind-the-scenes stuff."

"We've got bills." Leah highlighted another row in her spreadsheet, watching the numbers flash red. "And I'm not sure Connie will appreciate us turning her bar into content."

Tess waved a hand, nearly spilling her wine. "Details. Besides, this could be our breakthrough moment. Picture it: 'From Corporate Life to Island Time: Two Sisters' Journey to Paradise.' It's practically a ready-made reality show."

"More like a cautionary tale," Leah muttered, but she couldn't help smiling. Even their failures had style thanks to Tess.

"Anyway, I'm calling it a night. Big day tomorrow." Tess stood, stretching like a cat. "Should we practice making margaritas? I think we still have some tequila from the 'Cocktails and Crafts' phase."

"I think we should save the tequila for after our first shift," Leah said wisely. "Something tells me we're going to need it."

"By the way, tell me again what Kaitlyn said about coming here," Tess asked.

Leah shrugged, "Not much, only that she needed a place to stay and that she couldn't wait to see us. It's not the best timing now that we've got jobs."

"She's young, Leah. She doesn't need us hovering to have a good time in Key West. She'll be fine."

As Tess disappeared into her room, Leah stared at the spreadsheet, her mind drifting back to Paradise Harbor House. Something about that house seemed more like an important Key West establishment than just a bed and breakfast. The woman's purposeful movements, the neat rows of chairs, the sense of order amidst the chaos of Key West—it all meant something. She just wasn't sure what.

She typed in the name online and found more about the building.

Paradise Harbor House: Hope and Shelter for Southern Florida Families. Leah wondered why she didn't notice the proper name when she saw the building earlier, but now, it made sense why it didn't look like a bed and breakfast to her.

She closed the laptop and stood, stretching her stiff shoulders. The kitchen walls seemed to close in around her, yellow paint glowing softly in the evening light. Their "Life's Better in Flip Flops" sign hung slightly crooked above the sink, a testament to their early days of decorating with more enthusiasm than skill.

Maybe tomorrow would bring answers—or at least a distraction from the ever-present weight of their dwindling funds. Either way, it would be an adventure. And with Tess around, adventures were never in short supply. The trick was surviving them with their dignity—and their bank account—intact.

Through the window, she could see Ernest the rooster walking away, no doubt going off to his nesting spot for the night.

For a brief moment she thought about calling their older sisters, Chelsea and Gretchen. It pained her to think that she and Tess would have to go crawling back to their sisters on Captiva

Island looking for help. But, in time, if things didn't improve, they'd have little choice.

Tomorrow, they'd start their new jobs as bartenders, adding another chapter to their increasingly complicated Key West story. But tonight, in the quiet of their tiny kitchen, Leah allowed herself to feel hope once again and put any thought of failure out of her mind.

CHAPTER 3

The heat of the midday sun pressed down on the yellow bungalow as Leah wiped her hands on a dish towel, glancing at the clock for the third time in five minutes. Ernest strutted past the window, his feathers ruffled by the humid breeze, seemingly as anxious about their incoming guest as she was.

"You're going to wear a groove into the floor if you keep pacing like that," Tess said from her spot on the sofa, where she was sprawled with a magazine that had clearly been read one too many times. The latest issue of "Island Life"—their last remaining subscription from better days—featured a cover story about "Making Paradise Perfect." The irony wasn't lost on either of them.

"I'm not pacing," Leah replied, though she immediately stopped moving. She adjusted a shell-encrusted picture frame for the fourth time, wondering if their attempt at island decor looked charming or just desperate. "I just want everything to be... ready."

"It's not like the Queen of England is visiting," Tess said with a grin, tossing the magazine onto their thrift store coffee table. "It's

Kaitlyn. She'll be too busy taking selfies to notice if the place is clean. Remember Christmas at Gretchen's? She spent the whole time doing TikTok dances in the kitchen."

Leah gave her sister a look but said nothing. Tess had always had a knack for minimizing stress, even when it wasn't helpful. For Leah, the arrival of their niece was both exciting and nerve-wracking, not to mention ill-timed.

"Does Gretchen know her daughter is coming to stay with us?" Tess asked.

Leah shrugged. "Good question. I didn't ask, nor did I press her to explain why the last minute visit. I mean, it's short notice."

Leah felt uncomfortable about the whole thing, but didn't complain. Their niece was fun, yes, but she was also a whirlwind of youthful energy that Leah wasn't entirely sure they could keep up with. Especially now, when their own lives felt like they were held together with dental floss and optimism.

She'd spent the morning hiding evidence of their financial struggles—past-due notices tucked into drawers, their wall of failed business cards discreetly removed, the "vision board" relocated to Tess's room. The last thing they needed was for Kaitlyn to report back to her mother about their situation. Gretchen, their older sister, had already made her opinions about their "midlife crisis" quite clear.

A car horn beeped outside, and Tess shot to her feet, dropping the magazine. "Speak of the devil!" She practically bounced to the door, her enthusiasm genuine despite everything else going on in their lives.

Leah followed her to the door, where they found Kaitlyn climbing out of her car, her long blonde hair spilling over her shoulders. She pulled a floral suitcase from the trunk with dramatic flair, flashing the driver a smile that could have been plucked straight from a travel commercial. Everything about her screamed "influencer in training," from her perfectly coordinated resort wear to the professional-looking camera hanging around her neck.

"Aunties!" Kaitlyn exclaimed, her voice lilting with exaggerated enthusiasm as she bounded up the steps, managing to look both effortlessly casual and carefully composed—a skill that seemed to come naturally to her generation.

Tess opened her arms wide, pulling Kaitlyn into a hug that nearly toppled them both. The smell of expensive perfume—something with notes of coconut and vanilla—wafted between them. "Look at you, Miss College Graduate! All grown up and ready to take on the world."

Kaitlyn stepped back, laughing, though something flickered behind her carefully maintained smile. "Or at least ready to take on Key West. This place is so cute. I can already see my Instagram blowing up. My followers are going to love it." She gestured to the street, where a group of tourists on bikes pedaled past, their matching helmets bobbing in the sun. "It's like a movie set or something."

Leah smiled warmly as Kaitlyn leaned in to hug her. Up close, she could see the slight shadows under Kaitlyn's eyes, barely concealed by expensive makeup. Something about her sunny demeanor felt forced, like she was putting on a show for an invisible audience.

"How was the trip?" Leah asked, noting how Kaitlyn's designer sundress looked fresh despite the long drive. Some people just had a gift for appearing perfectly put together, no matter the circumstances.

"Long," Kaitlyn said, wrinkling her nose. "But worth it. I'm so excited to be here. Mom's been driving me crazy with all her 'responsible adult' lectures. It's like, hello, I just graduated. I need time to figure things out, you know?"

"Well, we're excited to have you," Leah said, helping with the suitcase that probably cost more than their monthly rent.

"Though I should warn you, it's not all beaches and cocktails. Key West has its own…rhythm."

"Why would you say something so cruel?" Tess teased, guiding Kaitlyn inside. "Let the girl live in bliss for a few hours before reality sets in. Remember how excited we were when we first got here?"

"That was different," Leah muttered, but neither of them seemed to hear her.

Inside, Kaitlyn's eyes darted around the living room, taking in the seashell decor and slightly worn furniture. Her expression was carefully neutral, but Leah caught the slight raise of her eyebrows—the same look Gretchen got when confronted with something she found beneath her standards. She plopped onto the sofa, kicking off her sandals with a carefree sigh that seemed practiced.

"This is perfect," Kaitlyn said, stretching her arms over her head. "It's so laid-back. Totally Key West vibes. Very…authentic." She pulled out her phone, angling it to capture the room's best features.

Leah exchanged a glance with Tess, who shrugged as if to say, "Just let her enjoy it." They'd both become experts at reading between the lines of polite comments about their living situation.

"How about some iced tea?" Tess asked.

"I'd love some," Kaitlyn responded, looking around the room. "So, where will I sleep?"

Leah smiled. "You're sitting on it. That's a pull-out."

"Oh, that's perfect. I hope I'm not putting you out."

"Don't be silly, we're thrilled to have you," Tess answered.

They moved outside to the small area with a table and four chairs. Kaitlyn shared stories about her college years and the endless drama of her sorority sisters. Each tale seemed crafted for maximum entertainment value, like episodes of a reality show.

"And then Madison—you remember Madison from my

Christmas posts, right?—she totally freaked out because Kyle liked someone else's photo from like, three years ago." Kaitlyn paused for dramatic effect, stirring her tea with a practiced flourish. "It was this whole thing. But honestly? I think she was just stressed about not having a job lined up. Everyone's so obsessed with having their lives figured out right after graduation."

Leah caught the slight tremor in Kaitlyn's voice. Maybe their niece wasn't as carefree as she wanted them to believe.

"So," Kaitlyn said, flipping her hair over one shoulder, "what's the plan for tomorrow? Beach day? Shopping? Maybe some nightlife? I need content for my travel highlights reel."

Leah hesitated, glancing at Tess. They hadn't exactly planned for entertainment—their budget barely covered groceries these days. "Actually, we have work tonight."

Kaitlyn's expression flickered with surprise, her carefully maintained facade cracking slightly. "Work? I thought you guys were, like, retired or something. Mom said you'd cashed out your retirement accounts to move here."

Tess laughed, though the sound was slightly forced. "Oh, sweetie, no. The island life isn't quite as glamorous as it looks on Instagram. We've taken a job at Margarita Max's."

"A bar? That's so fun!" Kaitlyn said, clapping her hands together, recovering her enthusiasm with impressive speed. "Can I come watch? I'll be your biggest cheerleader. Maybe we could do a behind-the-scenes series—'Key West After Dark' or something?"

"It's not exactly spectator-friendly," Leah said, softening her words with a smile. "But maybe another time. When we're more…settled in."

Kaitlyn leaned back, pouting slightly. "Well, if you're busy, I guess I'll have to explore on my own." She brightened suddenly. "Actually, that might be better for content. More authentic, you know?"

"Careful with that," Tess said, her tone light but her eyes

serious. "Key West might seem small, but it's easy to get lost in all the...distractions. It's not exactly like spring break in Miami."

Kaitlyn grinned mischievously. "I think I can handle it. Besides, what's the worst that could happen? It's not like I'm going to join a pirate crew or something." She paused, considering. "Although that would make amazing content."

Leah finally asked the question she'd been dying to ask. "Honey, does your mother know you're here?"

Kaitlyn frowned, clearly not thrilled to answer. "I haven't talked to my mother since graduation if that's what you're asking. You know how things are with her. We haven't always seen things the same way."

"I understand that, but maybe…"

She cut Leah off. "Do we have to talk about Mom right now?"

Leah shook her head. "No, we don't. Let's get you unpacked and set up a space for your things. How does that sound?"

Kaitlyn smiled. "It sounds perfect to me."

It wasn't long before Kaitlyn found a friend. Leah peeked out the window and saw her niece chatting animatedly with a man carrying a crate of bananas—likely one of the local vendors. Kaitlyn gestured wildly, her bright energy practically radiating off her, though Leah noticed she kept adjusting her pose to catch the best morning light.

"She's making friends already," Tess said, appearing beside Leah with a steaming mug of coffee. "Told you she'd fit right in. Though I'm pretty sure she's already posted more photos than we have in a year."

Leah nodded, though a small part of her couldn't shake the feeling that Kaitlyn's carefree attitude would clash with the reality of their lives here. The girl in those carefully filtered photos seemed worlds away from their soon-to-be, sticky-floored existence at Margarita Max's.

"I'm worried about her," Leah said.

"What? Why? She seems perfectly fine to me," Tess said. "And if you look at her photos online, you'd think she was the happiest young lady on the planet."

Leah nodded. "That's what I'm afraid of. I think those photos don't tell the whole story."

As the afternoon unfolded, Kaitlyn announced her intention to explore on foot, armed with her camera and what looked like a professional lighting attachment. She declined their offer to join her, insisting she wanted to "get a feel for the place" on her own first. "Sometimes you have to let a place speak to you," she said with the wisdom of someone who'd read too many travel blogs.

Leah and Tess spent the afternoon preparing for their shift at Margarita Max's, trading nervous jokes about surviving Trivia Tuesday. "Maybe we should warn Connie about our social media sensation niece," Tess suggested. "Before she tries to turn ladies' night into a viral moment."

"Remember," Connie said as she handed Tess and Leah their new name tags, "tonight's Trivia Tuesday. Should be easy enough for your first shift." She paused, eyeing their matching black shirts with the bar's logo. "Just don't let anyone convince you that 'Margaritaville' is the answer to every question."

Leah adjusted her shirt, already feeling the humidity seeping through the fabric. "How bad can it be?"

Two hours later, she had her answer. The bar was packed, mostly with a rowdy group wearing matching t-shirts proclaiming, "Linda's Last Brain Cell Before the Ring!" They'd taken over the trivia corner, and their answers were getting more creative with each round of drinks.

"The capital of Florida is…" the trivia host announced.

"MARGARITAVILLE!" the bachelorette party shouted in unison.

"That's wrong for the fifth time." The host sighed. "And it wasn't right for 'Who wrote the Declaration of Independence?' either."

Tess skillfully navigated through the crowd with a tray of elaborate cocktails, her former yoga instructor balance coming in handy. "You know what?" she called to Leah over the noise. "I think I've found my calling. Watch this!" She did a little spin, not spilling a drop. "Years of failed dance classes finally paying off!"

"The inventor of electricity was..." the host began.

"JIMMY BUFFETT!" came the enthusiastic response.

"That's not even close," the host muttered into his microphone.

The door chimed, and Leah looked up to see Kaitlyn entering with her camera ready. "Oh no."

"Oh yes!" Kaitlyn beamed, already framing a shot. "This is perfect! Raw, authentic Key West nightlife! My followers will love—"

She was cut off by a splash as one of Linda's bridesmaids accidentally backed into Tess, sending a tray of rainbow-colored shots in all directions. Tess managed to stay upright but now sparkled with what appeared to be several different flavors of vodka.

"I'm so sorry!" the bridesmaid gasped. "But wait...this is actually a great look for you. Very island chic!"

Connie appeared with a towel, barely concealing her amusement. "Welcome to Margarita Max's," she said dryly. "Where every night is an adventure, and somebody always ends up wearing the drinks instead of drinking them."

"The first person to walk on the moon was..." the host tried again.

"JIMMY BUFFETT!"

"I'm not even sure how to respond to that," the host said, looking at his cards in despair.

Kaitlyn had positioned herself in a corner, documenting

everything. "This is amazing! The authentic struggle of two women finding their way in paradise! I'm thinking of calling it 'From Corporate to Cocktails: A Key West Journey.'"

"If you post any of this," Leah warned, wiping what she hoped was just pineapple juice from her arm, "we'll tell your mother where you are."

Kaitlyn lowered her camera slightly. "You wouldn't."

"Try me," Leah said, just as Linda's party decided to start an impromptu conga line through the bar.

"Okay, final question," the trivia host announced, sounding relieved. "What is the chemical formula for water?"

"TEQUILA!"

"That's…actually more creative than Margaritaville," the host conceded. "Still wrong, but I appreciate the effort."

By the end of their shift, Tess had mastered the art of dodge-serving (a necessary skill when half the customers were doing the Macarena), Leah had learned seventeen different ways to say "No, we don't have Jimmy Buffett's private phone number, and besides, he's dead," and Kaitlyn had enough material for a full documentary series.

"See?" Tess said as they counted their tips. "This wasn't so bad!"

"You're still sparkling from the glitter in those bachelorette party shots," Leah pointed out.

"I know! Free body glitter. This job has benefits we never even considered."

Connie shook her head. "You two might actually survive here. After a few weeks, you should be able to work the eleven to four shift. Just remember—tomorrow is Wannabe Wednesday. The karaoke machines have seen things you can't unsee."

"Can I come document that too?" Kaitlyn asked hopefully.

"NO!" all three women responded in unison.

Kaitlyn shrugged. "Fine. I'm headed out to check out more on

Duval Street. I saw there's a haunted trolley ride. I might do that. Can I have the key to your place?"

Leah grabbed her purse and found her keys. Throwing them to Kaitlyn she yelled, "Catch! Have fun. We'll most likely be in bed by the time you come home."

"I'm starving. I know it's late but my stomach has been begging for food the last hour. Do you mind if we stay and eat an appetizer before heading home?" Tess asked.

"Sounds good to me. Let's sit in the corner out of the way though. I don't want anyone thinking we're working."

They had fried conch fritters and twice-baked potatoes and when Leah asked for the bill, Connie refused their money. "You earned those appetizers, but next time come to work with a full belly."

"I guess they don't want the help sitting out here with everyone else," Tess said.

Leah laughed, "Either that, or they don't want to keep giving us free food."

As they walked the few blocks to their house, Tess grabbed Leah's arm.

"By the way, did you hear Connie say eleven to four? Did I hear that right?"

Leah nodded. "Yup, you sure did."

"Oh, Leah, I don't know about this. Tonight was hard enough, I can't see myself staying awake until four in the morning. I think this job is meant for younger people. My feet are killing me."

Leah chuckled, "Let's just take this one shift at a time. Who knows? We might not even last a week."

When Tess and Leah returned home, exhausted but still sparkling slightly from the night's misadventures at Max's, they found Kaitlyn curled up on the sofa, fast asleep. Her phone had slipped from her hand, open to a draft of a post about "finding authentic island experiences."

"I thought she was going to check out Duval Street?" Tess said.

Leah smiled. "It was a long day for her, driving for hours. Her body gave out before her spirit did."

"What's this?" Tess asked, picking up a brochure from the floor.

"Let me see that," Leah said.

"This is that Paradise Harbor House we saw yesterday. It's a shelter for displaced families. I was reading about it online. How funny that she went there."

"Well, she wanted adventure, it looks like she's already found one," Tess whispered, draping a blanket over Kaitlyn. She brushed some leftover party glitter from her shirt, adding softly, "Though I'm not sure it's the one she was expecting."

Leah stared at the brochure, her thoughts swirling despite her exhaustion from their first shift. On the inside of the pamphlet was the same blue sign that had caught her attention earlier, the same sense of purpose she'd noticed in the woman on the porch. Despite Kaitlyn's earlier enthusiasm about documenting their bartending debut, she'd apparently found something else to capture her attention.

Tomorrow would bring another shift at Margarita Max's, another day of pretending they had everything under control. But for now, watching Kaitlyn sleep peacefully on their worn sofa,

Leah allowed herself to hope that their niece's arrival might be more than just another complication in their increasingly complicated lives. After all, if they could survive their first night of Trivia Tuesday, maybe anything was possible.

CHAPTER 4

The next morning, Kaitlyn awoke to the golden light of the Key West sun streaming through the blinds. She stretched, savoring the gentle hum of the ceiling fan and the faint scent of salt in the air.

The bungalow was quiet except for distant mockingbirds and the occasional shuffle of Ernest's feathers as he conducted his morning inspection of the withered herb garden.

On the kitchen counter, she found a note in Tess's looping handwriting: "Gone to the market—still recovering from Trivia Tuesday! Back soon with stuff for breakfast and lunch. DON'T post those photos from last night! T&L"

Kaitlyn smiled, scrolling through her phone to the unposted documentation of her aunts' first night at Margarita Max's. The images told quite a story—Tess doing her improvised serving ballet through the crowd, Leah's increasingly exasperated expressions at the trivia answers, and the infamous moment when the bachelorette party had started their conga line. She'd promised not to share them online, but they were too precious to delete.

Another notification buzzed—a message from her mother, probably another thinly veiled attempt to discover her whereabouts through questions about job applications and "real world plans." Kaitlyn ignored it, just as she'd been ignoring the LinkedIn notifications and emails from her college career center.

For the first time in months, she felt like she could breathe without the weight of expectations pressing down on her, away from her mother's constant stream of "suggestions" about law school applications and corporate internships.

Through the window, Ernest strutted past, his feathers gleaming in the morning light like he was posing for his own Instagram story. The rooster paused to eye his reflection in the window, adjusting his stance as if practicing for his close-up.

Kaitlyn tossed on a breezy sundress and sandals, pausing briefly to consider if the outfit would photograph well for her social media updates. The dress was new—a graduation gift to herself that had maxed out her credit card, but she'd justified it as an "investment in her personal brand."

Now, standing in her aunts' modest bungalow, the price tag felt slightly ridiculous. Like so many things in her carefully curated life, it was starting to feel more like a prop than a necessity.

Deciding to forgo breakfast, she grabbed her phone and a water bottle and stepped out into the morning heat. Looking left, she could see the streets were coming to life—tourists on bicycles wobbling their way through intersections, shopkeepers setting out racks of brightly colored dresses, and the occasional rooster strutting confidently across the road as if it owned the place.

She remembered seeing a cruise ship the day before and wondered if another wave of visitors seeking their own slice of paradise would descend upon the island.

Instead of immediately documenting everything for her followers, Kaitlyn found herself simply observing. A local coffee shop owner arranged chairs with practiced efficiency, nodding hello to passing neighbors.

The scent of fresh-baked Cuban bread wafted from a nearby

bakery. Two women in business attire power-walked past, deep in conversation about restaurant permits and health inspections. This was a different Key West than the one she'd imagined—less party paradise, more real community.

As she wandered, she let her curiosity guide her, snapping photos of quirky signs and tropical flowers. She passed a group of artists setting up their easels for the day, their canvases already alive with vibrant island colors. The morning light caught their palettes, turning simple blobs of paint into jewels.

A chef emerged from a tiny restaurant to water the herbs growing in wooden boxes along the sidewalk, the smell of basil and mint mixing with the salty air. He waved to her, offering a fresh sprig of mint that she tucked behind her ear instead of photographing.

Each corner revealed something new—a hidden courtyard draped in bougainvillea, a tiny bookshop just opening its doors, a cat sleeping in a sunny window display. Her camera captured some moments, but others she just let sink in, like the sound of wind chimes from a second-story balcony or the way the morning breeze carried snippets of conversations in multiple languages.

She turned down a quiet side street, away from the main tourist thoroughfare, and found herself in front of a weathered blue house with a hand-painted sign that read, "Paradise Harbor House: Hope and Shelter for Southern Florida Families." The name sparked a memory of the brochure she'd picked up the day before, the one she'd been studying when exhaustion had finally overtaken her curiosity.

Something about the house drew her closer. It wasn't just the cheerful blue paint or the neat row of rocking chairs on the porch, but the soft hum of voices and the occasional laugh filtering out through the open windows. The garden was well-tended, with neat rows of vegetables and herbs growing in raised beds. Wind chimes tinkled softly in the breeze, their gentle music a contrast to the raucous tourist bars she'd passed earlier.

Kaitlyn hesitated at the gate, unsure if she should intrude. Her mother's voice echoed in her head—"Always have a plan, always make connections that advance your career." This definitely wasn't part of the carefully curated Key West experience she'd imagined documenting for her followers. Her mother would probably say she was wasting her time, just like she'd said about most of Kaitlyn's choices lately.

Before she could decide, a warm voice called out, "Can I help you?"

She turned to see a woman standing on the porch. Mid-forties, with dark hair pulled into a sleek ponytail and a clipboard in hand, the woman exuded calm authority. Her clothes were simple but professional, a far cry from the tropical prints and flip-flops Kaitlyn had come to expect in Key West. Her eyes crinkled kindly as she descended the steps to meet Kaitlyn.

"Hi," Kaitlyn said, suddenly feeling awkward in her carefully chosen resort wear. "I was just walking by and saw the sign. I'm Kaitlyn." She resisted the urge to add her Instagram handle, a habit that had become almost reflexive.

The woman's smile widened, genuine warmth replacing professional courtesy. "Nice to meet you, Kaitlyn. I'm Elena Armstrong, Director of Paradise Harbor House. Are you looking for someone?"

Kaitlyn shook her head, her rehearsed social media personality falling away in the face of Elena's direct gaze. "Not exactly. I just…I don't know. This place seemed interesting." She gestured vaguely at the house. "It feels different from everything else around here."

Elena studied her for a moment, her expression thoughtful. Then she nodded toward the porch. "Why don't you come in? I'll show you around." She tucked her clipboard under her arm, making a small notation before giving Kaitlyn her full attention.

Kaitlyn followed Elena up the stairs. Inside, the house was bright and welcoming, with mismatched furniture that somehow worked together to create a cozy atmosphere. Children's artwork adorned the walls alongside inspirational quotes painted in cheerful colors. The effect should have been chaotic but instead felt intentional—a space designed to make people feel at home.

A few women sat in the living room, chatting softly while folding laundry. Their conversation paused briefly as Elena and Kaitlyn passed, but resumed naturally, creating a gentle backdrop of normalcy. In the corner, a toddler played with a stack of wooden blocks, carefully constructing and demolishing towers with equal enthusiasm.

"Paradise Harbor House provides transitional housing for women and children in the Southern Florida area who are trying to get back on their feet," Elena explained as they walked through the house. The hardwood floors creaked softly beneath their feet, telling stories of countless footsteps before them. "We offer counseling, job training, childcare—whatever support they need to rebuild their lives."

They passed a small library filled with books and comfortable reading chairs, then a computer room where two women were working on resumes. Everything about the space spoke of purpose and hope, so different from the chaos of Kaitlyn's college life.

"That's amazing," Kaitlyn said, genuinely impressed. "How long have you been here?"

"About ten years," Elena said, leading them into a sunny kitchen where the smell of fresh coffee mingled with something baking in the oven. "I came on as director five years ago. Before that, I was in corporate marketing, but...well, life has a way of steering you toward where you need to be."

Kaitlyn caught the subtle shift in Elena's tone, sensing there was more to the story. But something in the older woman's expression suggested that was a conversation for another time.

"Do you need help?" Kaitlyn found herself asking, surprising herself with the offer. "Like, volunteers?" She thought of all the carefully planned content she'd intended to create during her stay—the beach photos, the sunset videos, the carefully staged shots of tropical drinks. Somehow, they seemed less important now.

Elena raised an eyebrow, clearly intrigued. "We're always looking for people who want to contribute. Do you have any experience?"

"A little," Kaitlyn admitted, thinking back to her sophomore year. "I volunteered at a women's shelter in college. It was part of a service requirement for my sorority. I liked being able to help. It felt real, you know?"

Elena smiled, and Kaitlyn had the distinct impression she was seeing past the carefully constructed facade to something more authentic. "That's a great start. If you're interested, we could use help organizing donations and maybe working with the kids. Nothing too overwhelming to start."

"I'd love to," Kaitlyn said, surprising herself with how much she meant it. The idea of doing something meaningful, something that couldn't be captured in a perfectly filtered photo, appealed to her in a way she hadn't expected. "What should I do next?"

"Why don't I introduce you to a few people here right now. Then, you should come by tomorrow morning to get started," Elena said, handing her a small pamphlet from a neat stack on the counter. "We'll get you set up. The morning shift is usually quieter—good for getting to know the place."

"I will, thank you, Kaitlyn responded. "I'm looking forward to it."

"Ready to meet some compassionate and committed employees?"

Kaitlyn, smiled. "Lead on."

When Tess and Leah returned from the market, they found Kaitlyn sitting at the kitchen table, flipping through the Paradise Harbor House pamphlet. She'd read it cover to cover twice, drawn in by the stories of people who'd found their way to the shelter and, more importantly, found their way forward.

"You found it," Leah said softly, setting down the grocery bags. There was something knowing in her tone, as if she'd been waiting for this moment.

Kaitlyn looked up, surprised. "You know about Paradise Harbor House?"

"I did some research after we saw it the other day," Leah admitted, exchanging a glance with Tess. "We've been living here for over a year, and I don't ever remember seeing the place before."

Tess laughed. "I bet we've walked by it before but never paid much attention."

"It seems like they're doing important work there," Leah added.

"They are," Kaitlyn said, straightening in her chair. "I met Elena today—she's the director. I offered to volunteer, and she accepted."

"Really? You want to volunteer? I had no idea. I thought…" Leah didn't finish.

"You thought all I wanted to do was party, right?"

Leah felt ashamed to admit Kaitlyn was right. "Honey, there's nothing wrong with wanting to have a good time. You just graduated from college. You have every right to celebrate and take whatever time you need to figure out what you want to do with your life."

Tess pulled out a chair and sat down, her expression thoughtful despite the lingering effects of Trivia Tuesday evident in her slightly squinted eyes. "That could be good for you, Kaitlyn."

"You don't think it's weird?" Kaitlyn asked, a hint of defensiveness in her tone. "Me coming to Key West for vacation but wanting to do something serious?"

"Honey," Leah said, joining them at the table, "we all need to find our own way. Sometimes it just takes a while to figure out what that looks like." She paused, choosing her words carefully. "Does your mother know you're interested in this kind of work?"

Kaitlyn tensed slightly at the mention of her mother.

"Mom doesn't know a lot of things right now." The words hung in the air, heavy with unspoken meaning. "She has my whole life planned out—law school, corporate career. But maybe that's not what I want anymore."

"Well," Tess said, breaking the tension, "I think it's great. And who knows? Maybe while you're helping others find their way, you might find yours too."

Kaitlyn's face seemed to soften at the lack of judgment in her aunts' responses. "Thanks. I start tomorrow morning."

"Great. In the meantime, how about we have a little late breakfast? Do you like quiche?" Leah asked.

Kaitlyn smiled. "Yes, I love it, and I didn't realize it until now, but I'm starving."

CHAPTER 5

Tess leaned on the sticky bar at Margarita Max's, watching the crowd ebb and flow with the unpredictable rhythm of a Key West evening.

The overhead fans spun lazily, barely cutting through the humidity, while the jukebox blared an off-key rendition of "Sweet Caroline" courtesy of a karaoke enthusiast who had clearly peaked three margaritas ago. The neon signs cast a multicolored glow over everything, turning the usual chaos into something almost magical.

A group of sunburned tourists crowded the bar, their matching t-shirts proclaiming them part of "Ava's Last Fling Before the Ring." Tess had already memorized their drink order—five strawberry daiquiris and one virgin margarita for the designated driver. They'd been cycling through the same drinks for the past two hours, each round getting progressively louder and gigglier.

"Leah, table four needs another round," Connie barked from across the bar, her tone sharp but not unkind. She moved with military precision, mixing drinks while simultaneously keeping an eye on every corner of the establishment. Nothing escaped her notice—not the couple trying to sneak their own drinks in, not the wannabe musician attempting to adjust the sound system, and certainly not her new employees' growing competence.

Leah adjusted her tray and nodded, weaving through the tightly packed tables with practiced care. She'd mastered the art of dodging tipsy patrons and balancing drinks like a pro. Her corporate efficiency had translated surprisingly well to bartending, though the sticky floors and constant noise were a far cry from her former office. Still, it wasn't exactly the life she'd imagined when she'd moved to Key West.

"Watch your back," she called out to a server carrying a precarious tray of shots. The younger woman flashed her a grateful smile—they'd all learned quickly that survival at Max's depended on looking out for each other.

"How's it going?" Tess asked as Leah passed by, her voice loud enough to cut through the noise. She was arranging lime wedges with the same attention to detail she'd once applied to their failed craft projects.

"Great," Leah deadpanned. "I'm living my best life." She gestured to a spot on her shirt where someone's blue cocktail had left its mark. "The tourist from table seven wanted to show me his impression of a dolphin. It involved a lot of arm movement."

Tess grinned and returned to wiping down the bar, where a man in a Hawaiian shirt was gesturing wildly about "the best fish tacos on the island." She nodded along, throwing in the occasional "uh-huh" while her mind wandered to Kaitlyn.

Their niece's sudden interest in Paradise Harbor House had caught both of them off guard. Tess had expected beach days and bar hopping, not volunteering at a women's shelter. It was like watching a butterfly emerge from its social media cocoon.

The man in the Hawaiian shirt leaned forward, his enthusiasm for fish tacos apparently boundless. "You gotta try Rico's place—it's this little shack down by the marina. Changed my life!" He punctuated this declaration by accidentally knocking over his water glass, which Tess caught with newfound bartender reflexes.

"Nice save," Connie commented as she passed by. "You're getting better at this." Coming from Connie, it was high praise indeed.

As if summoned by her thoughts, Kaitlyn appeared in the doorway, her sundress fluttering slightly in the breeze.

The contrast between her fresh, put-together appearance and the bar's cheerful chaos was striking. She spotted Tess and waved, weaving her way through the crowd with the kind of youthful confidence Tess envied. Even the Ava's Last Fling crew paused their celebration to watch her pass.

"What are you doing here? Why aren't you out having fun?" Tess asked as Kaitlyn reached the bar. "Shouldn't you be out enjoying your night?" She gestured to the growing crowd of twenty-somethings gathering near the karaoke machine.

"I just came to say hi," Kaitlyn said, sliding onto one of the barstools. Her perfectly styled hair and careful makeup seemed at odds with the excitement in her eyes. "Plus, I wanted to tell you about my visit to Paradise Harbor House this morning."

"How did it go?" Tess asked, genuinely curious. She mixed a mojito on autopilot while keeping her attention on her niece. The change in Kaitlyn over the past twenty-four hours had been subtle but noticeable—like watching a script being rewritten in real time.

"Really well," Kaitlyn said, her face lighting up in a way that had nothing to do with the bar's neon signs. "I met with Elena Armstrong and she has some ideas where I can volunteer. We talked about a lot of things and she even introduced me to some people who are living there. You should see the inside. It's the coziest home. I mean it's a big house, but it still manages to seem small and welcoming. It's like going to visit at your grandmother's house. There's this little girl, Maria, and her mom. They're staying there because they had nowhere else to go after leaving a bad situation. Maria's only five, but she's so sweet. She showed me her collection of seashells—she keeps them in an old shoebox and knows all their names."

Tess's smile softened. "Sounds like a great place to volunteer." She remembered their own early days in Key West when everything had seemed possible. Maybe it still was, just not in the way they'd expected.

"I hope so," Kaitlyn said. She hesitated, her fingers tracing the edge of a napkin. "I was thinking about asking Elena if I could help with their communications. You know, social media, marketing, that kind of thing. It's what I studied, so maybe I could actually put my degree to use."

"That's a great idea," Tess said immediately, recognizing the spark of genuine passion in her niece's voice. "You're a natural at that stuff."

"Thanks," Kaitlyn said, her cheeks pinking slightly. "I'm nervous, though. I don't want to mess it up. This isn't like posting vacation photos or sorority events. These are real people with real stories."

Before Tess could respond, Leah appeared, her tray now empty but her shirt sporting a new stain. "What's this about messing up?"

"Kaitlyn's thinking about helping Paradise Harbor House with their marketing," Tess explained, already reaching for the soda gun to fill another order.

Leah's eyebrows lifted. "That's ambitious." Her tone carried the same cautious assessment she'd once used in board meetings.

"It's also something she's good at," Tess said pointedly.

Leah folded her arms, glancing at Kaitlyn. "Well, if you're serious about it, I say go for it. The worst that can happen is you learn something from the experience." A ghost of a smile crossed her face. "Heaven knows we've learned plenty from our experiences in Key West."

"Thanks," Kaitlyn said. "I'll talk to Elena tomorrow."

"So, what else have you been up to?" Leah asked.

"Well, after my visit with Elena, I went on a tour at the Ernest Hemingway Home and Museum. That was pretty cool. Did you know there are about sixty cats living there? They were everywhere. I petted a few that were friendly, but a few didn't want me to touch them. Right now, I thought I'd go check out the fish tacos at Seven Fish. My guidebook says they're really good. Then, I guess I'll head home." She dangled the house key in the air. "I've got my key. I'll catch up with you guys later."

Tess watched as another group of tourists stumbled through the door as Kaitlyn headed out.

The night wore on, a blur of drink orders and tourist stories. Before Kaitlyn left Tess found herself watching her niece as she sat at the bar, occasionally chatting with customers but mostly observing everything with new eyes. She wasn't just seeing potential photo opportunities anymore—she was seeing stories, connections, possibilities.

By the time their shift ended, the crowd had thinned, leaving behind only a few die-hard karaoke fans and a table of locals playing cards in the corner. The Linda's Last Fling group had departed hours ago, their matching shirts now adorned with various drink stains and their designated driver herding them into waiting cabs.

Tess and Leah wiped down tables, their energy drained but their spirits surprisingly high. The sticky floors seemed less annoying somehow, the karaoke less grating. Tess thought maybe they were finally finding their rhythm in this unexpected chapter of their lives.

"You know," Tess said as she stacked chairs, their legs

squeaking against the floor, "Kaitlyn's got more focus than I gave her credit for."

Leah nodded. "She's surprising me too. I didn't expect her to take an interest in something like Paradise Harbor House. I thought we'd be spending our days off chaperoning beach parties."

"Maybe she's just figuring out what matters to her," Tess said. "Kind of like we are." She paused to rescue a forgotten phone from under a table, making a mental note to add it to Connie's lost and found collection.

Leah gave her a look. "You think working here is us figuring things out?"

"I think it's a step," Tess said with a shrug. "And sometimes that's all you need. Remember when we first got here? We thought we'd be running sunset cruises and teaching beach yoga by now."

"Instead, we're mixing margaritas and cleaning up after spring breakers," Leah said, but there was more amusement than bitterness in her tone.

"At least we're doing it together," Tess pointed out. "And hey, we haven't had any more brilliant business ideas in four days. That's progress, right?"

Leah smiled. "I guess so."

The next morning, Kaitlyn stood on the porch of Paradise Harbor House, her heart pounding as she knocked lightly on the screen door before walking inside. She'd traded her usual resort wear for something more practical—neat shorts and a crisp white shirt.

Elena appeared swiftly, a clipboard clutched in her hand and a warm smile lighting her face. From behind her, the sounds of breakfast preparation spilled out—the clinking of dishes, children's laughter, and a symphony of cozy chaos signaling a home awakening.

"Kaitlyn! Good to see you. What brings you by so early?"

"I wanted to talk to you about...maybe doing more," Kaitlyn said, fidgeting slightly. Her carefully prepared pitch suddenly seemed inadequate in the face of the real work happening inside. "I have a degree in business communication, and I thought maybe I could help with your marketing. Social media, fundraising, things like that."

Elena's expression brightened, her clipboard lowering slightly. "Our online presence could use a refresh, and we're always looking for ways to boost donations. I'm not sure what else you were thinking of doing but we can explore ideas. We do amazing work here, but sometimes getting the word out can be challenging."

Relief flooded Kaitlyn's face. "Really? That's great. I can start whenever you need me. I've been thinking about some ideas already—ways to share success stories, highlight your programs, maybe even set up a regular donor newsletter."

"How about today?" Elena said. "We're planning a fundraiser in a couple of weeks. We're just now working on ideas for that. It would be wonderful to have your input. Lily helps me with marketing things, but perhaps you and she might brainstorm? Sometimes fresh eyes see opportunities we might miss."

Kaitlyn nodded eagerly. "I'm in."

She followed Elena inside, where Maria was carefully taking her seashells out of a shoebox and carefully arranging them on a windowsill, each one placed with deliberate care. She looked up and waved, her smile missing two front teeth.

Kaitlyn waved back. For the first time since graduation, she felt like she was exactly where she was meant to be. Not performing for an online audience or meeting someone else's expectations, but doing something real, something that mattered.

Through the window, she could see happiness everywhere.

Maybe her aunts weren't the only ones who'd come to the island looking for a fresh start. Maybe sometimes you had to get lost in paradise to find your way forward. She thought of Key West as the next stop on her journey to find purpose and meaning.

She smiled and reminded herself that there wasn't anything wrong with having fun now and then as well. And, with Aunt Tess and Aunt Leah, fun would always be just around the corner.

CHAPTER 6

*E*rnest strutted past the window, pausing to eye the kitchen activities with his usual literary criticism while Leah chopped vegetables for dinner.

Tess sat at the kitchen table, leafing through a tattered cookbook she'd found at a thrift store, her pencil scratching notes in the margins. The book had clearly been well-loved by its previous owner, with dog-eared pages and splatter marks telling stories of meals long past. She'd bought it on impulse last week, drawn to its vintage cover and promise of "Island Cuisine Made Simple."

"How about lime and honey glazed shrimp?" Tess suggested, holding up the book. The recipe's page was marked with one of their old business cards—"Island Inspirations" in faded gold lettering. "We could serve it over coconut rice."

"Sounds good," Leah replied, carefully dicing a bell pepper. "As long as we don't overdo the honey. Remember last time?" Their attempt at honey-garlic chicken had ended with a sticky mess in the kitchen.

Tess laughed. "Right. Sticky chaos. Got it. Though you have to admit, that sauce was pretty tasty once we got it off the counter. I'm going to shake some red chili peppers on mine."

The kitchen had settled into a comfortable rhythm lately, their evening meals becoming a time to decompress and plan, usually right before heading out to work. It was almost like their early days in Key West, before the pressure of failing businesses had started to weigh them down. There was something different now, a hint of hard-won wisdom in their conversations.

Kaitlyn burst through the door just then, her cheeks pink from the heat and her arms full of folders. Her usual perfectly styled appearance was slightly disheveled, but her eyes were bright with excitement. A few loose papers escaped her grip, scattering across the floor like confetti.

"You wouldn't believe the day I've had," she said, dropping her load onto the couch before flopping down beside it. Her enthusiasm was contagious, filling the small space with energy. "Elena said they're planning a fundraiser in a few weeks, and she's thinking about doing a sunset dinner cruise. She thinks it'll bring in some big donations."

"That's ambitious," Leah said, wiping her hands on a towel. She couldn't help but notice how different Kaitlyn seemed from the social media-obsessed niece who'd hadn't been in Key West for no more than two days. There was substance behind her excitement now, purpose in her planning.

"It is," Kaitlyn agreed, gathering up the fallen papers. "But I think it could really work. The tricky part is getting local businesses to donate or sponsor. We're meeting with some tomorrow. Elena's been introducing me to everyone— she knows practically every business owner in Key West."

"You've been here for what, two days? And you're already planning a major event?" Tess teased, her tone light but impressed. She closed the cookbook, giving Kaitlyn her full attention. "Looks like someone inherited the family's entrepreneurial spirit."

Kaitlyn grinned, but there was a hint of self-awareness in her expression that was new. "What can I say? I'm good at making things happen. Though this time it's different. It's not just about creating content or getting likes. These people really need help." She hesitated, looking between her aunts. "Speaking of which…I was wondering if you two might want to help? Just a little? Maybe with the food side of things?"

Leah blinked, caught off guard. The knife paused mid-chop. "You want *us* to help?"

"Why not? Aunt Tess, you're always coming up with creative dishes, and Aunt Leah, you're the most organized person I know. Plus, it's for a good cause." Kaitlyn sat up straighter, her expression earnest. "And honestly? I could really use your experience. Even the failed business attempts taught you both so much about what works and what doesn't in Key West."

Tess tilted her head, clearly intrigued. The vintage cookbook lay forgotten as new possibilities sparked in her mind. "A sunset dinner cruise fundraiser? That does sound fun. And I've always wanted an excuse to try a few new recipes. Maybe something with local ingredients, really showcase what makes the Keys special."

"I don't know," Leah said, hesitant. She resumed chopping, the rhythm slightly less steady now. "We're already working full shifts at the bar. Adding something else might be too much. Not only that, does the shelter have money for this? It's one thing to get donations, but up-front costs, we can't afford."

"It doesn't have to be a lot," Kaitlyn said quickly. She stood, moving to the kitchen counter with the energy of someone who refused to take no for an answer. "Maybe just brainstorming ideas or testing a dish or two. If it's too much, you can always back out. No pressure." She paused, then added softly, "But I really think you'd be good at this. It won't be a sit-down dinner, just appetizers or maybe a buffet. I'm not sure yet. Elena said she knows several restaurant owners who might help, but it would be great if you could help too."

Leah exchanged a glance with Tess, who raised her eyebrows in encouragement. There was something different about this opportunity—it wasn't about making money or finding their place in paradise. It was about helping others find theirs.

With a sigh that carried more acceptance than resignation, Leah nodded. "All right. We'll help where we can. But let's keep it manageable this time. And we're going to have to meet Elena at some point."

Kaitlyn beamed, her smile brightening the kitchen more than the setting sun. "Thank you! You're the best. Just wait until you meet some of the families at Paradise Harbor House, you'll understand why this matters so much."

Leah smiled. "I have no doubt."

The next morning, Kaitlyn arrived early at Paradise Harbor House, armed with a notebook full of ideas and a nervous excitement she couldn't quite shake. The morning air was thick with humidity, and the porch's rocking chairs moved gently in the breeze.

Elena greeted her with a warm smile, already holding a steaming mug of coffee. Her clipboard was tucked under one arm, several new pages added since yesterday. "Good morning, Kaitlyn" she said, holding the door open. "Ready to tackle the fundraiser?"

"Absolutely," Kaitlyn replied, following her inside. The house smelled of coffee and cinnamon, with a hint of fresh paint from where they'd been touching up the living room walls. "I've got a list of potential sponsors, and my aunts agreed to help with the food. They're actually pretty excited about it."

Elena's eyebrows lifted, pleasant surprise crossing her face.

"Your aunts are getting involved? That's wonderful. The more community support we have, the better. And from what you've told me about their creative ideas, they might bring exactly the kind of energy we need. I'd love to meet them."

"They want to meet you too," Kaitlyn responded. "I think they're afraid I'm getting in over my head."

Elena smiled. "Oh, I'm sure they just want to better understand what we do here. Tell them to stop by anytime."

Kaitlyn followed Elena into her small office, where a wall of photos told stories of Paradise Harbor House's successes—families smiling in front of new homes, women graduating from training programs, children celebrating birthdays in the backyard garden. Each image represented a life changed, a bridge built to a better future.

Kaitlyn and Lily spent the next few hours strategizing, contacting local businesses. Kaitlyn surprised herself with how smoothly the work came to her. She had always been good at organizing, but this felt different. It felt…meaningful.

Her social media skills, once used primarily for gathering likes and followers, now served a greater purpose as she crafted compelling messages about Paradise Harbor House's mission.

"What about approaching some of the sunset cruise companies sooner, rather than later?" Elena suggested, reviewing their sponsor list. "They might be willing to donate a boat and crew for the evening. It would save us a significant expense."

Kaitlyn nodded eagerly, already pulling up her notes. "I've researched a few options. There's one company that does charity events regularly—they might be interested."

By noon, they had secured three small sponsorships and piqued the interest of a local bakery that offered to donate desserts for the event.

Kaitlyn practically floated out of Paradise Harbor House, her confidence growing with each small success. The morning's work had shown her that her skills—even the ones she'd once dismissed as frivolous—could make a real difference.

Back at the bungalow, Leah and Tess were brainstorming menu ideas. The kitchen table was covered with cookbooks, notepads, and the beginnings of a shopping list. Their old vision board had been repurposed, now holding sample menus and recipe cards instead of failed business plans.

"Key lime pie is a must," Leah said, jotting it down. "But maybe with a twist—like a coconut crust or mango sauce."

"And definitely conch fritters for one of the appetizers," Tess added, comparing prices from different suppliers. "We could do a mini version, more elegant for a fundraiser."

"No way. With all the great conch fritters on the island, there is no way I'd want to tackle that. Besides, we're hardly fishermen or sea divers."

"What about a vegetarian option?" Tess asked, flipping through her thrift store cookbook. "We need to be inclusive."

Leah tilted her head, considering. "Stuffed peppers? They're easy and can be prepped ahead of time."

Tess nodded approvingly. "I like it. We'll need to test a few recipes." Her eyes sparkled with the same enthusiasm that had once led them to buy a coffee cart, but this time it felt grounded in reality rather than dreams.

"I hope Kaitlyn knows what she's getting us into," Leah said, though there was no real bite in her words. Instead, there was a hint of pride—both in their niece and in themselves for taking this step.

Tess grinned, reaching for another cookbook. "She's full of surprises. Maybe we are too. Who would have thought our failed catering business would come in handy?"

"Do you know if she's talked to Gretchen yet?" Leah asked.

Tess shrugged. "No idea. Why?"

"Because, although I hate to rain on her parade, she has to answer her mother's calls. Gretchen will be frantic and blow everything out of proportion. I'm going to have a talk with Kaitlyn. She can't put this off any longer."

Tess nodded. "I agree. Maybe we should meet with Elena before Kaitlyn calls Gretchen. You know how our sister is, she'll pounce on us and ask a million questions we can't answer. I don't feel like hearing another lecture about how irresponsible we are."

"You're right. We should see the place for ourselves."

Without letting Kaitlyn know they were headed to Paradise Harbor House, Tess and Leah walked several blocks to find Elena Armstrong. When they arrived, they saw a few children playing under the shade of a massive banyan tree, their laughter carrying across the yard.

As they climbed the porch steps, the screen door opened and a woman with long hair pulled back in a neat braid stepped out.

"Hello, can I help you?"

"We're Kaitlyn's aunts, I'm Leah and this is my sister, Tess."

"Welcome" she said warmly. "I'm Elena. Nice to finally meet you."

"Hope we're not interrupting anything," Leah said, but Elena was already waving them inside.

"Not at all. Come in, please. We just finished lunch—would you like some coffee?"

The interior of Paradise Harbor House was well-worn but immaculately kept, with comfortable furniture and walls covered in photos. Elena led them through a living room where two women sat sorting donated clothing, past a study space where another woman worked intently at a computer, and into a large, sunny kitchen.

"This is where most of our community happens," Elena said, gesturing to the massive kitchen table that could easily seat twelve. "Meals, homework, job applications, late-night conversations—it all happens here."

Tess ran an appreciative hand along the industrial-sized stove. "This is quite a setup."

"We serve three meals a day, plus snacks for the kids," Elena explained, pouring coffee into mismatched mugs. "Some of our residents are learning food service skills—basic cooking, food safety, that sort of thing."

"Kaitlyn mentioned that," Leah said, accepting a mug. "It's a wonderful program."

"Kaitlyn's told me about your various business ventures over the years."

"You mean our failures," Leah said dryly.

"I mean your persistence," Elena corrected gently. "That's something we understand here at Paradise Harbor House. Everyone deserves second chances, sometimes third and fourth chances too."

As if to illustrate her point, a teenage girl burst into the kitchen, making a beeline for the refrigerator. She pulled out a jug of juice, then noticed the visitors and froze.

"It's okay, Maya," Elena said. "These are Kaitlyn's aunts, the ones helping with the fundraiser." To Tess and Leah, she added, "Maya's our resident artist. She's helping us come up with design ideas for the fundraiser."

Maya's shy smile turned proud. "Want to see?" Without waiting for an answer, she darted out and returned with a sketch pad. The design she showed them was elegant but warm, featuring a sunset over water and simple, flowing text.

"This is beautiful," Tess said sincerely, and Maya beamed before disappearing again, juice forgotten.

"That's what we do here," Elena said after she'd gone. "We help people rediscover their talents, their worth." She pulled out a folder. "Now, about this fundraiser. Kaitlyn's been sharing your menu ideas…"

For the next hour, they discussed logistics, possibilities, and challenges. Elena's practical experience balanced their creative ideas, and slowly, a plan began to take shape. Through it all, Paradise Harbor House's daily life continued around them, women coming and going, children's voices drifting in from the yard, phones ringing with potential donations or new arrivals needing help.

When they finally stood to leave, both sisters felt differently than when they'd arrived. This wasn't just Kaitlyn's project anymore—it had become real, important.

"Thank you for coming," Elena said at the door. "And thank you for supporting Kaitlyn in this. She's brought such energy to our little community."

"Speaking of Kaitlyn," Leah said, "we need to convince her to call her mother."

Elena's expression turned understanding. "Ah, yes. She's mentioned being worried about that conversation. Perhaps remind her that we all need our support systems, even when those relationships are complicated."

Walking back to their bungalow in the late afternoon heat, Tess and Leah were quiet, both processing what they'd seen.

Finally, Tess spoke. "You know what this means, right?"

"That we're definitely going to need a bigger kitchen?"

"That, and we're fully committed now. No backing out."

CHAPTER 7

Kaitlyn's phone buzzed for the third time that morning as she climbed the steps to Paradise Harbor House. Her mother's name flashed on the screen again, accompanied by a photo from happier times—both of them smiling at her college graduation, before she knew the truth. Before she discovered the other family photos, the ones where her father smiled just as proudly beside a different daughter.

She silenced the phone and shoved it deep into her bag. The morning air was thick with humidity, promising another scorching Key West day. Through the open windows of the old Victorian, she could hear Elena's voice directing someone to the donation room, the familiar creak of floorboards under new feet.

"Perfect timing," Elena said as Kaitlyn entered, her clipboard tucked under one arm. "We have a new arrival I'd like you to meet."

The woman stood in the common room, three children clustered around her like satellites. Her dark hair was pulled back in a hasty ponytail, and she held herself with the rigid posture of someone expecting the world to strike at any moment. The oldest child, a girl around seven, kept one hand on her younger brother's shoulder while the toddler clung to their mother's leg.

"This is Carla," Elena said softly. "And her children—Christina, Dominic, and Jack. They arrived late last night."

Kaitlyn noticed the way Carla's eyes darted between them, measuring, assessing. The way she kept her children close, like a mother bird shielding her nest. The familiar ache bloomed in Kaitlyn's chest—the one that appeared whenever she thought about families and secrets, about the sister she had never known.

"Welcome to Paradise Harbor House," Kaitlyn said, keeping her voice gentle. "I'm Kaitlyn. I help out here with…well, whatever needs helping with."

Carla nodded curtly, her fingers absently stroking her youngest's hair. Dark circles shadowed her eyes, telling stories of sleepless nights and endless worry. "Elena said there might be clothes? For the kids?"

"Of course," Kaitlyn replied, recognizing the deflection for what it was—a mother focusing on practical needs to avoid darker thoughts. "The donation room's this way. We just got some new things in yesterday."

As they walked, Kaitlyn's phone buzzed again in her bag. She ignored it, but Carla's sharp glance told her the other woman had noticed. "Someone trying to reach you?"

"Just my mother," Kaitlyn said, the words tasting bitter. "I can talk to her later."

Something flickered in Carla's eyes—recognition, maybe, or understanding. Christina pressed closer to her mother's side, and Kaitlyn saw how the girl watched everything, absorbing the undercurrents of adult conversation like a small sponge.

The donation room was organized chaos—racks of clothes sorted by size, boxes of toys and books, shelves of essential supplies. Kaitlyn had spent time the day before organizing everything after the latest community drive.

"Take whatever you need," Kaitlyn said, gesturing to the racks.

"Christina, I think I saw some books over there that might interest you. And Dominic, we have a whole box of cars and trucks if you'd like to look."

The children glanced at their mother, waiting for permission. Carla nodded slightly, and they drifted toward the offerings, though Christina kept glancing back as if to ensure her mother hadn't vanished.

"They're good kids," Kaitlyn observed, watching as Dominic carefully showed his little brother a toy car.

"They've been through a lot," Carla said, her voice tight. "Their father…he left. Just disappeared one day. Cleaned out our accounts, canceled the cards. Turns out he had another life all set up, just waiting." Her laugh was sharp, brittle. "Funny how people can do that, isn't it? Just walk away like the life they're leaving doesn't matter."

The words hit Kaitlyn like a physical blow. Her phone buzzed again, the sound muffled by her bag. On the other side of the room, Christina was showing Dominic something in a book, her voice soft and nurturing despite her own youth.

"Yeah," Kaitlyn managed, her throat tight. "Funny how that works."

Carla began sorting through the clothes with efficient movements, checking sizes and conditions. Her hands shook slightly, but her voice remained steady. "I don't want pity. We just need… time. Space to figure things out."

"That's what Paradise Harbor House is for," Kaitlyn said, focusing on the practical to steady herself. "We have programs, resources. Ways to help you rebuild." She paused, then added more softly, "And sometimes just having someone listen helps too."

Carla's hands stilled on a small t-shirt. "Maybe," she said, but her shoulders relaxed fractionally. "The kids need stability first. Everything else can wait."

As if on cue, Jack toddled over, clutching a stuffed bear nearly as big as himself. His face lit up as he offered it to his mother, and for a moment, Carla's careful composure cracked. She scooped him up, bear and all, pressing a kiss to his curls.

Kaitlyn turned away, giving them privacy. Her phone had gone silent, but she knew there would be more messages waiting. Her mother never could take a hint. Just like she had never noticed—or never admitted—what had been happening right under her nose all those years ago.

Through the window, she could see the resident kitten strutting past, his bouncing amusing the children. The sight normally made her smile, but today it just reminded her of how appearances could be deceiving. How families could look perfect from the outside while hiding fault lines deep beneath the surface.

"Would you like help carrying things to your room?" she asked, turning back to find Carla had assembled a small pile of necessities.

"We can manage," Carla said quickly, then seemed to reconsider. "But…thank you. For not asking questions. For just…" She gestured vaguely at the room, at her children, at everything.

"That's what we do here," Kaitlyn said, and meant it. Even if her own wounds were still raw, maybe she could help someone else heal. Maybe that would be enough.

As she watched Carla and her children navigate the stairs with their selections, Kaitlyn's phone buzzed one final time. A text from her mother: "Please call me. We need to talk."

She deleted it without responding. Some conversations weren't ready to happen. Some truths needed time to settle, like dust after a storm. For now, there was work to be done, people to help, stories to tell that didn't include her own.

But watching Christina help her brother carry his treasures, Kaitlyn couldn't help but wonder about another girl, not so far away, who shared her eyes, her father's smile, and a life she would never know.

The bungalow was quiet when Kaitlyn returned, though the smell of Tess's latest culinary experiment lingered in the air. She found her aunts on the back porch, Leah working on paperwork while Tess jotted down menu ideas for the Paradise Harbor House event. Ernest strutted past, pausing to eye the remains of Tess's cooking with his usual literary criticism.

"How was your day?" Tess asked, looking up from her notebook. "Elena mentioned you had a new family arrive."

Kaitlyn dropped into the worn wicker chair, suddenly exhausted. "Yeah. A mother and three kids. The father left them." She pulled out her phone, deleted three more missed calls from her mother without looking at them. "Apparently he had a whole other life set up."

Leah's pen paused mid-sentence. "That must be hard on the children."

"The oldest girl, Christina—she's trying so hard to be strong for her siblings." Kaitlyn's voice caught slightly. "Kids shouldn't have to deal with stuff like that. She's what, seven? Eight? And she's already acting like a second mother."

"No, they shouldn't," Tess agreed softly, watching her niece with careful eyes. "Are you okay? You seem…"

"Fine," Kaitlyn said quickly. Too quickly. "Just tired. And Mom keeps calling. You know how she gets."

"Gretchen always was persistent," Leah said, using their sister's name in that particular way she had when disapproving of something. "Maybe you should talk to her. She worries."

"She worries when it's convenient," Kaitlyn muttered, then forced a smile. "Anyway, I should work on the Paradise Harbor House website. Elena wants to highlight our family support programs."

"Wait," Tess called as Kaitlyn started to rise. "I made key lime bars. New recipe for the fundraiser. You should try one."

"Not hungry." Kaitlyn's phone buzzed again. This time it was a text, and she caught a glimpse of the preview before deleting it: Mom: Sweetheart, please. We need to discuss…

"Have you had dinner?" Leah asked, her tone careful. The one she used when trying not to spook a nervous client. "And you're not sleeping well. We can hear you up late at night."

"I'm fine," Kaitlyn repeated, the words worn smooth from repetition. "Just…processing everything with Paradise Harbor House. Getting to know the families. It's emotional work, you know?"

Tess and Leah exchanged a look—the kind that had developed over decades of sisterhood, the kind that carried entire conversations in a single glance. Kaitlyn used to envy that connection. Now it made her stomach twist.

"We're here," Tess said simply. "Whatever's going on. Whenever you're ready."

"I know." Kaitlyn managed another smile, this one feeling like it might crack her face. "I just need to work on this website. The families deserve to have their stories told properly."

As she headed inside, Kaitlyn heard Leah whisper to Tess, "Something's not right with her."

"Give her time," Tess whispered back. "Whatever it is, she'll tell us when she's ready."

"But Gretchen…"

"Let it be, Leah. You know how complicated mother-daughter relationships can be."

Kaitlyn closed her laptop a little harder than necessary. If only they knew. If only they understood why every happy family photo on Paradise Harbor House's website felt like a knife twisting in her chest. Her phone buzzed one more time—not her mother now, but a social media notification. Her finger hovered over it, knowing what she'd find if she looked: another perfect family moment, another smiling photo of the sister she'd never known.

Some truths were better left buried, even if they refused to stay quietly in their graves. Even if they haunted every conversation, colored every interaction, turned even the simplest family moment into a minefield of unspoken words.

Through the window, she could see Ernest pecking at invisible treasures in the withered herb garden. At least his world was simple—food, sunshine, and the occasional literary criticism. He didn't have to worry about families and their secrets, about the way truth could split a life in two as cleanly as a knife through water.

Her phone lay silent now, but she knew it wouldn't last. Her mother never could take a hint. And now, with every passing day at Paradise Harbor House, watching families piece themselves back together, Kaitlyn felt the weight of her knowledge growing heavier.

She opened her laptop again, forcing herself to focus on the website. There was work to be done, stories to tell that didn't include her own. For now, that would have to be enough.

CHAPTER 8

Kaitlyn adjusted her camera settings, watching through the lens as residents moved through their daily routines. A mother helping her daughter with homework. Two women sorting donations. A toddler building a tower of blocks only to knock it down with delighted giggles.

"Just pretend I'm not here," she called out, though she knew it was impossible. The camera changed things, made people conscious of themselves in ways they usually weren't. She'd learned that during her influencer days, when every moment had to be perfectly staged.

Elena appeared at her elbow, clipboard in hand. "How's it going?"

"Good. I've got some nice candid shots for the website. Shows the real Paradise Harbor House, you know?"

"And Carla?"

Kaitlyn lowered her camera. "Still won't agree to be photographed. Says she doesn't want to risk him finding them through social media." She didn't need to specify which 'him' she meant. "I get it. Some people shouldn't be able to find you."

"That's not unusual. Besides, I'm only interested in exterior shots at this point. We have to protect the people who stay here."

Kaitlyn nodded. "Yes, I understand."

Her phone buzzed in her pocket—another call from her mother. She ignored it, just like she'd been ignoring the social media notification that had popped up earlier: *Sarah Miller just posted a new photo album: Family Beach Day!*

She hadn't looked, but she didn't need to. Moments like these made her regret creating her fake social media accounts.

Through her lens, she watched Carla move through the common room, efficient and wary. Christina followed close behind, carrying Jack while Dominic clutched a toy truck to his chest. They moved like a single unit, each attuned to the others' needs.

"Maybe we could just photograph the back of their heads?" Elena suggested. "Or focus on their hands doing activities? Something that shows their story without showing their faces?"

Before Kaitlyn could respond, Carla approached, her posture rigid. "I've been thinking about your website project."

"Oh?" Kaitlyn lowered her camera again, careful to point it away.

"Christina wants to draw pictures of Paradise Harbor House instead. She thought maybe you could use those. Show the place through a child's eyes."

Something in Kaitlyn's chest tightened. Here was Carla, trying to protect her children while still letting them be seen. Still letting them exist in the world on their own terms.

"That's…that's actually perfect," Kaitlyn said, her voice thick. "Way better than my photos."

Christina beamed, already reaching for her crayons. Dominic perked up too, truck forgotten as he scrambled for paper.

"Mama, can I draw our tree?" he asked, referring to the one visible through the window. It had become their special spot, where Carla would read to them in the evenings.

"Of course, baby." Carla's voice softened the way it only did with her children. "Draw whatever makes you happy."

Kaitlyn watched through her camera as the children settled at the craft table, their faces intent with concentration.

She caught the moment Dominic stuck his tongue out while coloring, the way Christina helped him pick just the right shade of green. Even Jack contributed, adding enthusiastic scribbles to his siblings' works.

These were the moments that mattered. Not the posed shots, not the carefully curated glimpses of perfect lives. Just real people finding their way together, one crayon stroke at a time.

Her phone buzzed again. This time, she turned it off completely.

Later that afternoon, Kaitlyn sat cross-legged on the floor beside Christina, watching the girl add careful details to her drawing. The paper was filled with colorful figures—residents, volunteers, even the little kitten bouncing across the page in vibrant crayon strokes.

"That's Miss Elena," Christina explained, pointing to a figure with a clipboard. "And that's Dominic and Jack, and Mama." She hesitated, then added in a smaller voice, "I didn't draw my dad. Mama says we don't have to think about him if we don't want to."

Kaitlyn's hand stilled on her camera. "Sometimes that's easier, isn't it? Not thinking about people who aren't here anymore?"

"Do you have someone you don't think about too?"

The question, innocent as it was, hit like a physical blow. Before Kaitlyn could respond, Carla appeared with Jack on her hip.

"Time for lunch, sweetheart," she said, but her eyes lingered on Kaitlyn's face. "You've been drawing for hours."

"Can I finish?" Christina held up her picture. "I want to add the flowers by the porch. The yellow ones that smell nice."

"Jasmine," Kaitlyn supplied, grateful for the distraction. "They bloom at night. My mother used to grow them."

Carla settled beside them, adjusting Jack in her lap. "You don't talk about your mother much."

"Not much to say." Kaitlyn focused on her camera settings, though she hadn't taken a photo in hours. "Sometimes the people closest to us are the ones we understand the least."

"Mama," Dominic called from across the room, "look what I made!" He held up another drawing—their tree, but with birds nesting in its branches. Safe. Protected. Everything a should be.

Kaitlyn's phone lay silent in her pocket, powered off against the weight of unanswered calls and unopened messages. On her camera's memory card, dozens of photos captured life at Paradise Harbor House—all carefully framed to tell stories of hope and healing. None showing the photographer's own fractured reflection.

"You're good with them," Carla said quietly as Christina added the last flower to her masterpiece. "Patient. Like you understand."

"Maybe I do." Kaitlyn managed a smile that felt only slightly cracked. "Sometimes the best way to heal is to help others do the same."

Later, as she uploaded the children's artwork to the Paradise Harbor House website, Kaitlyn found herself pausing on Christina's drawing. The figures stood together, holding hands, their crayon smiles bright against the paper. A family not perfect, but present. Real in all the ways that mattered.

Kaitlyn sat on a porch rocking chair, her camera beside her, reviewing the day's photos on her laptop.

The children's artwork had already been scanned and uploaded, but she found herself returning to one image—a candid shot she'd caught of Carla reading to her children under their tree.

The photo was taken from behind, showing only silhouettes against the setting sun. No faces, as promised, but the story was there in every line: the way Carla's shoulders curved protectively around her children, how Christina leaned into her mother's side while helping Dominic follow along with the words, little Jack's hands reaching for the pages. A family holding on to each other in the face of everything that had tried to pull them apart.

The screen of her phone lit up beside her—not a call this time, but an email notification. The preview showed her mother's name and a subject line that made her stomach clench: "Found some old family photos…"

She closed the laptop with more force than necessary, startling a gecko that had been watching from the railing.

"Careful with that," a voice said behind her. "Technology doesn't like rough handling."

Elena stood in the doorway, two mugs of tea sending steam into the cooling air. She handed one to Kaitlyn before settling beside her on another rocking chair.

"Long day," Elena observed, blowing on her tea. "But productive. The children's artwork idea was inspired. Shows exactly what Paradise Harbor House means to the people who matter most."

"It was Carla's suggestion." Kaitlyn wrapped her hands around the warm mug, anchoring herself in the present moment. "She's… she's trying so hard to give them stability. To let them still be children despite everything."

"Sometimes that's the hardest part," Elena said carefully. "Letting people hold on to their joy when the world seems determined to take it away."

She paused, studying Kaitlyn's profile in the fading light. "You understand that better than most, I think."

Kaitlyn's fingers tightened on the mug. "What do you mean?"

"Just that you have a way with our families. Especially the children. You see what they need—whether it's space to draw, or permission not to smile for a camera, or…" She trailed off as voices drifted through the screen door behind them.

Carla appeared, Dominic half-asleep against her shoulder. "He wanted to say goodnight," she explained. "And thank you for putting his tree picture on the computer."

"Of course," Kaitlyn said, managing a smile that felt almost real. "He's quite the artist."

"It's got birds in it," Dominic mumbled sleepily. "'Like a real family tree."

Something sharp and cold twisted in Kaitlyn's chest. Family trees. Branches that split and divided, roots that ran deeper than anyone could see. She stood abruptly, gathering her equipment. "I should go. It's getting late."

"Kaitlyn," Elena called as she reached the gate. "Remember what I said about joy? Sometimes we have to choose it, even when it's hard. Even when it feels impossible."

Kaitlyn nodded and twirled the ring on her right hand. "What do you do when impossible doesn't feel like a strong enough word."

Elena smiled. "Float…you just float."

The walk home was longer than usual, each step weighted with unspoken words. Through windows and over fences, Kaitlyn caught glimpses of other families ending their day—dinners being shared, children being tucked in, the comfortable rhythms of lives unfolding together.

Her phone buzzed again. Another email from her mother: "Please, sweetheart. We need to talk about what you found…"

But how could they talk about it? How could they discuss the photos she'd discovered, the sister she'd never known, the life her father had built while leaving his first family behind? How could any conversation bridge that kind of divide?

The bungalow was dark when she arrived, her aunts still at their evening shift at Margarita Max's. Ernest dozed on the porch railing, one eye cracking open at her approach. She envied him sometimes—his simple world of food and sunshine, unmarred by complicated family histories.

Inside, she put her laptop on the table and opened it. The screen glowed with the Paradise Harbor House website draft.

Christina's drawing smiled up at her—all those figures holding hands, connected by crayon lines and childish hope. Below it, Dominic's tree spread its branches wide, offering shelter to any bird that needed it.

She opened a new browser tab, fingers hovering over the keyboard. One click would take her to the profile she checked compulsively, show her another family's moments—birthdays and graduations, father-daughter dances and family vacations. All the memories that could have been hers in another life, another version of her story.

Instead, she clicked back to the Paradise Harbor House page. These were the stories she needed to tell—of families rebuilding, of hope taking root in unexpected places, of people finding their way forward despite the past's long shadows.

Tomorrow there would be more photos to take, more moments to capture. More chances to help others document their journeys while keeping her own carefully hidden. For now, she let the children's artwork fill her screen, their simple truths drowning out the complicated ones that threatened to overflow.

Through the window, she could see the stars emerging over Key West, each one a pinpoint of light in the gathering dark.

Somewhere out there, another family was ending their day, another sister was living her life unaware. But here, in this moment, Kaitlyn had her own purpose—helping others find their light, even if her own path remained in shadow.

CHAPTER 9

Kaitlyn adjusted the straps of her tote bag as she stepped out of the bakery, the scent of fresh Cuban bread and espresso still lingering in her nose. The bag was loaded with donated pastries for Paradise Harbor House, and the heat of the mid-morning sun made her wish she had grabbed an iced coffee for the walk.

As she turned onto the street leading to the shelter, she slowed at the sight of a man with a camera, crouched near the entrance of Paradise Harbor House. He was filming the building, panning up to catch the sign, then turning his lens toward the side lot where some of the women were tending the small community garden.

Kaitlyn's immediate reaction was suspicion. Her grip tightened around the tote. *Who is this guy? Some influencer trying to get content at the expense of vulnerable women?*

She approached him quickly, her sandals clapping against the pavement.

"Hey! What do you think you're doing?" she demanded, stepping into his shot.

The man glanced up, his striking blue eyes narrowing slightly as he pushed his shaggy brown hair, which fell just below his chin, out of his face. He had a little unshaven scruff—just enough to give him a rugged look, and when he smirked, Kaitlyn found herself momentarily thrown off by how gorgeous his smile was. Charming, irritating, and far too self-assured all at the same time. He wore a plain gray t-shirt and cargo shorts, a camera strap slung across his chest.

"Filming," he said simply.

Kaitlyn folded her arms. "Yeah, I can see that. But why? Because unless you're with the news or someone from the city, I don't think you have permission."

The man sighed and stood, adjusting his camera. "I'm Will. Will Moreno. I'm working on a documentary about the people who live and work in Key West beyond the tourism scene. You know, the ones who don't make it into the glossy brochures. I met Elena a few days ago, and she said it was okay for me to get some exterior shots."

Kaitlyn blinked. "Elena approved this?"

Will smirked. "Did you think I just showed up with a camera and started recording?"

"Honestly? Yes. That happens more than you'd think," she shot back. "Social media vultures love to exploit places like this for pity clicks."

Will's smirk faded. "That's not what I do. I don't chase feel-good stories to go viral. I tell real ones. I was actually about to head inside to talk to Elena again—unless you want to arrest me first."

Kaitlyn huffed but waved toward the door. "Fine. But I'm watching you."

Inside, the air-conditioning was a welcome relief. Elena was speaking with one of the volunteers when she spotted them.

"Will! Good timing," she said, smiling. Then she glanced at Kaitlyn. "I see you've met our skeptical volunteer."

Kaitlyn gave a sheepish shrug. "Sorry. I thought he was just some random guy trying to get content."

Will chuckled. "No hard feelings. I'd probably assume the same thing."

Elena gestured toward the seating area. "Will is interested in telling the story of Key West from a different angle—one that includes places like Paradise Harbor House. I think it could be a good opportunity for us."

Kaitlyn still wasn't convinced. "And how do we know this isn't just a one-off project that will get a few festival screenings and then disappear? These women don't need someone swooping in, putting a lens on their lives, and then leaving like they were some passing inspiration."

Will studied her for a long moment. "That's not how I work. I don't just drop in and grab a few soundbites—I stay. I follow through. That's why my last documentary took two years to make. It's about the people, not the footage."

Kaitlyn folded her arms. "Two years? That's a commitment."

Will nodded. "Yeah. And if I'm lucky, this project will take just as long."

Elena leaned in. "I really do think Will's work could help bring awareness in a way we haven't been able to. I've got to get to my office. Perhaps you can answer any questions Will has." Elena looked at Will. "I'm sure Kaitlyn will be happy to help."

Elena walked away and Kaitlyn looked back at Will. She hated when she was put on the spot, but she also hated the idea of dismissing someone just because she didn't trust easily.

Kaitlyn looked back at Will. "All right. Prove it. Show me your work."

Will didn't hesitate. He grabbed his phone and pulled up a website, scrolling until he found a link. "Here. My last documentary, *Under the Surface*, is about the fishing communities that are being priced out of Florida's coastal towns. No sob stories. Just real people trying to hold on to the life they've built."

Kaitlyn took the phone, watching the short preview video. The footage was raw but striking—stunning ocean shots juxtaposed with interviews of fishermen discussing rising costs, the struggle to keep their businesses afloat, and the impact on their families.

Handing the phone back, she tilted her head slightly. "Okay, so you're not a hack. What beach is that?"

Will smirked. "I'll take that as a compliment. That's Smathers Beach. Haven't you been there?"

Kaitlyn shook her head. "No. I haven't had a chance to check it out. I didn't think there were many good beaches here."

Will let out a soft chuckle, shaking his head. "Now that is a shame. It's one of the best around. I go there all the time. I'd be happy to show it to you."

"Thanks, but I've got too much to do to take a beach day." Her response came out sharper than she intended, and she immediately regretted the defensiveness in her tone. "Besides, I'm more than capable of finding it on my own."

He shrugged, unfazed. "Suit yourself."

Kaitlyn turned and strode from the room, but not before catching the flash of confusion that crossed Will's face. She told herself she couldn't trust him, yet found her gaze drawn to the window throughout the day, watching Will Moreno as he worked outside.

By the time she left Paradise Harbor House that afternoon, her thoughts were still tangled. Will Moreno was…interesting. He wasn't just another tourist chasing a cheap headline. He was thoughtful, and serious about his work, but it didn't change Kaitlyn's opinion that he was someone worth keeping an eye on. *For professional reasons, of course.*

The bell above the door chimed softly as Leah stepped into The Lost Anchor, the sound almost lost beneath the whir of ceiling fans.

The bookstore wasn't on her carefully planned route for the day, but she'd noticed it while walking back from another failed attempt to get local business support for Paradise Harbor House. A hand-painted sign in the window had caught her eye: "Books for every journey, maps for every soul."

The interior was a reader's dream—floor-to-ceiling shelves created intimate nooks and crannies, while comfortable chairs invited lingering. The air smelled of old books and fresh coffee, with something else underneath—salt air drifting in through open windows, reminding visitors they were still in Key West despite the literary sanctuary.

"We're not a tourist shop," a voice called from somewhere behind the shelves. "If you're looking for Hemingway merchandise, try Duval Street."

"Actually, I need books on nonprofit management and grant writing," Leah replied, following the voice. "Preferably something published this decade."

She rounded a corner to find a man sorting through a stack of books, his silver-streaked dark hair falling across his forehead as he worked.

He looked up, and Leah found herself caught by sharp green eyes behind wire-rimmed glasses. He had the kind of face that showed he smiled often, though right now he was studying her with amused skepticism.

"Nonprofit management?" He set down the book he was holding. "That's refreshingly specific. Usually people just want beach reads or local history."

"I like to be specific," Leah said, straightening her shoulders slightly. "It saves time."

"Ah, a pragmatist." He moved toward a different section of shelves with the easy familiarity of someone who knew exactly where everything belonged. "And what worthy cause brings you to the exciting world of grant writing manuals?"

"Paradise Harbor House. We're trying to expand our programs, but—" She paused as he held up a hand.

"Elena's place? The women's shelter?" His expression shifted from mild amusement to genuine interest. "Now that's a story worth telling. Though I'm guessing you're more interested in the funding chapters than the narrative ones."

Leah blinked, surprised by both his knowledge and his insight. "You know about Paradise Harbor House?"

"I know about most things that matter in Key West," he said, pulling several books from different shelves. "Jack Calloway, by the way. Former journalist, current purveyor of literary escapes and caffeinated salvation."

"Leah Lawrence." She found herself charmed despite her usual business-like approach. "Former corporate consultant, current… well, I'm still figuring that part out."

Jack's smile crinkled the corners of his eyes. "Aren't we all?

He handed her a stack of books. "Here, start with these. The green one's outdated on tax law but brilliant on program development. The blue one's new, good for modern fundraising strategies. And this one," he tapped a worn copy of 'To Kill a Mockingbird,' "is just because everyone involved in social justice should revisit it occasionally."

Leah glanced at the classic novel. "I'm not sure I have time for fiction right now. We have deadlines—"

"Always time for fiction," Jack interrupted, leading her toward the café area. "Stories remind us why we do the work in the first place. Coffee?"

She should say no. She had a schedule, a to-do list, three more businesses to visit about donations. Instead, she found herself settling onto a barstool at the counter while Jack moved behind it with practiced ease.

"Cuban roast," he said, starting the coffee maker. "Local blend.

Like everything else worth knowing in Key West, there's a story behind it."

"You seem to know a lot of stories," Leah observed, setting her stack of books beside her.

"Hazard of the former profession. Never lost the habit of collecting them." He placed a mug in front of her, the aroma rich and inviting. "So tell me about Paradise Harbor House. Not the grant version—the real story."

And somehow, in that quiet bookstore with afternoon light filtering through windows clouded by salty air, Leah found herself doing just that. She told him about Elena's tireless dedication, about Kaitlyn's work with the families, about their dreams of expanding services. Jack listened with the focused attention of someone used to finding the heart of a story, asking questions that made her see their work from new angles.

"You know," he said finally, refilling their cups, "I used to host author events here, before the tourist shops took over the local literary scene. Been looking for a reason to restart them. Paradise Harbor House might be just the cause we need."

Leah's practical nature surfaced through her unexpected enjoyment of their conversation. "A fundraiser?"

"Among other things." Jack's smile held a hint of challenge. "Sometimes the best support isn't just financial. Sometimes it's about creating spaces where stories can be shared, where people can connect beyond their immediate needs."

"That's…" Leah paused, realizing she'd completely lost track of time. The afternoon light had shifted, painting the bookshelves in gold. "Actually, that's exactly what we've been trying to articulate in our grant applications."

"See?" Jack tapped the copy of 'To Kill a Mockingbird.' "Fiction helps. Now, about that event—I was thinking we could start with local authors, maybe some readings from shelter residents, if they're interested. Create a real community dialogue."

Leah found herself nodding, her mind already organizing

possibilities. "We'd need to be careful about privacy, make sure everyone's comfortable with the format."

"Of course." Jack's expression turned serious. "I may be out of the journalism game, but I still understand the importance of protecting sources. We'll do it right."

"Thank you so much. We're working on a sunset cruise fundraiser as well. I hope you'll join us."

He smiled and the twinkle in his eye made her heart race.

"I'd love to. When is it?"

"We're still working on that. I'll get the information to you just as soon as I know more."

Looking at him in the warm light of his bookstore, Leah realized she'd completely abandoned her scheduled activities for the day—and for once, she didn't mind. There was something about Jack Calloway that made her want to set aside her spreadsheets and listen to more stories.

"I should go," she said reluctantly, gathering her books. "How much do I owe you?"

Jack waved away her reaching for her wallet. "Consider it an investment in the community. Just promise you'll come back and tell me how the grant writing goes. I may have some contacts from my reporting days who could help."

"I will." Leah turned to leave, then paused. "The coffee was excellent, by the way."

"Come by tomorrow," Jack called after her. "I'll tell you its story."

As she stepped back into the Key West afternoon, Leah realized she was smiling. Her carefully planned day had been thoroughly derailed, but somehow she felt more energized than ever. Maybe sometimes the best plans were the ones that left room for unexpected chapters.

CHAPTER 10

Kaitlyn slumped into her chair at the small kitchen table, exhaustion pressing down on her. She didn't feel much like talking.

Tess studied her for a moment before breaking the silence. "Do you want to talk about the fundraiser?"

Kaitlyn hesitated, then shrugged. "Sure…I guess."

Leah exchanged a glance with Tess before leaning forward. "I think it's time we look into renting the boat, don't you?"

The weight of the evening settled around them, thick and unspoken. Kaitlyn's fingers traced the rim of her water glass, her movements slow, deliberate. Across the table, Leah tapped impatiently against the wooden surface, the soft rhythm filling the spaces where words failed.

Another message from Gretchen lit up Kaitlyn's phone screen, and Leah finally had enough.

"Enough," Leah said, setting her own phone face down on the table. "Kaitlyn, what's really going on with you and your mother? She lived with us all last year. If something was wrong—"

Kaitlyn laughed. "She would have told you?" she interrupted, her voice tight. She stood at the sink, staring out at Ernest's evening patrols, her fingers gripping the edge of the counter as if steadying herself. "Because my mother is a liar."

Shocked, Leah was angry. "Stop that. Whatever is going on with you, your mother doesn't deserve that."

"Oh really? What do you know about what my mother deserves? If she cared about any of us, she would have explained it all. Each of us had a right to know."

Tess set down her spoon, her eyes narrowing. "Know what?"

Kaitlyn's knuckles turned white. The silence stretched long enough for Leah to shift uncomfortably in her seat.

"Kaitlyn," Leah said, her voice softer now, "talk to us."

For a moment, it seemed like Kaitlyn might shut down completely, but then she turned, the tension in her face finally cracking.

"That he has another family. That I have a sister."

The words hung in the air, sucking all sound from the room. Tess's mug stopped halfway to her mouth. Leah's spine straightened as if she'd been shocked.

"What are you talking about?" Leah asked carefully. "Your father and Gretchen divorced when you were in high school. If he had another family, Gretchen would have—"

"She *knew*, Leah." Kaitlyn turned, and there were tears in her eyes despite her fierce expression. "She's *always* known. Since before he left us."

Tess shook her head slowly, horror dawning on her face. "No. That's not…Gretchen would have told us. When she stayed with us, when she was going through the divorce—"

"She didn't tell you because she didn't want *anyone* to know. When he left, she already knew his mistress was pregnant," Kaitlyn said, her voice shaking now. "I found out by accident—right after college graduation. I was scrolling through my Instagram feed when I saw a 'suggested connection'—a woman named Joanna Miller. The name didn't mean anything to me at first, but when I clicked on her profile, I saw *him*. My father. Then I realized who she was. He was smiling in photos with her, holding their daughter at a birthday party, sitting front row at a school recital. Like some perfect family man. Years and years of photos telling a story I had no knowledge of."

Leah's face darkened. "Gretchen *knew*? And she said nothing?"

"She knew," Kaitlyn said, her voice breaking. "She *let it happen*. And not just that—she made sure I never had the chance to know my sister or to see my father. She kept him away from me, Leah. Not because he left, but because she *made* him leave. She punished him for cheating by punishing *me*."

Tess inhaled sharply, covering her mouth. "Oh, sweetheart…"

"She kept my sister from me. She knew about her the whole time, from the moment he walked away from us." Kaitlyn's voice grew stronger, more bitter. "She didn't want me to know I had a sibling. She didn't want me to know the truth. And when I confronted her, she just…she *admitted it* like it was nothing. Like it wasn't my life she was playing with."

Silence fell again, broken only by the whir of the air conditioner and the distant sound of Ernest greeting the evening. Each woman seemed lost in recalculation—of memories, of assumptions, of family bonds they thought they understood.

"Just like Mom and Dad," Tess whispered.

"Stop it, Tess," Leah insisted. "This is nothing like Mom and Dad."

Leah stood slowly, pressing her palm flat against the table as if grounding herself. "We have to talk to Gretchen."

"No!" Kaitlyn spun to face her aunts, her eyes flashing with something between panic and fury. "You *can't*. Please. I don't want her to know I'm here. It will destroy everything."

"Keeping this secret will destroy us more," Leah said softly. "Trust me, secrets like this…they don't stay buried. They rot everything from the inside out."

"Like they're rotting you." Tess spoke gently.

Kaitlyn's shoulders slumped. All the fight seemed to drain out of her at once. "I don't know how to face her. How do you face someone who has spent years lying to you? I don't even know what to say to her right now. I need time."

Tess and Leah exchanged a look—the kind of silent communication that came from years of sisterhood. But this time it carried the weight of their own shock and anger Gretchen had lied to them as well. She lied to Chelsea and now was living on Captiva Island to be near her, still holding on to her secret.

Leah's heart raced. How had they not known? How had they lived with Gretchen for a year and never suspected?

"All right, but Kaitlyn, send your mother a text and tell her you need time. Gretchen should understand that. Not answering her calls at all won't make her stop," Tess said finally. "We'll figure this out together, and when we do, we'll all confront this at the same time."

Leah added, finally moving to pull Kaitlyn into a hug, "Tonight we just…process."

Through the window, they could see the stars emerging over Key West. Somewhere in Miami, another family was ending their day, unaware that their lives were about to intersect with a truth long hidden. And in a small yellow bungalow, three women held on to each other, their own constellation of love and hurt and healing, trying to find their way forward in the face of a past that refused to stay buried.

Kaitlyn sat at her desk at Paradise Harbor House, sifting through a stack of donation receipts. The quiet hum of the morning surrounded her, broken only by the occasional rustle of paper.

She had come in early, hoping the routine would keep her mind occupied, but last night's discussion still pressed heavily against her thoughts. Sunlight streamed through the windows, illuminating dust motes in its path, a soft contrast to the restlessness churning inside her.

Her phone lay face down beside her, silent since she'd sent her mother the brief text Tess had insisted on: "I need time. Please respect that."

The sound of equipment being set up made her look up. Will was arranging his camera near the common room windows, talking quietly with Elena about lighting. The sight of his camera made something twist in her stomach. How many family photos had her father taken with his other daughter while Kaitlyn waited for even a phone call?

"Morning," Will called, noticing her. "The light's perfect for interviews today. Elena thought maybe we could talk about the community outreach program."

"No." The word came out sharp enough to make Elena glance over in concern. Kaitlyn softened her tone with effort. "No interviews. Not today."

Will's eyebrows rose slightly as he studied her. Gone was his usual easy confidence, replaced by something more careful. "Everything okay? You seem…"

"I'm fine." She gathered the receipts into a neat pile, needing order in something. "I just…I don't think we should be recording people's stories right now. Some things aren't meant to be documented."

Elena touched Will's arm lightly. "Maybe we should focus on the building today. The garden, the renovations…"

"Right," Will agreed, but his eyes stayed on Kaitlyn. "Though sometimes telling our stories helps us understand them better."

Kaitlyn's laugh held no humor. "And sometimes stories are just lies we tell ourselves to make the truth easier to swallow."

She thought of all those years her mother had fed her explanations about why her father stayed away, each one calculated to keep her from discovering Joanna, from knowing about her sister.

Will set his camera down entirely, an action that made her look up in surprise. "Want to talk about it? Off the record, obviously."

"Why? So you can understand the human condition better? Get some insight into family dynamics?" The bitterness in her voice surprised even her. "Sorry. That wasn't...I should go check on the donation sorting."

But as she turned to leave, his quiet voice stopped her. "You know what I've learned, doing this work? Everyone thinks their pain is unique. That no one could possibly understand. But sometimes sharing it helps us realize we're not as alone as we think."

Kaitlyn turned back slowly, seeing the genuine concern in his expression. For a moment, she almost wanted to tell him everything—about finding Joanna's Instagram, about her half-sister's life documented in perfect filtered squares, about her mother's years of careful deception.

Instead, she said, "Some stories aren't ready to be told." She gestured at his camera. "Not everything needs to be captured and shared."

Will nodded, accepting her boundary without pushing. "Fair enough. But if you ever want to talk—no cameras, no documentation—I'm a pretty good listener."

Something in his tone, the complete lack of pressure, made her throat tight. "I'll keep that in mind."

As she walked away, she could feel his gaze following her, seeing more than she was ready to show. Her phone buzzed in her pocket—probably another message from her mother—but she left it unanswered. Some truths needed time to settle, to find their own way into the light.

CHAPTER 11

Tess wiped down the bar at Margarita Max's, her movements automatic as her mind wandered back to the new revelations about Gretchen.

The familiar rhythm of Open Mic performances at dinnertime was a welcome distraction and easier to appreciate than the Wannabe Wednesday night karaoke that would begin a few hours later. The gentle clink of glasses, quiet conversations, and none of the tourist chaos that usually filled the place was a welcome change.

"We have to tell Chelsea," Leah murmured, refilling the salt rim tray beside her. A group of regulars waved from their usual corner table, and she acknowledged them with a smile that didn't quite reach her eyes. "She deserves to know what Gretchen's been hiding. They live ten minutes apart on Captiva now."

"One family crisis at a time," Tess replied softly, mixing a mojito for one of their regulars—an older woman who wrote mystery novels and always tipped in cash with a note about which character she'd named after her bartender that week. "Let's figure out how to handle Kaitlyn first."

She broke off as movement near the small stage caught her

attention. A man was settling onto the stool, guitar in hand. Tess found herself pausing in her work, drawn to something in his presence.

He looked to be in his forties, his dark brown hair just starting to silver at the edges, wearing a faded button-down with rolled sleeves that somehow made him look perfectly at home. His fingers moved over the guitar strings with the kind of familiarity that spoke of years of practice.

"Who's that?" Tess asked, unable to look away as he began tuning his guitar. The way his hands moved over the instrument made her think of stories waiting to be told.

Leah followed her gaze, then smiled slightly, the first real smile Tess had seen from her since Kaitlyn's confession. "Jameson Carter. Jamie. Connie said he used to be a regular performer here until…" She hesitated, lowering her voice. "Until his wife passed. He owns the restaurant Harbor Lights, that seafood place on Whitehead."

"The good one with the key lime pie I love?" Tess asked, remembering one of their failed attempts to network with local restaurants. Their 'Island Catering' business cards were still stuffed in a drawer somewhere, another dream that hadn't quite found its footing.

"That's the one. This is the first I've heard him play." Leah's expression turned thoughtful. "Connie says he used to write his own music. Love songs mostly. But after Emma—his wife—died ten years ago, he just…stopped. Packed away his guitar and focused on the restaurant."

"Ten years is a long time to stay silent," Tess mused, watching as he adjusted the microphone.

"It certainly is sad," Leah replied.

Before Tess could respond, Jamie's voice filled the bar, deep and rich as he addressed the crowd. "All right, folks. It's been a while, so go easy on me."

The regulars responded with warm encouragement—these

weren't the usual tourist crowds looking for Jimmy Buffett covers. These were the people who remembered him from before, who had watched his story unfold over years of Wednesday nights. Some even put down their phones, giving him their full attention—a rare sight in any bar these days.

Then he began to play, and Tess felt something shift in her body as his voice wrapped around the bluesy melody. It wasn't just skill—though he had plenty of that. It was emotion, raw and real, the kind that made you feel less alone with your own complicated feelings. She recognized the song—an old Tom Waits number about love and loss and finding your way home.

"Speaking of time healing all wounds," Leah said quietly, but Tess barely heard her. She was caught in the way Jamie lost himself in the music, in how his fingers moved over the strings like they were having a conversation only he could hear. There was something about a man willing to be vulnerable in public that made her breath catch.

When the song ended, the applause was genuine and warm. Jamie acknowledged it with a small, almost shy smile that made something flutter in Tess's stomach. He followed it with two more songs—one she recognized from the radio, and another she suspected was original, though he didn't introduce it as such.

"You're staring," Leah murmured, amusement temporarily replacing her worry about their family drama. "Like you used to stare at that street musician in Faneuil Hall Marketplace."

"I am not," Tess protested, but then Jamie was making his way to the bar, guitar still slung over his shoulder, and all her clever responses deserted her. He moved with an easy grace that spoke of someone comfortable in their own skin, even if that comfort had been hard-won.

"Whiskey?" he asked, his smile hitting her like a physical thing. Up close, she could see the laugh lines around his eyes, the way his hands still moved like they were keeping time to some internal rhythm.

"On the house," she managed, pouring him a glass. The good stuff—not the well whiskey they served to tourists. "That was… you're incredible."

His smile deepened, reaching his eyes. "Thanks. Wasn't sure I still had it. Been a while since I've played for anyone but my empty kitchen."

"Trust me, you do." She found herself leaning slightly closer, drawn in by the warmth in his voice. "So what made you decide to play again?"

Jamie traced the rim of his glass, thoughtful. The gesture reminded her of the way Kaitlyn had held her coffee mug the day before, both of them carrying weights they weren't quite ready to set down.

"Honestly? Something about tonight just felt right. Like maybe it was time to stop living in the past."

The words hit close to home, making her think of Kaitlyn, of Gretchen, of all the ways the past could hold you hostage if you let it.

"I get that," she said softly, meaning it more than he could know.

He met her gaze, something warming in his expression. "So what's your story? You don't seem like the usual Max's bartender."

Tess laughed, the sound surprising her with its genuineness after the tension of the past day. "That obvious?"

"Just a little. Most bartenders I've dealt with don't look at their customers like they're trying to write their stories in their heads."

She hesitated, then offered him a version of the truth. "My sister and I moved here thinking we had it all figured out. Turns out life has other plans sometimes." She gestured at the bar around them. "Though lately I'm starting to think maybe the plans find you, rather than the other way around."

"Best laid plans…" Jamie nodded, understanding in his eyes. "Sometimes you have to let go and see where the music takes you.

Everything I thought I had figured out ten years ago…" He shrugged, but there was peace in the gesture rather than resignation. "Life has its own rhythm."

"Says the man who hasn't played in a decade," she teased, surprising herself with her boldness.

He chuckled, the sound doing interesting things to her pulse. "Touché. Maybe we're both due for some new material. Although, to be fair, I started back up playing guitar several years ago, just not in public."

As if on cue, Leah's phone buzzed.

"It's Kaitlyn," Leah said. "Just checking on us to see if we're all right."

"That's sweet," Tess said, the weight of family obligations reminding her of their difficulties. For just a moment, looking into Jamie Carter's warm eyes, Tess felt like maybe there was room for more than one kind of healing in Key West.

"You should play again next week," she found herself saying. "The regulars would love it." She paused, then added more softly, "I would too."

His smile turned contemplative, a spark of something like hope in his eyes. "Maybe I will. Especially if the audience is this appreciative."

The way he looked at her made it clear he wasn't talking about the whole crowd, and Tess felt warmth spread through her body.

Maybe Leah was right—sometimes time was all you needed to find your way back to the music. Or maybe sometimes you just needed someone to remind you how to listen for it.

Leah, Tess and Kaitlyn went about the next two days feeling numb and unwilling to talk about what Gretchen had done. It wasn't that they didn't want to talk about it further, but rather, just as Kaitlyn had told her mother, they each needed time to process.

Tess was feeding Ernest leftover corn kernels when leah walked into the room.

"Did Kaitlyn go to the shelter?" Leah asked.

Tess shook her head. "Nope. She said she was going to take some quiet time at the beach. I think it will do her a lot of good. I think she finally realized how stressed she is."

Leah nodded. "She's wound so tight, I'm afraid she's going to do something drastic."

"Drastic?" Tess asked.

Leah sighed. "I'm as angry at Gretchen as Kaitlyn is, but I don't want to sever my relationship with my sister because of it. Kaitlyn needs her mother, and heaven help us, we're going to have to help her realize that."

Tess nodded. "I feel the same way. Sooner or later, though, we're all going to have to confront Gretchen, and I can't wait to hear what Chelsea is going to say about all this. She'll be furious."

Leah laughed. "It won't be the first time our oldest sister has been angry at Gretchen."

"Or us, for that matter," Tess added.

"Well, for now, let's let tempers cool. I'm headed to the shelter. I need to talk to Elena about something I've been thinking about," Leah said.

"Ciao!" Tess responded.

Leah found Elena in her office, surrounded by stacks of paperwork. Through the open door, they could hear children's laughter from the backyard, punctuated by the occasional adult voice giving gentle direction. A half-drunk cup of coffee sat forgotten among the papers, probably cold by now.

The walls of Elena's office told their own story—photos of successful transitions, thank-you notes written in careful handwriting, children's artwork preserved in dollar-store frames. A bulletin board overflowed with community flyers, business cards, and what looked like a carefully maintained calendar of appointments and deadlines.

"Do you have a minute?" Leah asked, noting how Elena's desk calendar was covered in scribbled notes and reminders. Red marks in several squares caught her attention—probably bills coming due.

"For you? Always." Elena gestured to the chair across from her desk, pushing aside a stack of donation receipts to create eye contact. "Kaitlyn's been telling me about your business background. Says you're some kind of financial wizard."

"I was hoping to talk to you about that, actually." Leah settled into the chair, trying not to disturb the precarious paper piles. "I've been looking at your website, the programs you offer. You're doing amazing work here, Elena."

"But?" Elena's smile was knowing. She'd clearly heard praise followed by suggestions before.

"But I noticed something. Have you ever considered applying for grants?"

Elena's pen stilled. She set it down carefully, like she was buying time to form her response. "Of course. But running this place…" She gestured at the paperwork surrounding her. A report had slipped partially off the desk—Leah caught the words "monthly expenses" before Elena tucked it away. "There's barely time to keep up with daily operations, let alone learn grant writing. And hiring a professional grant writer?" She shook her head. "That's a luxury we can't afford."

"But you have connections all over Key West," Leah pressed, thinking of how many local business owners seemed to know and respect Elena. "Surely someone—"

"Could help?" Elena's smile held a touch of weariness. "Yes. But asking for help means admitting how precarious our funding is. That could scare away donors, make residents worry about our stability." She met Leah's eyes. "Most of these women have already lost everything once. I can't risk them thinking they might lose this place too."

Understanding dawned. "So you've been handling it all yourself."

"Doing my best." Elena picked up her pen again, twirling it between her fingers. "Monthly donations keep us afloat, but barely. Every time a new family arrives, I wonder if we'll have enough. And now with the sunset cruise fundraiser..." She trailed off, glancing at a budget sheet that seemed to mock her from the corner of her desk.

A child's laughter floated in from outside, followed by what sounded like Carla reading a story. The sounds of life continuing, of healing happening, despite the financial strain evident in this room.

"Let me help," Leah said. The words came naturally, surprising her with their certainty. "I've written countless proposals in the corporate world. Grants can't be that different."

"They're very different," Elena warned, but something in her posture had shifted—a slight relaxing of her shoulders, perhaps. "More complicated in some ways, simpler in others. And the competition for funding is fierce. You're not just selling a product or service—you're asking someone to believe in possibility."

"Then I'll learn." Leah straightened in her chair, feeling that familiar spark she used to get before tackling a new project. "I'll need to brush up on current practices, but–"

"Check out The Lost Anchor, over on Fleming. The owner's an old friend—used to be an investigative journalist before..." She paused, something flickering across her face. "Well, that's his story to tell. But if anyone can help you navigate the world of grant writing, it's Jack Calloway."

Something in Elena's tone made Leah look at her sharply, but Elena was already turning to her filing cabinet, the moment lost.

"Here's our financial history for the past five years. Not pretty, but honest. And this–" She pulled out another folder, this one newer. "Research I started on potential grants before reality got in the way. I'd love to know what you think about the sustainability angle. Several foundations are focusing on that now."

She handed both folders to Leah, then hesitated. "There's something else you should know. We're not just struggling—we're approaching a crossroads. The building needs repairs, our programs need updating, and the demand for our services keeps growing. If we can't find sustainable funding soon…"

"You won't have to close," Leah said firmly. "We won't let that happen."

"We?" Elena's eyebrow rose slightly.

"Yes, we. You're not alone in this anymore." Leah stood, clutching the folders like a lifeline. "I may not know much about grant writing yet, but I know about building cases for support. And Paradise Harbor House? This place sells itself. We just need to tell its story the right way."

"About that storytelling," Elena said, a slight smile playing at her lips. "Jack's actually been working on a book about Key West's hidden communities. He has a way of seeing beyond surface appearances, finding the heart of things." She paused meaningfully. "Rather like someone else I'm getting to know."

"Elena…" Leah started, recognizing matchmaking when she saw it.

"What? I'm just suggesting a valuable resource." Elena's innocent look wasn't fooling anyone. "And Leah? Thank you. Not many people see beyond the surface here."

"I'm learning to look deeper," Leah said softly, thinking of Kaitlyn, of Carla, of all the stories Paradise Harbor House held. Her fingers traced the edge of the folders, feeling the weight of responsibility they represented.

As she left Elena's office, Leah heard the sound of small feet running past, followed by Carla's gentle reminder about indoor voices. A volunteer was teaching someone how to use the computer in the common room, their heads bent together over the keyboard. In the kitchen, someone was baking cookies, the warm smell wrapping around her like a promise.

This place was worth fighting for. And if that meant learning a whole new skill set, spending hours in a bookstore with a former journalist...well, there were worse fates. She smiled, tucking the folders into her bag as she headed toward Fleming Street, toward The Lost Anchor, toward whatever story was waiting to begin.

CHAPTER 12

The bell above the door chimed softly as Leah entered The Lost Anchor, Elena's files weighing down her tote bag. The morning light filtered through dusty windows, catching on book spines and creating warm patterns across worn wooden floors. A few early customers browsed the shelves, coffee cups in hand.

Jack looked up from behind the counter where he was sorting through a stack of new arrivals. His face brightened with recognition. "The nonprofit management expert returns."

"Hardly," Leah said, approaching the counter. "Though I do come bearing evidence of how much help we need." She lifted her bag. "Elena gave me Paradise Harbor House's financial records."

"And you thought reading depressing numbers would be more enjoyable with coffee?" His eyes crinkled with amusement, but she caught genuine interest beneath the teasing.

"Actually, I thought they'd be more manageable with expert guidance." She met his gaze directly. "Elena seems to think you know something about grant writing."

"Elena seems to think a lot of things lately." Jack's tone was dry, but warmth colored his expression. He gestured toward a quiet corner where two comfortable chairs faced each other across a small table. "Let's see what we're dealing with."

As Leah spread out the files, Jack disappeared behind the counter, returning moments later with two steaming mugs. "Cuban roast," he said, setting one beside her. "Brain fuel."

"You don't have to—"

"Rule of the house," he interrupted, settling into the chair opposite her. "Serious conversations require serious coffee." He leaned forward, studying the papers she'd arranged. "Now, show me what's keeping Elena up at night."

For the next hour, they pored over the documents together. Jack asked precise, thoughtful questions, his journalist's instincts zeroing in on key details. His hand brushed hers occasionally as they exchanged papers, each contact sending small sparks through her fingers.

"The story's in the numbers," he said finally, tapping a particularly revealing spreadsheet. "But it's not the whole story. What we need is…"

"The human element," Leah finished. When he looked up in surprise, she added, "That's what Elena said. We're not just selling a service, we're asking people to believe in possibility."

"Elena's smart." Jack leaned back, studying her. "And apparently a bit of a matchmaker these days."

Leah felt heat rise in her cheeks. "She means well."

"She usually does." His smile softened any sting from the words. "Though in this case, her interference might be…fortuitous. For Paradise Harbor House, of course."

"Of course," Leah agreed, trying to ignore how his gaze made her pulse quicken. "So, about these grants…"

"Right." Jack pulled a legal pad toward him, uncapping a pen. "First rule of grant writing—know your audience. Different foundations have different hot buttons. Some want innovation, others want proven track records. The trick is matching your story to their interests without compromising your truth."

As he talked, Leah found herself drawn in, not just by the information, but by his passion for the subject. His hands moved expressively as he explained concepts, his voice warm with enthusiasm. This was clearly more than just a favor for Elena.

"Why do you care so much about this?" she asked during a natural pause. "About Paradise Harbor House, about helping us?"

Jack was quiet for a moment, absently turning his coffee mug between his hands. His expression shifted, becoming more serious. "You know why I left journalism?"

The sudden change in direction caught her off guard. "Elena mentioned there was a story, but said it wasn't hers to tell."

"I was working on an exposé about corporate corruption. Big story, career-making stuff." He set his mug down carefully. "But I got so focused on chasing the story, I missed the human cost. A source I'd promised to protect…well, let's just say I learned the hard way that some truths come at too high a price."

Leah watched his hands, noting how they tensed around the mug. "What happened?"

"She lost everything. Her job, her home, her kids' college funds. All because I was too caught up in being right to remember I was dealing with real lives, not just headlines." He met her eyes. "Elena was running a smaller shelter then. She helped that woman rebuild her life while I was busy winning journalism awards."

"That's why you opened the bookstore?"

"Partly. I needed to do something that helped people find their own stories instead of just exposing others'. And when Elena mentioned what you're trying to do at Paradise Harbor House…" He smiled slightly. "Let's just say I understand what it means to need a fresh start. To have people believe in you when you're rebuilding."

Something in his honesty made Leah want to offer truth in return. "I know something about fresh starts. My sister and I came here with big dreams and no real plan. We failed at everything we tried."

"And yet here you are, trying again." His voice was soft with understanding. "That takes courage."

"Or desperation." She tried to make it sound like a joke, but Jack wasn't smiling.

"You know what I've learned from running this place?" He gestured at the shelves around them. "Every good story has moments of desperation. It's what characters do next that matters."

Their eyes met, and Leah felt something shift between them—a recognition of shared understanding, of walls carefully lowered.

"Besides," he added, his smile returning, "I'm a sucker for a good story. And Paradise Harbor House? That's a story worth telling."

Will stood on the yellow bungalow's porch, second-guessing his decision to come. He'd left his camera at home deliberately—a peace offering of sorts after yesterday's tension at Paradise Harbor House. The morning sun was already fierce, and Ernest the rooster eyed him suspiciously from the withered herb garden.

When Tess answered the door, her expression was curious but not unwelcoming. "Morning."

"Hey, we haven't been formally introduced. I'm Will Moreno. I'm working on a…"

Tess interrupted him. "I know who you are. Elena mentioned you, I'm Tess, Kaitlyn's aunt…well, her other aunt. I think you met Leah already."

Will nodded. "I'm sorry to barge in like this. I stopped by Paradise Harbor House," he said, feeling oddly nervous. "Elena said Kaitlyn hasn't been in. I wanted to apologize if I pushed too hard with the documentary stuff yesterday."

Something flickered across Tess's face—concern, maybe understanding. "She's taking a mental health day. Said something about needing to clear her head."

"Oh." He shifted his weight, debating whether to press further. Kaitlyn's reaction yesterday had suggested something deeper than just discomfort with cameras. "Is she okay? She seemed… off."

"That's not really my story to tell." Tess paused, then added with careful consideration, "But if someone wanted to find her, she mentioned going to Smathers Beach. The quiet end, away from the tourists."

His heart lifted slightly. "Thanks. I, uh, I actually recommended that beach to her."

"Did you now?" The knowing look in Tess's eyes made him want to explain, though he wasn't sure what he'd say.

"It's not…I mean, I just thought…"

"Will?" Tess interrupted his fumbling. "The quiet end of Smathers. That's all I'm saying."

He nodded, already turning toward the steps. "Right. Thanks."

The quiet end of Smathers Beach was exactly as Will remembered it—a stretch of sand far enough from the tourist spots to feel almost private.

He spotted Kaitlyn immediately, sitting near the water's edge, her knees pulled up to her chest. Her blonde hair danced in the breeze, and something about her stillness made him catch his breath.

He approached slowly, making sure his footsteps were audible in the sand. "This spot taken?"

Kaitlyn looked up, surprise flickering across her face before settling into something more guarded. "How did you find me?"

"Your aunt Tess said you might be here." He gestured to the sand beside her. "Mind if I sit?"

She rolled her eyes. "Aunt Tess, of course." She patted the sand which he took as permission.

"I'm glad to see you followed my recommendation. It's a great place to chill."

Kaitlyn nodded but said nothing.

For a while, they just watched the waves, the rhythm of water meeting shore filling the silence between them.

He had a million questions, but he'd wait for Kaitlyn to lead the conversation. For now, he was content just to sit beside her and enjoy the moment.

Kaitlyn had chosen the spot carefully, far enough from the tourist chaos to hear herself think. The waves provided a steady backdrop to her churning thoughts, memories of her father mixing with images from Joanna Miller's Instagram feed— birthday parties, graduations, family vacations she'd never been part of. And now, the family drama was about to blow up into something more than she could handle.

Will's arrival should have annoyed her, but something about his quiet presence felt steadying. He hadn't brought his camera, she noticed. Hadn't tried to turn this into content.

She found herself acutely aware of him sitting beside her—the subtle scent of his soap mixing with the salt air, the way his blue linen shirt pulled across his shoulders as he leaned back on his hands, how his hair caught the morning light. Even with her world in chaos, she couldn't help but notice how attractive he was, especially now, with his usual swagger replaced by genuine concern.

"No camera today?" she asked, more to distract herself from these thoughts than anything else.

"Figured we could both use a break from documenting things." His voice was gentle, free of its usual teasing edge, and something about its warmth made her pulse quicken. "Sometimes it's okay to just…be."

The simple permission in those words—to exist without performing, to hurt without having to explain why—made her fight back tears. She looked out at the horizon, where the ocean met the sky in an endless blue line, very aware of how close he was sitting, how easy it would be to lean into him.

"I used to think everything important needed to be captured," she said finally, sneaking glances at his profile. She'd never noticed before how blue his eyes were or how expressive his hands were when he talked. "Every moment had to be filtered and shared and made perfect. But some things…" She swallowed hard. "Some things shouldn't be pretty. Some truths are messy."

Will was quiet for a moment, letting her words settle between them. His shoulder brushed hers, sending little sparks of awareness through her body.

"You know what I've learned doing documentaries? The real story isn't in the perfect moments. It's in the spaces between them. The quiet truths people carry."

She turned to look at him then, really look at him. His usual confident demeanor had softened into something more authentic, and the combination of strength and vulnerability in his expression made her heart twist. For the first time, she wondered what quiet truths he might be carrying. For the first time, she wanted to know his story as much as she wanted to hide her own.

"Does it get easier?" she asked. "Telling the hard stories?"

"No," he admitted. "But maybe it's not supposed to. Maybe the hard part is what makes them worth telling."

Another wave rolled in, erasing other footprints from the sand. Kaitlyn felt something shift inside her—not healing exactly, but perhaps the beginning of understanding how healing might be possible. And underneath that, a growing awareness of Will as more than just the annoying documentarian who'd challenged her defenses.

"I'm not ready to tell my story yet," she said softly, fighting the urge to reach for his hand.

Will nodded, his shoulder brushing hers again as he leaned back. This time, neither of them moved away from the contact.

"That's okay. Sometimes the best stories need time to find their way into words."

They sat there as the morning grew warmer, two people learning to be comfortable with silence, with the space between what could be documented and what needed to simply be felt.

For the first time in days, Kaitlyn felt like she could breathe—even if her heart was beating a little faster every time Will smiled at her.

After several quiet moments, Will spoke again. "You know, when I first started doing documentaries, I thought it was about capturing perfect moments. Getting the right shot, the perfect lighting, the most emotional soundbite."

He drew patterns in the sand beside him. "Took me a while to learn that real connection happens when the camera's off."

Something in his voice made Kaitlyn turn to him. "What changed?"

"I was filming this story about a fishing community in the Keys. Had all my shots lined up—the weathered boats, the sunrise over the water, all the typical stuff." He smiled, but it held a touch of self-deprecation. "Then one day, my camera broke. Couldn't film anything. I thought the day was wasted, but..." He paused, choosing his words carefully. "That was the day they actually started talking to me. Real talking, not just giving me what they thought I wanted to hear."

Kaitlyn hugged her knees closer, understanding exactly what he meant. How many times had she crafted the perfect Instagram post, trying to tell a story that looked better than it felt? "It's easier to hide behind a lens sometimes."

KEY WEST PROMISES

"Yeah," Will agreed softly. "But harder to really see people that way."

"And harder for people to see you."

Their eyes met, and Kaitlyn felt seen—not as a story to document or an image to capture, but as someone trying to make sense of her own messy truth. She could tell that her words hit him hard. His usual confidence had given way to something more genuine, more vulnerable, and she found herself trusting it in a way she hadn't expected.

"Sometimes I wonder," she said, surprising herself with her honesty, "if I spent so much time documenting the perfect life that I missed the real one happening around me. All those carefully filtered photos, trying to prove something…"

"To yourself or to others?"

The question hit home. "Both maybe." She watched a seabird dive into the waves. "It's funny, I came to Key West thinking I'd document every moment, turn it into content. Instead…"

"Instead, you found something that matters more than likes and followers?"

She thought about Paradise Harbor House, about the women and children finding their way forward, about how none of their healing moments would make for good social media content.

"Yeah. But it's scary too, you know? Being part of something real instead of just observing it."

Will's hand shifted in the sand, his pinky finger barely touching hers—a gesture so subtle it might have been accidental, except for how deliberately still he held himself afterward.

"Scary can be good though. Means you're growing."

The simple touch, combined with his words, made her heart race. Because he understood—really understood—what it meant to step away from the safety of observation and risk being part of the story.

"Will?" She waited until he looked at her. "Thank you. For

coming to find me." She smiled. "And for not bringing your camera."

Nodding, he laughed and then looked at her. "Thank you for letting me stay."

They sat in silence, watching the waves reshape the shoreline, each lost in thought but somehow less alone with their reflections. And if their hands stayed touching in the sand between them, neither felt the need to document or explain it.

CHAPTER 13

Kaitlyn walked alongside Will, their feet leaving parallel tracks in the damp sand. They'd fallen into a routine over the past few days—meeting where the quieter end of the beach offered a refuge from the chaos of their lives.

No cameras, no pretenses, just two people finding comfort in shared silence. A group of early morning joggers passed in the distance, their figures silhouetted against the brightening horizon.

Kaitlyn had barely slept the night before, tossing and turning as memories and possibilities warred in her mind. The weight of her situation felt heavier with each passing day, pressing against her chest until she could hardly breathe. She'd spent hours scrolling through Sarah's Instagram again, memorizing the details of her half-sister's life through carefully filtered squares—volleyball tournaments, coffee shop meetups with friends, family dinners that should have included her.

Will seemed to sense her mood, matching his pace to hers without comment. He'd left his camera behind again, a gesture that meant more to her than she could express.

A small crab scuttled across their path, disappearing into a tiny hole, and Will pointed it out with a quiet smile that made her heart flutter despite her troubled thoughts.

"I have a sister," she said finally, the words tumbling out before she could reconsider. "A half-sister I've never met. That's why...that's why I've been so weird about your documentary stuff. About families and recording everything. It's complicated."

Will stopped walking, turning to face her. The morning breeze ruffled his hair, and his expression held none of its usual playful confidence—just quiet attention. A seabird flew overhead, its cry punctuating the moment.

"Tell me," he said simply.

So she did. Standing there with waves lapping at their feet, Kaitlyn told him everything—about finding Joanna's Instagram, about discovering her father's other life, about her mother's years of deception. The words poured out like a tide finally breaking through a dam.

"Her name is Sarah," Kaitlyn said, her voice catching. "She's sixteen now. She plays volleyball and loves photography—I can tell from her posts. She has my father's smile. Our father's smile. And she has no idea I exist."

She described the moment she'd first seen Sarah's photo—a casual family snapshot at a beach bonfire, their father's arm around her shoulders, both of them laughing at some private joke. How she'd spent hours comparing their features, looking for shared traits, wondering if Sarah had inherited their father's terrible dancing or his love of spicy food.

"The worst part?" Kaitlyn continued, running her fingers through her hair in frustration. "Mom knew. All those years when I was asking about Dad, wondering why he traveled so much, why he seemed to disappear completely—she knew he had another family. She knew I had a sister out there, and when she'd finally had enough and divorced him, she just...she let me think I wasn't worth staying for."

Will listened without interrupting, his presence comforting.

When she finally fell silent, he asked, "Have you thought about reaching out to her?"

"Every day since I found out. And then I think about what it would do to my mom, to everyone..." She picked up a shell, turning it over in her hands. "How do you tell someone their whole life has a chapter they never knew about?"

"Maybe," Will said carefully, "that's exactly how you tell them. As a new chapter, not a revision of everything that came before."

The insight struck her with unexpected force. She looked at him—really looked at him—and felt something shift in her chest. Here was someone who understood the power of stories, who knew how they could hurt and heal in equal measure.

"I'm scared," she admitted, the words barely audible above the surf.

Will's hand found hers, warm and solid. "That's okay. Fear means it matters."

They stood there as the sun climbed higher, hands linked, watching pelicans dive into the waves. For the first time since discovering Sarah's existence, Kaitlyn felt the knot in her throat begin to loosen.

"You know what's weird?" she said finally. "Working at Paradise Harbor House, seeing all these families trying to rebuild, trying to find their way forward...it's made me realize maybe there's no such thing as a perfect family. Maybe it's all just people doing their best with what they have."

Will squeezed her hand gently. "That sounds like wisdom to me."

"Or maybe just exhaustion," she tried to joke, but her smile felt more real than it had in days.

"Want to get coffee?" Will asked, seeming reluctant to let go of her hand. "I know this great little Cuban place that makes the best café con leche in Key West."

Kaitlyn hesitated, then nodded. Maybe it was time to take a

break from the drama and just enjoy her time with Will. There was still plenty of time to figure things out. "Lead the way."

Across town at The Lost Anchor, Leah sat surrounded by grant applications and financial records, Jack's steady presence beside her as they worked. The familiar scent of books and coffee wrapped around them like a comforting blanket, and Leah loved spending time with Jack.

"Look at this," Jack said, pointing to a passage in the guidelines. "They're specifically looking for programs that bridge community divides. Paradise Harbor House's work with local businesses could be the angle we need."

Leah leaned closer, acutely aware of how his shoulder brushed hers. The contact sent a small shiver through her that had nothing to do with the air conditioning. She'd noticed lately how often these small touches occurred—casual brushes that felt anything but casual, moments of contact that lingered just a heartbeat too long.

"Elena's been building those relationships for years," she mused, trying to focus on the words rather than his proximity. "The job training program with local restaurants, the literacy partnership with schools…"

"Exactly." Jack's eyes lit up with that journalist's spark she was coming to recognize. "It's not just about providing shelter—it's about weaving people back into the fabric of the community. That's the story these grant makers want to hear."

He reached for another file, his hand brushing hers in the process. Neither of them commented on the contact, but Leah felt her pulse quicken. They'd been dancing around this growing attraction for days now, each interaction charged with unspoken possibility.

"You're good at this," Leah observed, meaning more than just grant writing.

"At what?"

"Seeing the story beneath the story."

His smile warmed. "Years of practice. Though lately I find myself more interested in being part of the story than just observing it."

The implication hung between them, delicate as a page turning. A customer approached the counter then, breaking the moment, and Jack stood to help them. Leah watched him move through his bookstore with easy grace, noting how he seemed to know exactly what each browser needed—whether it was book recommendations or just space to browse in peace.

When he returned, he carried fresh coffee and a plate of Cuban pastries. "Brain food," he explained, setting them down. "Can't write grants on an empty stomach."

"You're spoiling me," Leah said, but she reached for a pastry anyway.

"Maybe that's the plan." His eyes held hers over the rim of his coffee cup, and Leah felt heat rise in her cheeks.

Hoping he didn't see her reaction, she asked, "Can I ask you a somewhat personal question?"

"Of course."

"Do you smoke cigars? I only ask because I remember my father smoked cigars. Of course, that was a long time ago, but some smells linger."

"Guilty as charged. I learned to enjoy a good cigar the first year I moved to Key West, and I never looked back. I hope the smell isn't offensive."

Leah shook her head. "No, not at all. In fact, I like it."

They worked through the morning, their heads bent together over budget sheets and program descriptions. Jack's expertise in crafting narratives helped transform dry statistics into compelling stories of transformation and hope. Every so often, their hands would brush, or their eyes would meet, and the air between them would grow thick with possibility.

"Tell me something," Jack said during a natural break in their work. "What made you decide to help Paradise Harbor House? Besides Kaitlyn's involvement?"

Leah considered the question carefully. "I think I needed to believe in something again. After all our failed business ventures, after watching our savings disappear chasing dreams that weren't really ours..." She trailed off, surprised by her own honesty. "Paradise Harbor House is different. It's real. The work they do matters."

"And that matters to you," Jack observed softly.

"Yes." She met his gaze. "Doesn't it to you?"

"More than I expected." His voice held a weight that suggested he wasn't just talking about Paradise Harbor House.

Evening found Tess wiping down the bar at Margarita Max's, the usual Wednesday night crowd settling in.

The regulars had their routines—the retired teacher who always ordered a mojito and worked on her crossword puzzle, the local fishermen who gathered to swap stories about the day's catch, the young couple who came in for one drink and always stayed for Jamie's entire set.

Her movements slowed as Jamie took his place on the small stage, guitar in hand. He'd been playing regularly now, each week bringing new songs that seemed to carry messages just for her.

He'd begin right around dinner time when the atmosphere was more relaxed, leaving just before karaoke began. Tonight, he looked different somehow—more nervous than she'd seen him since his first performance back.

"Ladies and gentlemen," he said into the microphone, his voice carrying that slight tremor she'd come to recognize as genuine emotion rather than stage fright. "Got something new for you tonight. Something that's been working its way out for a while now."

He started playing, and Tess felt her breath catch. The melody was gentle but insistent, like waves reaching for shore.

As his voice filled the room, she recognized pieces of their conversations woven into the lyrics—subtle references to fresh starts and second chances, to finding music in unexpected places. There was a verse about a woman who helped someone remember how to smile, and Tess felt tears prick at her eyes.

"New song," Connie commented, passing behind her with a tray of glasses. "Wonder what inspired that."

Tess felt heat rise in her cheeks but didn't respond. She knew exactly what—or who—had inspired it. Just as she knew that Jamie's growing repertoire of original music marked his own kind of healing, his own journey back to the person he used to be.

The song ended, and Jamie's eyes found hers across the room. In that moment, surrounded by the warm glow of neon and the quiet murmur of regulars, Tess felt something settle into place—like a melody finding its harmony.

Later, as Jamie packed up his guitar, Tess approached the stage. The bar had quieted, most customers having drifted out into the night, leaving them in a bubble of privacy.

"That new song…" she began, not quite sure how to express what it had meant to her.

"Yeah?" His smile held a hint of vulnerability she hadn't seen before.

"It was beautiful. Real."

"Been feeling more real lately," he said softly. "Something about the company, I think."

Tess didn't know what to say to that, so she didn't respond.

"You know, I hadn't written anything new in years before… well, before you started working here."

The admission touched something deep in her chest. "And now?"

"Now the music won't stop coming." His free hand found hers, squeezing gently. "Funny how that works."

As she walked home that night, Tess thought about how healing happened in layers—like waves reshaping a shoreline, like music building note by note. Some changes you could see coming, like Kaitlyn's growing trust in Will or Leah's deepening connection with Jack. Others caught you by surprise, like finding your heart opening to new possibilities just when you thought it was permanently closed.

The yellow bungalow glowed welcomingly as she approached, Ernest dozing on his usual perch. Inside, she found Leah at the kitchen table, grant paperwork spread around her like confetti, a soft smile playing at her lips as she read something on her phone—probably a message from Jack.

"Good night?" Tess asked, though she already knew the answer.

"Getting better," Leah replied, looking up. "You?"

"Yeah," Tess said, thinking of Jamie's new song, of the way his eyes held hers as he played. Somehow she didn't want to speak, instead wanting to hold on to the memory of the last few hours, keeping it to herself. So much changed around them, and much of it felt out of their control but wonderful, nonetheless.

Tess had no idea what tomorrow would bring but for now, in their small corner of Key West, hope felt as steady as the lighthouse beam sweeping across the darkness, guiding them all home.

CHAPTER 14

Chelsea Marsden-Thompson stepped out of her car into the humid Key West morning, her designer sundress already wilting in the heat. She hadn't warned her sisters she was coming—hadn't really planned to come at all until Gretchen's increasingly frantic calls about Kaitlyn had pushed her to action.

As the eldest of the Lawrence sisters, Chelsea had long ago accepted her role as family mediator, but lately the weight of that responsibility felt heavier than usual.

After checking in at a small Airbnb a block away from her sisters' place, she dropped her suitcase on the bed and then drove to the yellow bungalow on Fleming Street.

It looked smaller than she remembered from her last visit, its cheerful paint seeming almost defiant against the weathered homes surrounding it. Ernest strutted past eyeing her with what she could have sworn was literary judgment. Some things, at least, hadn't changed.

Before she could reach the door, it swung open to reveal Tess, still in her pajamas, coffee mug frozen halfway to her lips.

"Chelsea?" Tess blinked rapidly, as if her older sister might be a heat-induced mirage. "What are you—how did you—"

"Surprise," Chelsea said, attempting a smile that felt more like a grimace. "Why is it you don't look happy to see me?"

"Don't be silly, of course we're happy...I mean, I'm happy... but..." Tess's eyes narrowed with sudden suspicion. "Did Gretchen send you?"

"No one sends me anywhere, little sister." Chelsea followed Tess inside. The air conditioning hit her like a blessing. "But yes, she's been on my front porch several times in the last two weeks. Something about Kaitlyn not answering her phone and you two harboring a runaway."

"Gretchen knows Kaitlyn is here? How is that possible?"

"Yes, our sister knows. She was ready to high-tail it down here until I stopped her. I'm not going to be able to keep her away from Key West for much longer, though. I figured it was best I come down ahead of her and find out what in the world is going on. All Kaitlyn had to do was contact her mother and I'd be home on Captiva enjoying the beach and eating Maggie Moretti's scones."

"It's more complicated than that," Tess said, her voice carrying an edge Chelsea hadn't heard before.

"It usually is." Chelsea sat down, taking in the eclectic decor—the mix of thrift store furniture and beach-themed accessories that somehow worked together. "Where's Leah?"

"Paradise Harbor House. She's helping with some grant applications." Tess hesitated. "And Kaitlyn's there too, volunteering."

"Paradise Harbor House? What's that?"

"It's a women and family shelter. They do really good work, Chelsea. You'd be proud of Kaitlyn…"

Chelsea held up her hand to stop Tess mid-sentence. "I don't care if she's pretending to be Mother Teresa. Get her out of there and back home where I can talk to her." Chelsea seemed to suddenly understand the change in her niece. "Wait, did you say Kaitlyn is volunteering at a shelter?"

Tess nodded. "That's right."

Chelsea raised an eyebrow. "Our Instagram-obsessed niece is volunteering at a shelter?"

"People change," Tess said quietly. "Sometimes because they have to."

Before Chelsea could respond, the screen door banged open and Leah burst in, her face flushed with urgency. She stopped short at the sight of Chelsea, emotions flickering across her face too quickly to read.

"Chelsea? What are you—never mind. We have bigger problems." She turned to Tess. "The shelter's main air conditioning unit just died. In July. Elena's trying to get emergency repairs, but…"

"But it's hurricane season and every AC company is already booked solid," Tess finished, understanding dawning. "What about the fundraiser planning money?"

"We can't touch that," Leah said. "It's barely enough for the cruise deposit as it is."

Chelsea looked between her sisters, noting the way they communicated in half-sentences and shared glances. Something had shifted in their dynamic—a new purpose that hadn't been there during their failed business ventures.

"How much?" she asked.

Both sisters turned to her. "What?"

"The air conditioning repairs. How much?"

Leah named a figure that made Chelsea wince. "But it's not just about the money," she added. "We need someone who can do it immediately. The shelter has children, elderly residents—they can't wait in this heat."

Chelsea was already pulling out her phone. "Give me two minutes. I know someone who knows someone." At her sisters' surprised looks, she shrugged. "What? You think you're the only ones with Key West connections? I've been coming here for art shows for years."

Chelsea made the call, and when she hung up, Kaitlyn walked in, deep in conversation with a tall man carrying camera equipment. She stopped abruptly at the sight of her aunt, color draining from her face.

"Aunt Chelsea?"

"Surprise number two," Tess murmured.

Will, who Chelsea assumed must be Kaitlyn's new boyfriend, spoke up. "I should go. Kaitlyn, call me later?"

Kaitlyn nodded, her eyes never leaving Chelsea. As Will left, the tension in the room thickened like storm clouds gathering.

"Did Mom send you?" Kaitlyn's voice was tight, defensive.

"Why does everyone assume I'm Gretchen's messenger?" Chelsea sighed, sinking into the sofa. "I came because something's obviously wrong, and unlike your mother, I've learned that sometimes you have to show up in person to understand the whole story. Besides, and you need to trust me on this, you do not want to see your mother right now."

The words hung in the air, heavy with unintended significance. Kaitlyn's face crumpled slightly before she caught herself.

"You want the whole story?" She pulled out her phone, fingers shaking slightly as she pulled up an Instagram page. "Here's the whole story. Meet Sarah Miller, my half-sister. The one Mom never told me about. The one she never told you or Aunt Tess or Aunt Leah about. The one she's been hiding for years."

Chelsea took the phone, her breath catching as she looked at the photo on the screen. The resemblance to Kaitlyn was unmistakable.

"That's not possible," she whispered, but even as she said it, memories began realigning themselves—Gretchen's peculiar behavior during the divorce, her insistence on handling all communication with her ex-husband, her sudden move to Captiva Island when her time in Key West fell apart.

"Oh, it's possible," Kaitlyn said bitterly. "Mom knew the whole time. She knew he had another family, knew I had a sister out there, and she just…she let me think he abandoned us for no reason." She corrected herself. "Well, not for no reason. There was obviously another woman. I understood that, but I had no idea she'd been in the picture for years. And Mom just lived with it."

Chelsea looked at her sisters, seeing the truth in their faces. "You knew about this?"

"Found out recently," Leah said softly. "We've been trying to figure out how to tell you, and how to deal with Gretchen. Apparently, Kaitlyn only recently found out about it through the internet."

"Because Gretchen now lives ten minutes from you on Captiva," Tess added, "we weren't sure…"

"Weren't sure if I was in on it too?" The hurt in Chelsea's voice was genuine. "I would never—" She stopped, taking a deep breath. "I would never keep something like this from any of you. But why in the world would Gretchen?"

The sound of a phone ringing cut through the tension. Leah grabbed it, relief washing over her face. "It's Elena." She listened for a moment. "Yes, he's there now? We'll be right there."

She hung up, turning to the others. "The AC repairman Chelsea called is at Paradise Harbor House. We should go back and see if Elena needs help with the families. Maybe we just take them to the beach or something until it's repaired."

"That was fast," Kaitlyn said.

Tess smiled. "Have you forgotten how your aunt Chelsea gets things done?"

"Well, that and apparently the guy was already next door having a beer. He didn't have to walk far," Leah added.

"I'll come too," Chelsea said, standing. "I'd like to see this place that's got you all so invested." She turned to Kaitlyn. "Honey, we'll figure this out. Why don't you come along and show me where you volunteer. I want to see what's more important than being an Instagram influencer."

They all walked to Paradise Harbor House, each woman lost in her own thoughts. The large Victorian house came into view and several adults and children sat outside on the porch. Chelsea thought the place seemed cheerful and welcoming, despite the peeling paint in spots.

Elena met them at the door, her relief evident as she led them to where the repairman was already working.

"It'll take a few hours," the man said, wiping sweat from his brow, "but I can fix it. Might want to move some of your more vulnerable residents somewhere cooler in the meantime."

"They can come to our place," Tess offered immediately. "It's not huge, but the AC works."

Elena's grateful smile was interrupted by a crash from upstairs, followed by the sound of running feet. Carla appeared at the top of the stairs, her youngest child on her hip.

"Sorry!" she called down. "Dominic was trying to help pack up some toys and knocked over some books. Everything's fine!"

Chelsea turned to Leah. "I don't know what you mean when you say your place isn't huge. You must have meant to say that it's the tiniest house in Key West." She then turned to Elena. "Why don't we all have a nice lunch over at The Pizzeria…my treat!"

Kaitlyn laughed. "Seriously, Aunt Chelsea? All of us?"

Chelsea smiled. "You bet. We can all have ice cream after and by then, I'm sure the air conditioning will be fixed."

Elena sighed and extended her hand. "That's very kind of you, thank you. We haven't been formally introduced. I'm Elena Armstrong. I'm the Director of Paradise Harbor House."

Chelsea shook Elena's hand. "Chelsea Marsden-Thompson, but please, call me Cheslea."

As they all walked to The Pizzeria, Chelsea's phone buzzed. Gretchen's name flashed on the screen, and for the first time in their lives, Chelsea hit 'ignore' on her sister's call.

Some revelations required space to process. Some betrayals needed time to heal. And sometimes, she was learning, the strongest thing a big sister could do was step back and let the truth find its own way forward.

Later, as they sat around the bungalow's kitchen table, fans whirring against the evening heat, Chelsea looked at her family—at Leah's determined focus as she worked on her paperwork, at Tess's quiet strength as she prepared salads, and at Kaitlyn's vulnerable courage as she showed her aunt more photos of the sister she'd never met.

"What do we do now?" Kaitlyn asked softly.

Chelsea reached across the table, taking her niece's hand. "Now? Now we figure out how to move forward. We're going to have to try our best to listen to what your mother has to say, and why she did what she did. We'll make no progress if we all keep talking about how angry we are. There has to be a reason your mother wouldn't, or couldn't, tell us the truth. You know," Chelsea said, watching Ernest strut past with his usual literary dignity, "sometimes things have to break completely before they can be fixed properly."

"Is that your artistic wisdom talking?" Tess teased, but her eyes were serious.

"No," Chelsea replied, thinking of Gretchen, of Sarah, of all the broken pieces waiting to be reassembled. "That's just life. We have no idea if Sarah and her mother want anything to do with our family. We can't put everything on your mother. We need to get to the truth. We need to get everything out on the table. It's the only way this family heals."

CHAPTER 15

Chelsea sat on the bungalow's porch in the early morning light, coffee growing cold beside her as she scrolled through Sarah Miller's Instagram feed for the third time.

Each photo felt like a punch to the gut—not just because of the girl's uncanny resemblance to Kaitlyn, but because of what these images represented. Years of family gatherings, holidays, and milestones that should have included both sisters. Years of Gretchen's careful deception.

Ernest strutted past, pausing to eye her coffee cup with his usual literary criticism. The rooster had become an odd source of consistency in the chaos of the past twenty-four hours.

"Don't even think about it or you'll be taking a nap on a plate tonight," Chelsea warned. "How'd you like to be thought of as the main course?"

"He prefers 'literary consultant,'" Leah said, appearing in the doorway with her own coffee. "We thought about naming him Hemingway but decided Ernest was a better fit. And he's very particular about proper coffee appreciation."

Chelsea managed a weak smile. "How long did it take you to process this? About Sarah, I mean?"

Leah settled into the chair beside her, considering. "Still processing, honestly. Every time I think I've wrapped my head around it, I remember something else—some conversation with Gretchen, some moment that means something entirely different now."

"I feel the same. That whole mess when you all came to Captiva the first time and I came running after you to give you money to get started. And then, my wedding. I can't stop thinking about it all. She's moved to Captiva and we've become close, at least closer than we have in years. She's had plenty of time over these last few months to tell me."

Leah nodded. "I know. The whole thing is crazy. Why would she do this? It's one thing not to tell us, but her own daughter? What could she have been thinking?"

"I was thinking about when Kaitlyn came to stay with me right after high school. She didn't want to go to college, and I think she spent that summer on Captiva to get away from her mother. Gretchen could have told both of us then. It would have been the perfect opportunity."

Leah nodded. "I'd forgotten about that. You know what I love? I love that our sweet niece runs to her aunts when life gets too tough. I hate to see her hurt, but it warms my heart to know that she runs to us when she is."

Chelsea laughed. "Leave it to Kaitlyn to come to three childless women for advice."

Leah chuckled. "You've got a good point there. I guess she gets all our undivided attention because of that. Kaitlyn's the daughter we never had."

"Have you called her?" Chelsea asked, though she already knew the answer. None of them had responded to Gretchen's increasingly frequent attempts at contact.

"What would I say? 'Hey sis, remember all those times you talked about honesty and family? Funny story…'" Leah shook her head. "I'm not ready."

Chelsea shrugged. "Well, by now, she's got to realize that we all know the truth. She'll be in Key West any day now. You mark my words."

Chelsea and Leah watched as a delivery truck backed up to Paradise Harbor House. The shelter was coming back to life after yesterday's air conditioning crisis, its routines returning to normal even as their family's foundations shook.

Leah nodded toward the street where Will approached with his camera equipment. "Kaitlyn agreed to let him document some of Paradise Harbor House's programs today. Elena thinks it'll help with grant applications."

Will waved to them as they watched him set up his tripod, his movements careful and precise. Kaitlyn emerged from the house, and even from the porch, Chelsea could see how her niece's whole demeanor changed around him—softening, opening up.

"He's good for her," Chelsea observed. "Her face lights up when he smiles at her."

"Wouldn't you if you were her? The guy is gorgeous, and sweet," Tess said, joining them with a plate of Cuban bread from the bakery. "Will gets her. He's kind and patient with everyone. You should see how he handles the shelter residents—always asking permission, always making sure they're comfortable with being filmed."

Kaitlyn looked more put-together than she had yesterday, though shadows still lingered under her eyes.

"Morning," she said cautiously, her gaze flickering between her aunts. "Will's going to interview Carla today. She finally agreed, as long as we don't show the kids' faces."

"That's huge," Tess said. "She hasn't wanted to talk to anyone about her story."

"I know." Kaitlyn's pride was evident. "She's starting training at Harbor Lights today too. Jamie created a position specifically for her."

Chelsea raised an eyebrow at Tess, noting her sister's slight blush at the restaurant owner's name. Clearly, there were other developments she needed to catch up on.

"Who's Jamie?" Chelsea asked, staring at Tess, who blushed and walked away.

Leah smiled. "That's a topic for another day," she whispered so she didn't disturb Elena's phone call.

"Yes, I understand the importance of proper permits," Elena said, her tone professionally pleasant despite the tension in her shoulders. "But surely there's some way to expedite…I see. Yes, thank you anyway."

She hung up, managed a smile, and said, "Good morning, everyone. Will, Carla's ready whenever you are. She's in the garden with the children."

As Will and Kaitlyn headed toward the back of the house, Chelsea found herself drawn to the bulletin board in the common room. It was covered in success stories—photos of women holding apartment keys or job offers, children's artwork, thank-you notes written in various hands. All these lives touched by this place, all these stories of healing and hope.

"Impressive, isn't it?" Elena appeared beside her. "Sometimes I look at this board when funding falls through or bureaucracy gets overwhelming. Reminds me why we keep fighting."

"Is that what the phone call was about? Fighting bureaucracy?"

Elena sighed. "Building permits for some necessary repairs. Everything takes twice as long and costs three times as much as it should. But we'll figure it out. We always do."

Through the window, they could see Will setting up his equipment in the garden. Carla sat on a bench nearby, watching her children play while answering his preliminary questions. Her posture was tense but determined.

"She's come so far," Elena said softly. "When she first arrived, she wouldn't even let us take her photo for our files. Now she's willing to share her story to help others."

In the garden, Dominic was showing Will his collection of toy cars, explaining something with great enthusiasm while his mother looked on with a mixture of pride and protective concern. Christina helped Jack arrange his blocks, her natural caregiving instincts evident even in play.

"Jamie's taking a risk," Elena continued. "Training someone with no restaurant experience, working around school schedules for the kids. But he believes in second chances. She'll start tonight, and I know everything will work out for her and her family with all of us helping and believing in her."

"Seems to be a lot of that going around," Chelsea observed, thinking of her sisters' own journey of reinvention. "Jamie? Is he a good guy?" she asked, wondering how important he was to Tess.

Elena nodded. "One of the best. Jack's a good man too. We're lucky to have such support."

Inside, the shelter hummed with activity. Women attended job training workshops, worked with counselors, or simply found quiet moments to breathe and plan. Children's laughter echoed from the playroom where volunteers led activities. It was organized chaos, but chaos with purpose.

Chelsea watched as Leah spread grant paperwork across a table, Jack beside her offering guidance. Their heads bent close together as they worked, and Chelsea didn't miss the way their hands brushed "accidentally" as they reached for the same document.

"Your sisters have become integral parts of our community," Elena said, following her gaze. "Sometimes the right people find us exactly when we need them."

Chelsea marveled at how much her sisters had changed in such a short time. The self-absorbed women she had once known were long gone. She had always believed that Gretchen was the stable, responsible sibling, stuck in a marriage with a husband who didn't appreciate her. But now, Chelsea wasn't so sure which of her siblings were truly the stable ones.

At Harbor Lights, Carla stood in the gleaming kitchen, taking in the professional equipment with wide eyes. Jamie moved around the space with practiced ease, explaining procedures and safety protocols while Will filmed discreetly from the corner.

"We'll start you on prep work," he said, "then move on to basic cooking techniques. The hours work around your kids' schedules, and there's room for advancement if you're interested."

Carla nodded, her fingers twisting the edge of her apron. "I've never...I mean, I cook for my family, but nothing like this."

"Everyone starts somewhere," Jamie said kindly. "And you've got something that can't be taught—determination."

Tess appeared in the doorway then, and Chelsea noticed how Jamie's whole demeanor brightened. Another piece of the puzzle clicking into place.

"Thought we'd stop by and see how everything's going," Tess said, though her eyes were fixed on Jamie.

"Perfect timing," Jamie replied. "We're about to start Carla's training with the world's most important kitchen skill—organizing everything before you begin preparations."

"Everything in its place," Tess translated, smiling at Carla.

Will finished taking photos of Carla at Harbor Lights and walked back toward Kaitlyn's place. He'd parked there earlier hoping he'd have some quiet time with her. So much was going on around them, unless they escaped to the beach, they weren't getting much time to spend, just the two of them.

When he reached her house, he packed up his equipment and then spent a few minutes cleaning the inside of his car before knocking on her door.

Kaitlyn and her aunts were gathered around the kitchen table with takeout from Harbor Lights. The day's events had left them all quietly contemplative.

"I've been thinking," Chelsea said finally, setting down her fork. "About Sarah."

Kaitlyn tensed slightly but nodded for her aunt to continue.

"She deserves to know about you, Kaitlyn. I think after all this time, your mother won't fight you on that."

"I know," Kaitlyn said softly. "But how? How do you just appear in someone's life and say, 'Surprise, I'm your secret sister'?"

"First of all, what makes you so sure she doesn't know about you? Just because your mother kept this from all of us doesn't mean your father or his new wife kept you a secret from Sarah."

"That's right, Kaitlyn. It's possible she already knows about you," Leah added.

"I don't know," Kaitlyn said. "I don't know how to…"

"Carefully," Chelsea replied. "With support. With understanding that her world is about to shift just as much as yours did." She paused, choosing her next words carefully. "And maybe with the help of someone who knows how to tell difficult stories with sensitivity."

They all looked toward the window where Will was hanging around his car looking like a lost puppy. His camera gear packed away after a day of documenting other people's journeys toward truth and healing, Chelsea could tell he was waiting for the right time to come inside.

"He'd help," Tess said quietly. "If you asked."

Kaitlyn nodded, tears gathering in her eyes. "I'm just…I'm scared. What if she hates me? What if she blames me somehow?"

"Then we'll deal with that together," Leah said firmly. "That's what family does—the real kind, not the Instagram perfect version."

Through the window, they could see Ernest settling in for the night, his silhouette regal against the darkening sky.

Chelsea's phone buzzed again—Gretchen, still trying to reach them. She silenced it, knowing she'd answer her sister soon.

"You know what else family does?" she said, reaching for her niece's hand. "Family shows up. Even when it's hard. Even when it's scary. Even when the timing isn't perfect."

"Even when you're not sure you're ready?" Kaitlyn asked softly.

"Especially then," Chelsea confirmed, thinking of her own impulsive flight to Key West, of all the ways love made you brave even when you didn't feel ready at all. "But right now, there's a young man outside who, if you don't go out and talk to him, might start talking to Ernest."

They all laughed, and for a moment all negativity was put aside, in favor of watching two young people find joy in the simple act of holding hands.

CHAPTER 16

*L*eah's phone rang just before dawn, Ernest's early morning strut temporarily halted by the unexpected sound. She knew who it was before she even looked at the screen. After days of avoiding her sister's calls, something told her it was time to answer.

"Leah?" Gretchen's voice crackled through the line, tight with tension. "Please don't hang up."

Leah stepped onto the porch, closing the screen door softly behind her. "I'm here."

"You all know, don't you? About Sarah?" A pause, heavy with unspoken words. "About everything?"

"Yes." Leah watched Ernest resume his morning routine, trying to keep her voice steady. "How could you, Gretchen? How could you keep this from us? From Kaitlyn?"

"I was trying to protect her—"

"From what? From knowing she has a sister? From having a relationship with her father?" Leah's whispered words carried years of accumulated hurt. "Do you have any idea what this has done to her? The rest of us are old enough to understand how difficult divorce can be. No one will judge you for that, but

Kaitlyn is different. You've made her feel that she can't trust you. Was it worth it? Do you not understand how damaging this is?"

"Of course I do!" Gretchen's voice cracked. "I've watched her Instagram posts, seen how she's changing, how she's…For Heaven's sake, Leah, she's working at a women's shelter? My daughter, who used to care more about followers than people, is helping families rebuild their lives. Don't you think that's killing me? Knowing she had to run away from me to find herself?"

"She didn't run away from you," Leah said softly. "She ran away from the lies and didn't know what to do with the pain. You should feel proud of her for not doing something far worse than running to her aunts."

The silence stretched between them, filled only by the sound of early morning Key West stirring to life.

"I'm coming to Key West," Gretchen said finally. "The car is already packed. I should get there by dinnertime. I appreciate that Chelsea went down ahead of me, but I can't wait one minute longer. She's my daughter and I need to be with her."

"Gretchen—"

"No, listen. Thanks to the internet, I know about the fundraiser cruise, and all the work you all are doing. I know you're all involved now—you and Tess and Chelsea. I know about the guy with the camera who looks at my daughter like she's the answer to every question he's ever had. I know about Jamie and Jack and how you're all building lives there while I've been…" She took a shaky breath. "While I've been hiding from the truth."

"How do you know all that?"

"I've spent every minute searching the internet for anything I can find about what's going on down there. I've started following Paradise Harbor House and have seen the photos, read about the work you're doing. And I've seen Kaitlyn… really seen her, maybe for the first time. I'm so proud of her."

Leah sank into one of the porch chairs, suddenly exhausted.

"Does Jeffrey know what's going on? You're going to have to tell him."

"I called him last night." Another pause. "He wants to come too. With Sarah."

"Are you kidding me?" Leah pressed her free hand to her forehead. "You can't just ambush Kaitlyn like that."

"I know. That's why I'm calling you first. I need help doing this right. For once."

The sun was properly rising now, painting the sky in shades of pink and gold. Through the window, Leah could see Chelsea moving around the kitchen, starting coffee for everyone.

"The fundraiser's important," Leah said finally. "To all of us, but especially to Kaitlyn. Don't make it about our family drama."

"I won't. I just...I need to see her. To explain. To try to fix what I did."

"Don't rush things, Gretchen. Give it time. What you have to realize is that it isn't just Kaitlyn you need to think about. Sarah is a young woman who is about to learn she has a sister. Not to mention, I have no doubt you're going to have to deal with his wife. Be patient with everything and build back trust with your daughter."

"When did you get so wise?" A hint of the old Gretchen surfaced in her voice—the sister who used to tease them about their dreams.

"Around the same time I started tending bar and writing grant proposals," Leah said dryly. "Life's funny that way."

After she hung up, Leah sat watching the morning unfold. Chelsea's phone dinged inside—no doubt Gretchen texting her next. The text would be brief but decisive: *I'm coming to Key West. Today. Don't try to talk me out of it.*

Kaitlyn's face was buried in her pillow as she slept on the sofa. Leah signaled to Chelsea and Tess to join her outside.

"She sounded different," Leah said. "Scared, maybe. I've never heard Gretchen scared before."

"Good," Tess muttered, but there was more worry than vindication in her tone. "Maybe now she understands what Kaitlyn's been going through."

"It's not that simple," Chelsea said, making both sisters jump. "You know Gretchen—she probably thinks she's been protecting everyone all these years."

"By lying?" Tess's voice rose slightly. "By letting Kaitlyn think her father just forgot about her? Moved on without a backward glance?"

"Lower your voice," Leah warned, glancing toward the house "Kaitlyn's still sleeping."

"Actually, I'm not."

They turned to find Kaitlyn in the doorway, still in her pajamas, phone clutched in her hand like a lifeline. She looked younger somehow, vulnerable in a way that made Chelsea's heart ache.

"How much did you hear?" Chelsea asked gently.

"Enough." Kaitlyn moved to the coffee pot, her movements mechanical. "Mom's coming. Today. And you're all trying to figure out how to handle it without upsetting me further."

"Honey—" Tess started, but Kaitlyn shook her head.

"Don't. Please. I can't handle anyone else trying to protect me right now." She turned to face them, gripping her empty mug. "Did she say anything about Dad? About Sarah?"

Leah exchanged a glance with Chelsea before answering. "She called him last night. They want to come too."

The mug slipped from Kaitlyn's hands and landed on the steps, and she started to cry. Tess was there instantly, steadying her niece with an arm around her shoulders.

"I can't," Kaitlyn cried. "I can't do this today. The fundraiser…"

"Is exactly why you can do this," Chelsea said firmly. "You'll be surrounded by people who love you, who support you. The whole community will be there."

"That's worse!" Kaitlyn pushed away from the counter, starting to pace. "Everyone will see. Everyone will know."

"Know what?" Leah asked quietly. "That families are complicated? That sometimes people make mistakes and have to find their way back to each other? Isn't that exactly what Paradise Harbor House is all about? Besides, you don't have to tell anyone about anything. You just focus on the people who need your help. But even if anyone asks what's going on, they'll understand."

"That's different. Those families…they're trying to rebuild. They're trying to move forward. This is just everyone's lies catching up to us. This is self-inflicted drama."

"Then maybe it's time," Tess said. "Maybe it's time for the truth to have its say. You can't live your life in a bubble. Not if you want it to be authentically yours."

Kaitlyn's phone buzzed in her hand—Will, checking in as he did every morning. She stared at the screen, not reading the message.

"What if I'm not ready?" she asked, her voice small. "What if Sarah isn't? What if we're all just pretending we can fix something that's been broken for years and needs to stay buried?"

Chelsea moved to her niece, taking the phone gently from her trembling hands. "Honey, look at me. You've spent all this time helping other people face their fears, rebuild their lives. Maybe it's time to let people help you do the same."

"But the fundraiser—"

"Will happen," Leah said firmly. "With or without the family drama. Paradise Harbor House's work is bigger than our problems."

"And you won't be alone," Tess added. "We'll all be there.

Jamie's helping us handle the catering, Jack's bringing his publishing contacts and will make sure it gets promoted the way it should, Will's documenting everything…"

At Will's name, Kaitlyn's expression shifted slightly. "Will. Oh no, he can't film this. He can't—"

"He won't," Chelsea assured her. "He cares about you, Kaitlyn. The real you, not the story. This is hardly something to be documented."

"What about Mom? She's coming here for a confrontation. It isn't the time or the place."

"You leave your mother to us," Chelsea said. "We'll make sure she understands what's at stake. We're not going to let her control the narrative."

"Not this time," Leah added with a chuckle. "This time, she's going to have to listen to her sisters, even the younger ones."

There was much work going on at Paradise Harbor House to prepare for the fundraiser, and although Chelsea was certain she could handle Gretchen, she silently worried about the drama that was about to unfold.

Will arrived as they were clearing breakfast, his camera conspicuously absent. He took one look at Kaitlyn's face and seemed to understand immediately.

"Want to take a walk?" he asked softly. "We should look around the block to see if there are additional photos I can take for the setup."

It was a transparent excuse to get her out of the house, but Kaitlyn accepted gratefully. As they left, Chelsea watched the way Will's hand found the small of her niece's back, steadying her without constraining her.

"He's good for her," Tess observed, echoing Chelsea's thoughts.

"Speaking of good for people," Chelsea couldn't resist adding, "when do I get to properly meet this Jamie I keep hearing about?"

Tess blushed but was saved from responding by Elena's entering the room. She looked harried but determined, clipboard in hand.

"The cruise captain needs final numbers," she said, then paused, noting the tension in the room. "What's wrong?"

"Our sister's coming," Leah explained. "Kaitlyn's mother. It's complicated."

Elena's expression softened with understanding. "Family usually is. Is this going to be a problem for Kaitlyn or the fundraiser? Anything I can do?"

"Thanks, but no," Chelsea said firmly. "We're not letting family drama derail something this important. Besides," she added with a slight smile, "sometimes the best way to handle difficult conversations is with witnesses around."

"And an open bar," Tess muttered.

"I heard that," Leah said. "And no—we're keeping our heads clear throughout the entire party. There's too much at stake."

Through the window, they could see Will and Kaitlyn walking slowly toward Paradise Harbor House, their heads bent close in conversation. Even from a distance, the intimacy between them was evident.

Chelsea's phone dinged. Another text from Gretchen: *I've booked a room at the Cypress House. Please don't tell them I'm coming. I need to do this my way.*

"Too late," Chelsea murmured, but she didn't respond to the text. Some conversations needed to happen in person, face to face with nowhere to hide, and she was tired of the constant lying.

By late afternoon, the humidity had thickened to an almost visible haze. Chelsea sat with Elena in her office, discussing last-minute details for the fundraiser, when Carla appeared in the doorway.

"There's a woman asking for Kaitlyn," she said. "Says she's her mother."

The words seemed to stop time for a moment. Through the window, Chelsea could see Gretchen standing on the porch, looking smaller and more uncertain than Chelsea had ever seen her sister appear.

"Well," Elena said softly, "I guess it's time."

Chelsea stood, smoothing her dress in an automatic gesture. "I'll get Kaitlyn. She's in the garden with Will."

But before she could move, Kaitlyn appeared behind Carla, as if some sixth sense had alerted her to her mother's presence. Will stood just behind her, close enough to support but far enough to give her space.

"Mom," Kaitlyn said, her voice carrying down the hallway. "You're early."

Gretchen stepped into view, her carefully maintained composure cracking slightly at the sight of her daughter. She looked at Chelsea, realizing that her sister didn't keep her arrival a secret.

"Kaitlyn, honey. We need to talk."

"Yes," Kaitlyn agreed, and something in her tone made Chelsea's heart ache. "We do, but not here."

The two women stared at each other across the entrance hall of Paradise Harbor House, years of secrets and silence stretching between them like a chasm. But before either could speak further, the screen door banged open again.

"I brought the extra—" Tess stopped abruptly, nearly colliding with Jamie who was carrying boxes of supplies. "Gretchen?"

Behind them, Leah appeared with Jack, more fundraiser materials in their arms. The hallway suddenly felt very crowded with all the people who had become part of this story.

Gretchen looked around, taking in the scene—her sisters, the significant others they'd found, the shelter that had somehow become the center of everything. Her gaze landed on Will's protective stance behind Kaitlyn, and something in her expression shifted.

"I see I have a lot to catch up on," she said quietly.

"Yes," Chelsea said, moving to stand beside Kaitlyn. "You do. I suggest we all go back to our place. And then," she met her sister's eyes steadily, "then we all need to talk."

CHAPTER 17

The yellow bungalow felt smaller than usual with all five Lawrence women gathered in the living room. Ernest watched from his perch on the porch railing, his literary criticism apparently extending to family drama.

Chelsea automatically moved to make coffee—a Lawrence sister tradition when facing difficult conversations.

"So," Chelsea said finally, passing out mugs. "We're all here."

"Yes," Gretchen replied, perched on the edge of the sofa like she might flee at any moment. "I suppose we are."

Kaitlyn stood by the window, arms crossed, looking more like her mother than she'd probably want to acknowledge. Tess and Leah sat together on the loveseat, presenting a united front as they always had during family crises.

"I didn't plan for any of this," Gretchen began, but Kaitlyn's sharp laugh cut her off.

"Really, Mom? You didn't plan to hide my sister from me for years? To let me think Dad just…what? Forgot about me? Moved on without a backward glance?"

"I was trying to protect you."

"Don't." Chelsea's voice was quiet but firm. "Don't say that,

Gretchen. That's exactly what Mom used to say when she made us keep her secrets. When she turned us against each other to hide her own choices."

The comparison seemed to hit Gretchen like a physical blow. She pressed her hands to her face, shoulders shaking. "I've become her, haven't I? I've become exactly what I swore I never would."

"We all did, in different ways," Tess said softly. "Remember those Sunday dinners? How Mom would make us all dress up, pretend everything was perfect while Dad drank himself numb in his study?"

"And if anyone slipped," Leah added, "if anyone showed a crack in the perfect facade…"

"The silent treatment," all four sisters said in unison, then shared a pained laugh at the shared memory.

Kaitlyn turned from the window. "Is that what this is about? Your childhood trauma bleeding into my life?"

"Kaitlyn," Chelsea started, but her niece wasn't finished.

"No, I want to understand. You all sit here talking about how terrible it was, being forced to keep secrets, to maintain appearances. Meanwhile, I've spent my whole life doing exactly that—crafting the perfect social media presence, pretending everything was fine, never knowing there was a whole other family out there. A sister who probably doesn't even know I exist."

"She does," Gretchen said quietly.

The room went still.

"What?" Kaitlyn's voice cracked.

"Sarah knows about you. Jeffrey…your father…he told her last night. That's why—" Gretchen swallowed hard. "That's why he wants to come to Key West. They both do."

"No." Kaitlyn started pacing. "No, absolutely not. I can't…I can't handle that right now. The fundraiser's in three days, and I have responsibilities, and I just…I can't."

"Breathe, honey," Chelsea said, moving to intercept her niece's nervous movement. "No one's saying it has to be now."

"Actually," Gretchen admitted, "Jeffrey wanted to come right away, but I told him to wait. After the fundraiser. To give us time to...to figure out how to do this right."

"Do what right?" Kaitlyn demanded. "Have some awkward family reunion where we all pretend the past sixteen years didn't happen?"

"No pretending," Leah said firmly. "That's what got us here in the first place."

"But how would this even work?" Kaitlyn sank onto the sofa, though notably not next to her mother. "Practically, I mean. Where would they stay? What would we do? Just sit around sharing family stories that half of us weren't part of?"

"They could stay at the Cypress House," Tess suggested. "Neutral territory. And we could plan some structured activities—maybe start with lunch somewhere public but quiet."

"And Joanna?" Chelsea asked. "Where does she fit in all this?"

"She's..." Gretchen took a deep breath. "She's actually been more understanding than I deserve. She's the one who encouraged Sarah to be open to meeting Kaitlyn. She said secrets had already cost both girls too much time."

"That must have been hard to hear," Chelsea observed. "Another woman being more generous than you could be."

"Everything about this is hard," Gretchen admitted. "The thought of facing Jeffrey again, of watching him with both his daughters while I stand there knowing I'm just as much to blame for keeping them apart...But I can't keep making choices based on my pride. That's what Mom did and look what it did to us. We missed out on so many years together."

"We need to think about Sarah too," Leah said practically. "She's sixteen—this is huge for her. What did Jeffrey say? How did Sarah take it?"

Gretchen shrugged. "Surprisingly well. I don't know if it's being young and not seeing the drama in it all or…"

"Or maybe she likes the idea of having a sister?" Chelsea asked. "I mean, far be it from me to put my two cents in but…"

Everyone stared at Chelsea as if she had two heads.

"You without an opinion?" Leah teased.

"Very funny. I mean it, haven't any of you wondered about that possibility?" She looked at Kaitlyn. "And, what about you? I know you're upset with your parents over this, but what does it mean to you to have a sister? I remember a time when you used to beg your mother to have another child."

Gretchen's face lit up. "That's right. I remember you not only begged me to have another baby, but you also insisted it be a girl because you wanted a sister."

Kaitlyn shook her head. "Mom, that was years ago. It's not that I don't want Sarah in my life. I'd like to get to know her, but it's not the same as growing up side-by-side, sharing everything together. We missed out on that."

Tess, ever the optimist, looked around the room. "Aren't you all tired of focusing on what you don't have instead of the gifts you've been given? Hasn't being around the families at Paradise Harbor House taught you anything?"

They all sat in silence at Tess's words, and Kaitlyn walked over to her aunt and wrapped her arms around her. "You're the wisest one in the room, Aunt Tess. What would we do without you?"

Tess laughed and Kaitlyn turned to her mother. "I guess we shift our attention to the logistics of how we do this."

"Maybe we start small? Coffee or lunch, just Kaitlyn and Sarah at first?"

"With support nearby," Tess added. "But not hovering. Give them space to find their own way."

"I'm scared," Kaitlyn confessed quietly. "What if she hates me? What if she blames me somehow for disrupting her perfect family? What if—" She stopped, swallowing hard. "What if Dad loves her more? He stayed for her, after all."

"Oh, honey." Gretchen ran to her daughter. "Your father's choices were about his own weakness, not about either of his daughters' worth."

"Tell me about her?" Kaitlyn asked after a moment. "Sarah? What did Dad say?"

"She's been following your social media the last couple of years," Gretchen said softly. "Apparently, when your father told her, she already knew. Don't ask me how. I'm guessing the internet had something to do with it."

Kaitlyn suddenly felt a weight lift from her shoulders. "Really? What did she say?"

"She's just as angry with Jeffrey as you are. My guess is she's going to be excited to meet you. I think you can stop worrying about whether she's going to like you. Based on what your father said, Sarah thinks you're a rock star."

The mood in the room changed with this news. Kaitlyn was still angry at her mother, and it had been a long time since she'd felt anything but resentment toward this entire situation. Now, for the first time, something else crept in—curiosity.

"She really said that?" Kaitlyn asked, her voice quieter, less defensive.

Gretchen nodded. "She did. And I think…I think she's been waiting for this as much as you have, even if you didn't know you were waiting."

Kaitlyn exhaled, staring down at the floor. "I don't know what to do with that."

"You don't have to do anything right away," Chelsea said gently. "Take a breath. Let it settle."

Leah, ever the pragmatist, leaned forward. "We should still talk about what happens next. If Sarah's already been following you online, she probably has a version of you in her head. This first meeting should be about making space for reality, for both of you."

Kaitlyn glanced up, hesitating. "I think I'd like to meet her. But I don't want a whole family circus around it. No big, dramatic setup."

"Then we keep it simple," Tess said, her voice soothing. "I have the perfect idea. Why don't they make reservations at The Gardens Hotel? We certainly don't have room here. It's a perfect place for them to stay, and an ideal spot to have quiet conversation, just the two of you, somewhere comfortable but neutral."

Kaitlyn chewed on her bottom lip. "And if it's awful?"

"Then you take it one step at a time," Tess replied. "But what if it isn't awful? What if it's good?"

That was the real question, wasn't it? What if Sarah wasn't some awkward extension of a past Kaitlyn resented, but instead, a person she could come to care about? What if she wasn't a reminder of all the things their father had done wrong, but instead, a chance to build something new?

Kaitlyn exhaled. "All right. But what about the fundraiser? This is crazy timing."

Gretchen nodded. "Why don't I call Jeffrey and tell him the plan. They can make reservations for after the fundraiser."

Chelsea smirked. "Remember, Kaitlyn. When you do meet, we'll be nearby. Not hovering," she added when Kaitlyn shot her a look. "Just within bolting distance."

That earned a half-smile from Kaitlyn. "Okay. Let's do this."

Gretchen looked at Kaitlyn and spoke softly. "What about us? What can I do to earn your trust again?"

The room settled into an unexpected stillness, as if everyone was holding their breath at the shift in energy.

"Give me time, Mom. I'm learning the hard way that none of us are perfect, and the things we do to run away from pain can be drastic. Can we please start by not lying to each other ever again?"

Gretchen smiled. "Never again, honey. I promise."

"I know it's practically a closet, but we've got a tiny room in the back. You can use the air mattress," Leah offered.

"My rental is pretty small, but you can stay with me if you'd rather," Chelsea added.

Gretchen shook her head. "No, I'd rather stay here to be near Kaitlyn, if she doesn't mind."

Kaitlyn shrugged. "That's fine, Mom, but I don't want to talk about this all the time."

Gretchen nodded. "Of course. I understand."

Kaitlyn smiled. "Well, then. I know we have lots to do in the next few days, but I really could use at least a morning at the beach." She looked at her aunts and smiled. "Anyone with me?"

"Absolutely," Chelsea said. "I didn't come all the way from Captiva to sit in this living room."

The tension in the room hadn't disappeared completely, but it had softened, replaced by something fragile and uncertain—hope.

Leah stretched and stood, rolling her shoulders as if physically shaking off the weight of the conversation. "Well, that was a lot for one night."

"No kidding," Chelsea said, rubbing her temples. "I don't know about you all, but I need something stronger than coffee after that. How about we all go over to Margarita Max's? We can introduce Gretchen to Connie and who knows, maybe Jamie is playing tonight." Chelsea looked at Tess and winked, then glanced at Kaitlyn. "You in?"

Kaitlyn hesitated, then let out a breathy laugh. "Honestly? Something tropical sounds perfect. We can toast to new beginnings."

"Now that's my niece," Chelsea said with a smirk.

Gretchen hesitated. "Kaitlyn, are you sure you want me to join, or would you rather just have time with your aunts?"

Kaitlyn looked at her mother, the walls between them still

standing but no longer impenetrable. "You can come," she said after a moment. "But no heavy talks, okay? Just…pina colada, pie, and maybe some bad storytelling if Aunt Chelsea gets chatty."

Chelsea clutched her chest. "How dare you."

Laughter rippled through the room, lightening the air in a way that felt long overdue.

Tess nudged Kaitlyn's shoulder. "And tomorrow morning, we hit the beach."

Kaitlyn nodded, a small smile curving her lips. "Yeah. That sounds nice."

For the first time since she'd arrived in Key West, the weight pressing down on her chest didn't feel quite so heavy. Maybe nothing had been fully resolved, and maybe there was still a long road ahead, but for tonight, this was enough.

And tomorrow? Tomorrow, she'd let the ocean wash some of the uncertainty away.

CHAPTER 18

Waves rolled gently onto the shore, their rhythmic motion a steady backdrop as Tess, Leah, Chelsea, Gretchen, and Kaitlyn strolled along the beach. Their footprints trailed behind them, vanishing with each retreating tide. The salty breeze carried the scent of the ocean, cooling the warmth of the morning and making everything feel light and unburdened. Leah tilted her head back to feel the sun on her face.

"I don't think I realized how much I needed this," Leah admitted, adjusting the brim of her straw hat. "Just the ocean, the sand, and no drama for a few hours."

Chelsea chuckled, stretching her arms over her head. "Don't say it too loud. The universe might take that as a challenge."

Tess shook her head with a smile. "Then let's not invite trouble. Let's just enjoy the moment. When was the last time the four of us did this?"

"All four of us? I'm thinking Chelsea's wedding weekend," Gretchen said.

"It was all a blur for me. I kept worrying that the tent was going to fall on top of everyone. There were moments of fun though. It was good having you all there to celebrate with me."

Chelsea added, "But I agree that we all need to do this more often. We can take turns hosting. One year you guys come to Captiva and the next Gretchen and I will come to Key West."

"Sounds good to me," Tess added.

"Well, I have no idea where I'll be. For now, Key West is my home and that feels right, but a year from now? Who knows."

Kaitlyn, a few steps ahead, dipped her toes in the foamy surf. "I know I should be stressing over the fundraiser, but right now, I just want to pretend I have nothing to do but lie on this beach."

"Pretend all you want," Leah said, smirking. "But at some point, we have to talk about appetizers."

Tess groaned. "Maybe we should let one of the other restaurants handle everything? I'm starting to feel like we're taking on more than we can handle. It seemed like a good idea at the time, but now, I don't know…"

Leah gasped, clutching her chest. "Bite your tongue! We are women of culinary distinction, Tess."

Chelsea laughed. "Distinction? More like desperation. You two cooked your way through every bad financial stretch you ever had."

"Exactly," Leah said. "Which is why we're going to make appetizers for the fundraiser. Jamie's restaurant is handling most of the food, but we'll contribute some homemade stuff. We promised Elena."

Tess sighed. "And where exactly are we doing all this? Our kitchen is the size of a closet."

"Elena said we can use the kitchen at Paradise Harbor House," Kaitlyn said, grinning. "It's huge—plenty of counter space, professional-grade ovens. No excuses."

Tess crossed her arms. "Fine, but I'm not making anything fussy. No tiny, bite-sized, 'stacked' things."

"Agreed," Leah said. "I was thinking bruschetta, maybe some kind of dip and homemade crackers. Stuff we can make ahead."

"And don't forget the mini key lime pies," Chelsea added. "Everyone will expect them."

Tess sighed dramatically. "I should've kept my mouth shut."

"You never keep your mouth shut," Leah said, nudging her.

Kaitlyn laughed, shaking her head. "Well, at least the big stuff is settled. Thanks to Jack, the sunset cruise is locked in. Apparently, the boat's captain is an old friend."

Chelsea lifted an eyebrow. "Of course he knows a boat captain. The man knows everyone."

Kaitlyn smirked. "I think he knows someone in every zip code."

"True," Leah agreed. "But hey, it works in our favor. The sunset cruise is going to be the highlight of the fundraiser. Between that, the auction, and the donations from local businesses, we should be able to do a lot for Paradise Harbor House."

"I've seen some of the flyers that Elena did. They look amazing," Kaitlyn said. "I think the fundraiser will be a big success. I know so many families are excited to see Paradise Harbor House getting the attention it deserves."

There was a pause as they all let that sink in. It wasn't just about planning an event; it was about changing lives.

Tess gave Kaitlyn a sideways glance. "This whole thing was your idea, you know. You should be proud."

Kaitlyn hesitated, then shrugged. "I just wanted to do something that mattered."

Leah linked arms with her niece. "Well, you're doing it. And you're not alone."

"We couldn't be prouder of you, sweetheart," Gretchen said.

"I'm ready to dive into the water. Who's with me?" Chelsea asked.

They all got up and walked toward the water, the easy rhythm of the ocean settling over them. Eventually, Leah attempted an impromptu yoga pose in the sand, only to topple over, sending a spray of sand onto Tess and Chelsea.

"I'm just testing the softness of the beach," Leah said, sprawled on her back. "It passes."

Chelsea snorted. "I swear, you were a circus performer in a past life."

Kaitlyn ran into the water first, her head diving into a large wave.

"Look at her," Gretchen said. "That's my daughter."

Chelsea smiled. "No matter how bad you feel about Jeffrey and Sarah, you should be proud of the way you raised Kaitlyn. She's an incredible young lady."

"She's all grown up. It's hard knowing what my place is in her life now."

Chelsea laughed and slipped her arm through Gretchen's.

"Don't you worry about it. She'll always be your baby, and from the looks of things, she's going to need her mother."

Kaitlyn looked back at her mother and her aunts and smiled. It wasn't perfect—there were still unspoken tensions, unfinished conversations—but here, now, there was peace.

She hated to admit it, but with everything that was about to happen in Key West, she imagined that peace wouldn't last much longer.

The sound of footsteps in the sand behind her made Kaitlyn glance over her shoulder. Will was walking toward her, his hands in the pockets of his board shorts, his easy stride making it look like he had all the time in the world.

"Hey, stranger," he said, stopping beside her.

Kaitlyn smiled slightly. "Hey yourself."

"I saw your aunts heading back up the beach. Figured you might still be out here."

She nodded, wrapping her arms around herself. "I wasn't ready to leave yet."

Will studied her for a moment before stepping closer. "What's on your mind?"

Kaitlyn let out a breath and ran a hand over her ponytail, her fingers toying with the ends of her hair. "Everything. Too much." She huffed a small, humorless laugh. "You ever feel like you're standing in the middle of a storm, but everyone else is just going about their business like it's a sunny day?"

Will tilted his head. "Yeah. I've felt like that a time or two."

She nodded, staring out at the water. "My father and my sister are coming to Key West next week."

Will didn't react immediately, giving her space to continue.

"I don't even know how to process any of this. One minute, I'm furious at my parents for keeping this from me. The next, I'm overwhelmed by the idea that I have a sister who might actually want to know me."

She could tell his silence meant that he was letting her work through her thoughts.

"And my dad…he stayed for her, you know? He left me behind but stayed for Sarah. I try not to think about what that means, but it's hard not to."

"So, your dad stayed with you and your mother when he already had another child?"

Kaitlyn shrugged. "For a while. I imagine it became too much for him. I have no idea about his new wife, but she must have put pressure on him for years to leave us."

"Not to mention how hard it was for your mother. I mean it had to be difficult to try to save her marriage, knowing what he'd done."

Kaitlyn hadn't thought of how her mother must have felt, but now, hearing Will say it, she suddenly felt sick to her stomach at the way she'd treated her mother.

"She must have finally given up when he left," she responded, her voice barely a whisper.

Will shifted slightly. "Have you talked to him?"

"No. Not yet. I don't know what I'd even say." She rubbed her arms like she was cold, even though the late afternoon was warm. "And it's not just that. The fundraiser is days away, and everything has to go perfectly. We need it to be a success, not just for the money but because Paradise Harbor House deserves it. I need to do something that matters."

Will nodded slowly. "You already are."

Kaitlyn let out a short laugh. "I don't know about that."

"I do." He turned slightly, facing her. "Look at what you've done since you got here. You found a way to take everything you're feeling—about your family, about where you come from—and turn it into something good. That says a lot about who you are."

She swallowed. "And what if it all falls apart? What if the fundraiser doesn't go the way we need it to? What if Sarah doesn't want anything to do with me? What if my dad…" She hesitated, her voice quieter now. "What if he never really wanted me in the first place?"

Will chuckled and then reached for her hand, threading his fingers through hers. "My love, you have a lot of 'what ifs' to keep you up at night. Why not let it all go and stop worrying? You're putting too much on yourself. Besides, you are not alone. I'm here."

Kaitlyn looked up at him.

"I mean it," he said, his voice steady. "I'll be there for you. However you need me to be. If you need someone to listen, I'll listen. If you need to vent, I'll let you yell at me. If you need to walk away for a while, I'll be the guy standing at a safe distance, waiting for you to be ready." His fingers squeezed hers gently. "But you won't go through this alone."

Something in her chest loosened at his words, at the certainty in his voice.

"Will…" She hesitated, shaking her head slightly. "I don't know what to say to that."

"You don't have to say anything." He exhaled, glancing down at their joined hands. "But there is something I need to say."

She felt his fingers tighten around her's before he looked back up at her, his expression unreadable, like he was sorting through his own emotions.

"I might as well come clean here. I'm getting in deep with you, Kaitlyn."

Her breath caught.

"I know neither of us is ready to slap a label on this," he continued, his voice quiet but firm. "But this thing between us? It's not casual for me."

She swallowed hard, her pulse racing.

"I need you to know that," he added. "Whatever's happening here, I'm in it for the long haul. I don't take it lightly."

Kaitlyn searched his face, trying to find the right words, but nothing felt big enough to match what he was giving her in that moment.

Finally, she just nodded. "It's not casual for me either."

A small, almost relieved smile flickered across Will's face before he reached up, his fingers brushing lightly against her cheek.

Kaitlyn stilled as his hand settled against her face, his thumb grazing her cheekbone, his touch warm and steady. She didn't pull away.

His gaze locked onto hers, searching, waiting—giving her the space to decide.

Kaitlyn's breath caught, and then she leaned in, closing the distance between them.

His lips met hers, softly at first, testing, but when she didn't hesitate, the kiss deepened—slow and sure.

When they finally pulled back, Kaitlyn exhaled shakily, her forehead resting lightly against his.

Will smiled, his voice a little rough. "I think we just crossed into deep waters."

Kaitlyn let out a soft laugh, her fingers curling into his shirt. "I think we did."

They stood there, the waves rolling over their feet, the rest of the world fading away.

Whatever this was, wherever it was going—they were in it together, and nothing felt more perfect.

CHAPTER 19

The next two days disappeared in a blur of preparations, to-do lists, and the occasional minor disaster. Paradise Harbor House's kitchen had transformed into command central, with Elena wielding her iPad like a general coordinating troops while Tess and Leah churned out trays of appetizers under her watchful eye.

The only problem was Gretchen wanted so desperately to connect with her daughter, she was driving everyone crazy, especially Chelsea.

"The bruschetta needs more basil," Gretchen announced, reaching past Tess to adjust the seasoning. "And honestly, have you thought about doing a test batch with sun-dried tomatoes instead? I saw this lovely recipe…"

"Gretchen," Leah said through gritted teeth, "I've been making this bruschetta since before Kaitlyn was born. The recipe is fine."

"I'm just trying to help." Gretchen rearranged the serving platters for the third time. "Speaking of Kaitlyn, has she mentioned her plans after the fundraiser? I mean, working at a shelter is wonderful, but it's hardly a career path. And about that young man with the camera."

Chelsea appeared in the doorway, arching an eyebrow at her sister. "Gretchen. A word?"

In the hallway, Chelsea crossed her arms. "You need to dial it back about ten notches."

"What? I'm being supportive!"

"You're being overwhelming. The bruschetta police routine? The not-so-subtle questions about Kaitlyn's future? You're trying so hard to make up for everything that you're suffocating everyone."

"I just want…"

"To help. I know. But maybe focus on the tasks Kaitlyn actually asked you to do instead of critiquing everyone else's work. And for heaven's sake, stop dropping hints about her career path. This isn't the time to talk about that. Besides, she'll figure it out."

Gretchen deflated slightly, leaning against the wall. "I don't know how to do this, Chelsea. Every time I see her taking charge of something, being so…capable, I want to jump in and be part of it. But then I remember why she's keeping me at arm's length, and I don't know how to…"

"Try harder?" Chelsea finished dryly. "Which makes her pull away more, which makes you try even harder. It's like watching someone dig themselves deeper while insisting they're building stairs. Maybe stop trying so hard and let things evolve naturally."

Through the kitchen door, they could hear Kaitlyn directing volunteers, her voice confident and sure. "The silent auction items need to be arranged by category. Maybe put the restaurant gift certificates together? And can someone double-check the display cards for typos?"

"Did you hear that?" Gretchen whispered. "When did she get so organized? And why didn't I know she could be like this? It feels like only yesterday I was telling her to clean her room."

Chelsea laughed. "Maybe because you were too busy planning her life to see the one she was building." Chelsea's voice softened at her sister's flinch. "Sorry. That was harsh. But Gretchen, you have to give her space to be who she is now, not who you thought she should be. No amount of pushing her right now is a good idea. She's got a lot on her plate. Try to be patient."

"I saw her looking at real estate listings," Gretchen blurted. "On her phone last night. Here in Key West. And Will mentioned something about a documentary series he's planning about local businesses. He wants her to help produce it."

"And?"

"And she's my daughter! She should be thinking about graduate school or a corporate job or—"

"Or maybe," Chelsea interrupted, "she should be thinking exactly what she's thinking. Which, by the way, is none of your business unless she chooses to share it."

Inside the kitchen, something clattered, followed by Tess yelling

"Gretchen! What did you do to my bruschetta? You didn't spread them out the way I told you to."

Chelsea smothered a laugh. "Come on. Let's find you something constructive to do that doesn't involve critiquing anyone's cooking or career choices. I think Elena needed help organizing the donation records."

"But—"

"No buts. The only way you're going to rebuild trust with Kaitlyn is by showing her you can respect her choices. Even the ones you don't understand. Even the ones that terrify you because they don't fit your plan."

Gretchen squared her shoulders, a gesture so like Kaitlyn's that it made Chelsea's heart twist. "I just want her to be happy."

"I know. But maybe it's time to let her show you what that looks like instead of telling her."

"By the way, I sent a text to Jeffrey and he and Sarah are definitely coming to Key West," Gretchen added.

"That's great. When?"

"He said they'd get here two days after the fundraiser."

"Let him know that I'll make reservations for them at The Gardens Hotel. I think it will be the perfect spot for Kaitlyn and Sarah to get acquainted in private."

Gretchen nodded. "Will do."

At that moment, Will walked in with his camera equipment, and Gretchen's entire body tensed like a guard dog spotting an intruder.

"Don't even think about it," Chelsea warned under her breath.

"I just want to ask him—"

"No."

"But his documentary work can't possibly provide a stable—"

"Gretchen. No."

They watched as Will set up his equipment with practiced efficiency. Kaitlyn emerged from the office, her face lighting up when she saw him. He matched her smile with one of his own, and even Gretchen couldn't miss the way the entire room seemed to fade away for them.

"The chairman of the arts foundation is here," Kaitlyn told him, consulting her clipboard. "Elena thinks it would be good to get some footage of their involvement. Show how the whole community supports Paradise Harbor House."

"Perfect," Will replied. "And I was thinking we could interview Jamie about the local restaurant partnerships."

"Already scheduled for this afternoon," Kaitlyn finished. "After he drops off the catering contracts."

Gretchen's fingers twitched toward her iPad. "You know, when I was organizing the hospital fundraiser last year and…"

"Nope," Chelsea interrupted, steering her sister toward the door. "Come on. Donation records. Now."

"But I have experience with that."

"What you have is boundary issues. Let's go."

As they left, they could hear Will asking Kaitlyn about camera angles for the silent auction setup. Her response was confident, professional, showing a depth of understanding that made Gretchen's steps falter.

"She's good at this," Gretchen whispered, half to herself. "Really good."

"Yes, she is. And that terrifies you, doesn't it?"

"What do you mean?"

Chelsea stopped in the hallway, turning to face her sister. "Because if she's good at this—if she's found her place here—then you have to accept that her life might look very different from what you planned. That she might choose Key West and Will and documentary filming over law school and corporate jobs and whatever else you had mapped out in your head."

"I just want her to be secure. To have opportunities."

"Look around, Gretchen. She's creating her own opportunities. She's building something meaningful. And if you're not careful, you're going to miss it because you're too busy worrying about what it isn't."

Before Gretchen could respond, Leah poked her head out of the kitchen. "Has anyone seen the backup list of auction items? The one with the donor contact information?"

"Blue folder!" several voices called out.

"No," Kaitlyn corrected, not looking up from her conversation with Will. "Mom reorganized everything into color-coded digital files this morning. Check your email."

The simple acknowledgment—"Mom"—made Gretchen's eyes fill with tears. It was the first time Kaitlyn had referenced her that way since the truth came out.

"Baby steps," Chelsea said softly, squeezing her sister's arm. "Now come on. Those donation records aren't going to organize themselves. Though I'm sure you have thoughts about their filing system too."

"Actually," Gretchen said, wiping her eyes, "I was thinking

maybe I should just observe for a while. See how they do things here. I just want to be close by and help if anyone needs me."

Chelsea's smile was approving. "Now that's the smartest thing you've said all day."

Leah sat at the welcome desk, updating donor lists and trying not to check her phone every five minutes. Jack had texted earlier about meeting with the cruise captain, promising to stop by afterward with details. She told herself her anticipation was purely professional—after all, the cruise was a crucial part of the fundraiser—but even she wasn't buying that excuse anymore.

"If you stare any harder at that door, you might burn a hole through it," Chelsea commented, passing by with an armload of auction items.

"I'm just waiting for information about the cruise," Leah protested.

"Mmhmm. Information. Is that what we're calling him now?"

Before Leah could respond, the door opened and Jack walked in.

"Good news," he announced. "Captain Mike's throwing in an extra hour at no charge. Says it's the least he can do for Paradise Harbor House."

"That's wonderful!" Leah stood, shuffling papers to hide her flustered reaction to his smile. "Did he mention anything about—"

"The sunset timing? Already worked out. The lighting will be perfect for photos right as we serve dinner." He stepped closer, lowering his voice. "Though I was thinking maybe we could do our own sunset cruise sometime. After all this is over."

"Are you asking me on a date, Jack Calloway?"

"Depends. Are you saying yes?"

Their eyes met, and Leah felt that now-familiar warmth spread through her body. "I might be. If you ask properly."

"In that case…" He leaned against the desk. "Leah Lawrence, would you do me the honor of having dinner with me? Preferably on a boat, definitely involving sunset, absolutely no grant writing allowed."

"No grant writing? You drive a hard bargain." She tried to keep her tone light despite her racing pulse. "But I suppose I could manage that."

His smile deepened, reaching his eyes in that way that made her forget about spreadsheets and donor lists and everything else. "I should warn you—I have ulterior motives. I've been looking for someone to help me test out all the coffee shops in Key West. For research purposes, of course."

"Of course. Very professional."

"Extremely. Could take weeks of careful investigation."

"Months, even," Leah suggested, playing along.

"Exactly what I was thinking."

The promise of future possibilities hung between them, sweet and unhurried. For once, Leah didn't feel the need to plan everything out. Some things, she was learning, were better left to unfold naturally.

"So," Jack said, pulling something from his messenger bag, "I brought you something. A special edition I found at the shop."

He handed her a beautifully bound copy of "Pride and Prejudice." Leah ran her fingers over the embossed cover, touched by the thoughtfulness of the gift.

"You mentioned it was your favorite," he explained. "And this one has some interesting margin notes from a previous owner—a literature professor from the 1960s. Thought you might enjoy another perspective on Elizabeth and Mr. Darcy's story."

"You remembered that conversation?" They'd discussed books during one of their late-night grant-writing sessions.

"I remember all our conversations," he said quietly. "Even the ones about proper comma placement in funding requests."

Chelsea chose that moment to walk by again, this time not even trying to hide her knowing smile. "Don't mind me. Just passing through. Repeatedly. Because I work here."

Jack chuckled. "Maybe we should continue this conversation somewhere else? The coffee shop down the street has great Cuban pastries. Unless you're too busy with fundraiser prep?"

"She's not," Chelsea called from across the room. "We've got it covered."

"I can spare thirty minutes," Leah said, trying to sound professional despite the warmth in her cheeks. "The donor lists can wait."

"Leah Lawrence, putting off paperwork? I'm shocked," he said.

"Don't get used to it." She grabbed her purse, then hesitated. "Though…maybe we could make this a regular thing? Coffee and books?"

"Careful," he teased, holding the door for her. "First it's coffee and books, then before you know it, we're discussing first editions and rare manuscripts. Could be dangerous."

"I think I'm ready for a little danger," Leah replied, surprising herself with her boldness.

His smile softened into something that made her heart skip. "You know what? I think I am too."

CHAPTER 20

In Elena's office, Gretchen found herself oddly soothed by the simple task of entering donation records into spreadsheets. The focus on numbers helped calm her constant urge to rush out and "help" with everything else.

Through the window, she could see Will filming Kaitlyn as she directed the setup of auction displays. Her daughter moved with a confidence Gretchen had never noticed before, pausing occasionally to adjust a display or consult with volunteers. The camera followed her naturally, as if Will instinctively knew where she would move next.

"They work well together," Elena observed, glancing up from her desk.

"They do," Gretchen admitted, then couldn't help adding, "But a documentary filmmaker? Really?"

"As opposed to what?"

"I just always thought…I mean, with her business degree…"

"You know what I see?" Elena set down her pen. "I see someone who understands how to tell stories that matter. Both of them do, in their own ways. Will with his camera, Kaitlyn with her way of connecting people to causes." She smiled. "That's a rare gift."

The sound of laughter filtered in from the kitchen—Tess and Chelsea's voices mixed with Jamie's deeper tones. Something crashed, followed by good-natured bickering about whose fault it was.

"Oh my," Gretchen muttered, half-rising. "I should—"

"Stay right here," Elena finished firmly. "They've got it handled."

"But—"

"You know what the hardest thing is about running this place?" Elena asked, gesturing to the shelter around them. "Learning when to step in and when to step back. These women come to us needing everything, and it's tempting to try to fix it all for them. But that's not what they really need."

"What do they need?"

"Space to fix things themselves. Support without suffocation. Someone who believes in them enough to let them stumble sometimes."

"I guess there is something to the saying 'Give a man a fish, and you feed him for a day. Teach a man to fish, and you feed him for a lifetime.'"

"Something like that. In this case, it's a woman, but I think it applies to everyone," Elena responded.

The parallel wasn't lost on Gretchen. She sank back into her chair, watching as Kaitlyn effortlessly resolved a conflict between two volunteers over table placement.

"When did she grow up?" Gretchen whispered. "How did I miss it?"

"You didn't miss it," Elena said kindly. "You just had a different version of it playing in your head. Maybe it's time to see the real story instead of the one you thought you were supposed to tell."

A small commotion from the hall interrupted them—the caterers had arrived with sample hors d'oeuvres for approval.

Gretchen's fingers itched to take charge, to rush out and organize everything, but she forced herself to stay seated.

Through the doorway, she watched Chelsea and Tess work together. Jamie appeared with additional platters, his easy competence in the kitchen matching Tess's.

They worked in seamless coordination, sharing small smiles and casual touches that spoke of growing comfort. Gretchen noticed what a gentle man he was and wondered when Tess might share his story with her.

"Mom?" Kaitlyn appeared in the office doorway. "Would you mind looking over these auction item descriptions? You're better at catching typos than I am."

The simple request—and the acknowledgment of her skill without pushing her away—made Gretchen's throat tight. "Of course."

"Thanks." Kaitlyn handed her a stack of papers. "Do me a favor and don't reorganize everything, okay? We have a system."

The gentle teasing in her daughter's voice was new, a tiny bridge across the chasm between them. "I'll restrain myself," Gretchen promised.

As Kaitlyn turned to leave, she hesitated. "Oh, and Mom? Will's going to film some interviews with the families later. The ones who are comfortable sharing their stories. Would you sit in? Maybe help them feel more at ease? You've always been good at that."

The request stunned Gretchen into momentary silence. This wasn't just busywork to keep her occupied—this was something real, something that mattered.

"I'd like that," she managed.

Kaitlyn nodded and left, immediately drawn into another discussion about table arrangements. Will caught her attention from across the room, and Gretchen watched as her daughter's entire face softened at whatever silent communication passed between them.

Standing nearby, Elena smiled. "You see?" Elena said softly. "Sometimes the best way to be needed is to wait until you're asked."

Gretchen chuckled. "I'm not very good at waiting, but I guess I'll have to learn."

"No one said growth was easy." Elena's smile was knowing. "But from what I hear, that's something of a family trait. You Lawrence women don't do anything the easy way."

A crash from the kitchen made them both jump, followed by Tess's voice: "Chelsea! That was the last sample of the crab puffs!"

"Not my fault! One of the children bumped me!"

Gretchen started to rise again, but Elena's raised eyebrow stopped her. Through the chaos, she could hear Kaitlyn's laugh—bright and real and so grown up—as she went to handle whatever crisis her aunts had created.

"She doesn't need me to fix everything anymore," Gretchen said softly.

"No," Elena agreed. "But she'll always need you. I can promise you that."

"Do you have any children of your own?" Gretchen asked.

Elena shook her head. "No, I wasn't able to have children. After my husband died, I didn't want to remarry. How do you get married again when you've already had your love story?"

Gretchen smiled. "I'm not sure. I'll let you know when it happens to me."

Elena chuckled. "Paradise Harbor House is where I get to be around children." She lifted her hand in the air. "This is where I was meant to be. This is where my maternal instincts kick in."

"Paradise Harbor House is lucky to have you," Gretchen said after a moment.

Elena smiled. "I think it's the other way around. This place saved me as much as I've helped others."

Gretchen nodded, letting the thought settle. *Maybe that's what I need—something bigger than myself to hold on to.*

A group of children ran by their laughter filling the air. Elena's face lit up as she waved to them, her joy unmistakable. Gretchen followed her gaze, watching Kaitlyn crouch beside a little girl, tying a loose shoelace with the same gentle patience she had once shown her dolls as a child.

"She belongs here," Gretchen murmured, a mix of sadness and pride welling inside her.

"She does," Elena agreed. "But that doesn't mean there's no place for you."

Gretchen sighed. Maybe she'd spent too long thinking about what she'd lost instead of what she still had.

"Maybe," she said, the word tasting like a possibility.

Elena smiled knowingly. "You'll figure it out."

And for the first time in a long while, Gretchen believed she just might.

Chelsea could feel the beat of Key West's nightlife in her bones as she sat in the beach chair behind Tess and Leah's yellow bungalow, the music from Duval Street carrying on the evening breeze. Though she'd visited her sisters here before, the rhythm of the island still felt wonderfully foreign compared to the quiet shores of Captiva where she and Gretchen lived. But tonight, her attention wasn't on the distant revelry—it was on her little sister, who sat beside her in uncharacteristic silence.

Taking a sip of her iced tea, Chelsea studied her sister's profile. Gretchen had that look on her face, the one she'd worn since they were kids whenever something big was weighing on her mind.

"You're awfully quiet," Chelsea said, breaking the evening silence.

Gretchen exhaled softly. "Just thinking."

"That's dangerous." Chelsea couldn't help but smirk as she

took another sip of tea. Some things never changed—like her need to tease her sister whenever she got too serious.

Gretchen huffed out a small laugh but didn't argue, which only confirmed Chelsea's suspicions. Instead, she wrapped her arms around herself, and Chelsea recognized that defensive posture immediately. Whatever was on her mind, it was big.

Setting her glass down on the table between them, Chelsea turned to face her sister fully. "You're thinking about moving here, aren't you?"

The way Gretchen's lips parted in surprise told her she'd hit the nail on the head. "What?"

"You heard me." Chelsea kept her tone gentle, knowing how easily Gretchen could spook when confronted with her own thoughts. "You've been looking at this place differently. Now that Kaitlyn is here, I can see the wheels turning in your head."

Gretchen shook her head, letting out that soft chuckle she always used when she felt exposed. "You always did know me too well."

"So, is that it?" Chelsea pressed, even as a knot formed in her stomach. As much as she loved visiting Tess and Leah, something about the idea of Gretchen moving here felt wrong. "Are you thinking of coming back here to live? I know Kaitlyn is here, but remember how unhappy you were when you were down here before?"

Gretchen sighed, rubbing a hand over her face—another childhood gesture Chelsea remembered well. "For a minute, I thought about it. I really did."

Chelsea waited, watching her carefully. Over the years, she'd learned that Gretchen needed space to work through her thoughts. Sometimes, being a good big sister meant knowing when to stay quiet.

"And…" Gretchen trailed off before shaking her head. "As much as I love visiting here with Kaitlyn, as much as I love seeing Tess and Leah so happy, Key West isn't where I belong."

The knot in Chelsea's stomach loosened slightly. Her sister was right, she'd known it from the moment she'd spotted Gretchen watching the sunset crowds on Mallory Square with that overwhelmed look in her eyes.

"This town is exciting, and I get why Kaitlyn loves it," Gretchen continued. "The energy, the people, the work she's doing at Paradise Harbor House, it's all part of something bigger than herself." She let out a breath. "Don't get me wrong, I'm still a work in progress, and I think finding something that really matters to me is in my future. It's just that right now, Key West isn't what I need."

"What do you need?" Chelsea asked, though she already knew the answer. She'd watched her relax in Captiva, and Chelsea could see how the quieter pace suited her.

Gretchen's gaze softened as she spoke. "Home. Quiet. Stability. Peace." She turned to Chelsea. "Captiva has that. I need that. I feel like I belong there."

Relief flooded through Chelsea. "You sure?"

"I'm sure." A genuine smile spread across Gretchen's face. "Captiva is slow mornings with coffee on the lanai. Long walks on empty beaches. A town that winds down at sunset instead of revving up. I laugh when I think that just as Captiva is going to bed, Key West is starting the party."

Chelsea couldn't help but laugh. "Yeah, Key West is definitely not Captiva, and I'm grateful for that," she said.

"No, it's not." Gretchen smiled wryly. "I love visiting here. I love spending time with Tess and Leah, and now with Kaitlyn. But I don't belong here the way they do."

Chelsea nodded slowly, thinking about how different their lives were from their sisters'. While Tess and Leah thrived on Key West's endless energy, its vibrant art scene, and even its tourist-filled streets, she and Gretchen had found their peace in Captiva's gentler rhythms.

"Did you hear yourself?" Chelsea couldn't help pointing out.

"'The way *they* do? Does this mean you're finally accepting that this might be where Kaitlyn will settle?'"

Gretchen smiled, catching her meaning. "I see you're using my words against me."

"Of course I am. It's my way of pointing out the obvious." Chelsea leaned back in her chair, feeling more relaxed now that they were on the same page. "I'm happy you're staying in Captiva. If you'd said you were moving here, I was worried I'd have to talk you out of it."

Gretchen's laugh echoed in the night air. "Oh really?"

"Yes, really," Chelsea said, crossing her arms. "I was already thinking about how I'd have to convince you that Key West is too much for you. That you'd hate the tourists, the late-night noise, the endless energy." She grinned, remembering their first morning here. "And don't even pretend you'd survive in a neighborhood with rooster wake-up calls every morning."

Gretchen wrinkled her nose in that familiar way that always made her look twelve again. "No way. I can barely handle the seagulls back home."

"Exactly." Chelsea felt a surge of affection for her sister. "Captiva suits us both. The quiet, the community. And I like knowing we'll still be neighbors."

Gretchen reached over and squeezed her hand, her grip warm and familiar. "Me too. I couldn't imagine living anywhere else. Before moving there, I felt untethered. Of all the places I've lived, and for the first time in a long time, Captiva feels like home."

Chelsea squeezed back. "Then it's settled."

Gretchen exhaled, and Chelsea could almost see the weight lifting from her shoulders. "Yeah. It is."

The wind rustled through the palm trees, mixing with the distant sounds of music and laughter from Duval Street. Chelsea smiled, knowing that sometimes the best part of finding where you belong is being secure enough in your choice to resist the pull of somewhere else.

A faint cheer erupted from somewhere down the street, followed by the upbeat strains of a Jimmy Buffett song.

The sisters caught each other's eyes and both laughed, the sound mixing with the nighttime symphony of Key West. Let Tess and Leah have their endless party, Chelsea thought. She and Gretchen had found their own kind of paradise in Captiva's quiet sunsets, and both of them were exactly where they needed to be.

CHAPTER 21

The afternoon unfolded in controlled chaos. Gretchen stayed in Elena's office, methodically working through the auction descriptions while watching the activity through the window. Every instinct screamed at her to intervene when things went wrong, but she forced herself to observe instead.

When Leah dropped an entire tray of canapés, Kaitlyn handled it with calm efficiency, already on the phone with Harbor Lights to arrange replacements.

When two volunteers disagreed about the silent auction layout, she mediated with a diplomatic touch that reminded Gretchen, achingly, of herself at that age—before life had made her rigid with the need to control everything.

"You survived," Chelsea commented, appearing with coffee. "Two whole hours without trying to reorganize anyone's system. I'm impressed."

"I'm learning," Gretchen said, accepting the cup. "Though it's killing me a little. Did you see how they're arranging the auction item? If they just—"

"Nope," Chelsea cut her off.

"I'm just kidding," Gretchen said. "I'll be good."

Through the window they could see Will interviewing Jamie about his restaurant's involvement with Paradise Harbor House. Kaitlyn stood behind the camera, occasionally making suggestions about angles or lighting. The easy synchronization between her and Will was obvious even from a distance.

"They look like they've been working together for years. She's really good at this," Gretchen said quietly. "All of it. The organizing, the people skills, even the technical stuff with Will's filming."

"Finally noticed that, did you?"

They watched as Will wrapped up the interview. He said something that made Kaitlyn laugh, her whole face lighting up in a way Gretchen hadn't ever seen before.

"When did she fall in love with him?" Gretchen asked.

"Probably around the same time she fell in love with this place, this work." Chelsea's voice was gentle. "When she stopped trying to be who everyone expected and started being herself. I think Will gravitated toward her like a moth to a flame. Kaitlyn is special, and he recognized that the first time he laid eyes on her."

Before Gretchen could respond Kaitlyn appeared in the doorway. "Mom? The first family is ready for their interview. Are you still up for helping?"

"Of course, just tell me what you need me to do."

"Great. Here's how it will go. We're interviewing Melanie, who is here with her daughter Hailee. They've been staying at Paradise Harbor House for several months. Her husband passed away unexpectedly, and without his income things unraveled fast. Melanie's been working hard to get back on her feet, but it hasn't been easy."

Gretchen nodded. "Poor thing. I can't imagine how hard that must be for her and her daughter. What can I do to help?"

"I need you to keep Hailee out of the frame. That's not going to be easy because she'll want to stay close to her mother. Melanie is happy to tell her story, but she's also a little nervous. The other volunteers are helping to keep the other children from running into the camera, but I need you to keep your eye on Hailee and also guard the door and make sure the other children don't slip through."

"Got it."

"Here is a coloring book and crayons. See if you can color with her. Okay, let's go."

They walked out into the courtyard. Hailee was tucked close to Melanie's side, clutching a worn stuffed bunny.

"Hi, Hailee," Gretchen said. "What a cute little bunny you have there. What is the bunny's name?"

"Yellow," Hailee said.

"Yellow? That's my favorite color.

Hailee smiled. "Me too."

"I was wondering if you'd like to color with me? I think there might even be a bunny in the book. We can color it yellow," Gretchen added.

Hailee nodded and walked to the table and chairs on the porch while Kaitlyn began talking to Melanie.

"There's no wrong way to tell your story," Kaitlyn assured her, sitting across from Melanie. "This is about what you've been through and how Paradise Harbor House has helped you. Take your time, and we can pause if you ever need a break.

Melanie let out a breath, her shoulders easing slightly. "Okay."

"Ready to roll?" Will asked from behind the camera.

Kaitlyn nodded.

Will raised his hand. "All right. Rolling in three…two…one."

Kaitlyn turned slightly toward Melanie, keeping her voice gentle.

"Melanie, thank you for being here today. Let's start at the beginning. Can you tell us a little about what brought you to Paradise Harbor House?"

"I lost my husband about six months ago. He worked construction, and when he died on the job…everything fell apart. We didn't have much saved, and I'd been staying home with our daughter, so when his income stopped, we had nothing to fall back on. We tried to get by but it wasn't enough. We lost our apartment and for a while… we didn't have anywhere to go. We had been living in our car for a few days when someone suggested we try a shelter. We didn't know where to go or what to do."

Kaitlyn nodded, her expression compassionate but calm, giving Melanie space to continue.

"Another woman who was also living in her car told us that she knew a good place in Key West that was helping families. She told me about Paradise Harbor House," Melanie said. "I wasn't sure what to expect, but the moment we got here, I knew it was different. It wasn't just a place to sleep. It felt…safe, you know, like a home."

"How has Paradise Harbor House helped you and your daughter since then?"

Melanie smiled. "In so many ways. Of course they gave us a warm bed, and meals but more than anything they've given us a sense of community. My daughter has made friends here, and I had time to get back on my feet. They helped me find job leads, taught me how to update my resume, and even made sure my daughter was cared for when I went to interviews."

"That's wonderful. And you recently found a job, is that right?"

"Yes, I'll be working in Miami, and thanks to Paradise Harbor House, we found an affordable apartment close to the bus line. Plus the job where I'll be working has child care right in the building, so I can see my daughter during the day. There is a good school nearby too, so we're now talking with them about that. There were financial issues to resolve with insurance, and the people here helped us navigate that as well. Mostly, I feel a sense of hope for the first time since my husband died. I don't know what we would have done without Paradise Harbor House."

Kaitlyn reached over and gave Melanie's hand a gentle squeeze. "What would you say to someone who might be struggling like you were?"

Melanie's eyes softened. "I'd tell them not to be afraid to ask for help. There are people out there who want to help—you just have to be willing to take that first step. And when you find a place like Paradise Harbor House, see it as a blessing."

"Thank you so much for sharing your story with us today, Melanie," Kaitlyn said, nodding to Will who lowered the camera.

"You did great," Kaitlyn said, looking over at her mother and Hailee. "It looks like Hailee's having a good time with my mom."

Melanie smiled. "Hailee loves it here. I hope she won't be too sad to leave."

"I know she's going to make a lot of new friends in Miami, and you'll have to come visit when you can."

"What about you, Kaitlyn? Will you stay in Key West?"

Kaitlyn smiled and she could feel Will's eyes on her, waiting for her answer.

"There's a very good chance I will," she answered.

"That's good. I think everyone will be happy to hear that."

Kaitlyn smiled and then looked at Will. Whether Key West was in her future or not, she knew there was one person she was now sure she couldn't live without.

After Melanie and Hailee left, Kaitlyn and Gretchen remained on the bench in the courtyard.

"That was beautiful," Gretchen said softly. "The way you handled the interview. You knew exactly how to make her feel comfortable, how to let her story unfold naturally."

"Thanks, Mom. I appreciate it."

"Kaitlyn..." Gretchen's voice caught. "I owe you an apology. A real one."

"Mom—"

"Please. Let me say this." Gretchen turned to face her daughter fully. "I was so busy trying to protect you that I forgot to listen to you. To see you. I thought if I could just control everything, keep all the messy parts of life away from you…" She shook her head. "I became exactly what I swore I never would."

"Like Grandma," Kaitlyn said quietly.

"Yes. Making choices for everyone, thinking I knew best." Her voice trembled. "I'm so sorry, honey. For all of it."

"I've spoken with your father, and it looks like he and Sarah will come to Key West right after the fundraiser. How do you feel about that?"

Kaitlyn nodded. "I think I'm ready, or at least I will be after all this is done. I think I felt a bit overwhelmed with everything happening at the same time."

Kaitlyn was quiet for a moment and then sighed. "Mom, do you know what hearing Melanie's story made me realize? How incredibly strong you were. Going through the divorce, dealing with Dad's betrayal, raising me alone, and you never let me see how much you were hurting."

"That was my job as your mother."

"No," Kaitlyn interrupted gently. "That was you trying to carry everything alone. And I didn't help, did I? Running around focused on my social media perfect life, never seeing what it cost you to maintain the facade of everything being okay."

"You were being a teenager," Gretchen said softly. "That was your job, by the way."

"I was old enough to see that you were struggling. I just didn't want to." Kaitlyn's voice caught. "It was easier to be angry, to blame you for Dad leaving. I'm so sorry, Mom. For not understanding how hard it all was. For not being there for you the way you were always there for me."

"Oh honey." Gretchen reached over, taking her daughter's

hands. "You were dealing with your own pain. Your father left both of us."

"But I made everything about me." Kaitlyn's voice cracked. "After high school, I refused to go to college, ran away to Aunt Chelsea on Captiva instead. Even when you came to live with Aunt Tess and Aunt Leah last year—I barely called. I was so wrapped up in my own life, my own drama." She squeezed her mother's hands. "You were so brave, Mom. Trying to save your marriage even after you knew about Joanna. Trying to keep our family together."

"Not brave." Gretchen shook her head. "Terrified. Of losing everything. Of failing you."

"But you didn't fail me, Mom. You protected me the only way you knew how." Kaitlyn's voice softened. "I understand that now, working here. Sometimes people make choices out of fear, out of love, out of desperation—and they're all tangled up together. I think you and I aren't that different after all."

"How do you mean?"

"The passion you had to keep our family together is the same passion that's inside me. I think it's why it's so important for me to meet Sarah. She's my sister and I want to be in her life and share my life with her."

"When did you get so wise?"

Kaitlyn shrugged, tears glistening in her eyes. "I'm not so wise, but I'm starting to understand the choices women have to make in the name of love. I hope I'm half the woman you are in my life."

Gretchen watched her daughter, feeling the weight of all they'd been through. Though she hated what Jeffrey had put them through, she was grateful for the struggle that had brought her daughter back to her—not just as her little girl, but as a grown woman with an incredible heart.

Whatever the future held, their relationship had evolved into something deeper: a friendship built on understanding and truth.

CHAPTER 22

Inside the community room at Paradise Harbor House, Elena, Kaitlyn, and Will sat around a table, reviewing the footage from the interviews earlier in the day.

"That was amazing," Kaitlyn said as the last clip played. "Melanie told her story so beautifully. It felt real, honest."

"She did great," Will agreed, clicking through his editing software. "I'll clean up the audio and add some soft background music, but the footage is solid. We'll have it ready before the fundraiser tomorrow."

Elena leaned back, nodding in satisfaction. "This is exactly what we needed. The community needs to see the heart behind Paradise Harbor House, not just statistics. Real stories connect people."

Kaitlyn smiled, but there was a trace of nervousness in her expression. "Do you think this will help push the fundraiser over the edge? I mean, we need every dollar we can get."

"The numbers are looking great so far. I appreciate what your Aunt Leah is doing regarding funding through grants. It's very forward-thinking of her. We do take things one day at a time, but we still need to think long-term if we want to stay afloat for many years to come. "

"I know she loves to work with numbers," Kaitlyn offered. And, she's good at this."

"I don't know much about the finance and investments, but if you're worried about money, your aunt Leah might have the answer for that. I realize that grant writing takes time, and it might be another year before we see any money. But, it's still important to diversify our outreach."

Kaitlyn nodded. "I understand."

"You'd be surprised how many people see a place like this and have no real idea the impact it has on a community. We're doing good work here, and that's what counts."

Elena reached for Kaitlyn's hand, giving it a reassuring squeeze. "I think this will remind people why they're here. And when they see what their donations can do, they'll give from the heart."

Will shut his laptop with a soft click. "Then let's make sure tomorrow night is everything it needs to be."

Kaitlyn took a deep breath and then smiled. She didn't want to measure the success of the fundraiser just by the numbers. What she worried about but couldn't say to anyone was that she was afraid of disappointing Elena.

This was the first time she'd put herself out there after college. She did her best to push her worries away and focus on being herself, a young woman finding her way in the world, one step at a time.

The door chimed, and Jack appeared, his messenger bag slung over one shoulder. "Hope I'm not interrupting."

"Perfect timing," Elena said. "We just finished reviewing the interview footage."

"Good, because I come bearing news." He dropped into the chair beside Leah, who'd been quietly working on donor packets in the corner. "Mike—the captain—wants to do a morning walk-through of the boat. Thought you might all want to see where everything will be set up."

Kaitlyn's eyes lit up. "Really? That would be incredible. Will, we could plan our camera angles ahead of time."

"Exactly what I was thinking," Jack smiled. "Nine a.m. work for everyone?"

"I'll text Mom and Aunt Chelsea and Tess," Kaitlyn said, already reaching for her phone. "They should see this too."

Jack looked at Leah and smiled.

"Thank you, Jack. I'm guessing you had something to do with that."

"I might have mentioned it. I can't remember."

Kaitlyn, Elena and Will looked at each other and smiled.

The twinkle in Jack's eyes told them everything they needed to know. That Leah was falling in love, and Jack Calloway was the reason.

The next morning dawned clear and perfect, with just enough breeze to ruffle the flags along the marina. Will and Kaitlyn arrived with her mother and aunts to find Jack already waiting at the dock, coffee carrier in hand.

"Cuban roast," he announced, passing out cups. "Brain fuel for party planning."

"You're a lifesaver," Chelsea declared, accepting hers. "Some of us needed this after staying up late sorting auction items."

"Where's Elena?" Kaitlyn asked.

"She wanted to stay back at the house to get breakfast ready for everyone, so she said she trusted us to handle this."

The boat was magnificent in the morning light, its white hull gleaming. Captain Mike met them at the gangway, his weathered face creased in a welcoming smile.

"Thank you so much for helping us with this fundraiser," Kaitlyn said.

"Jack's told me all about Paradise Harbor House," he said, shaking hands. "My daughter volunteers at a women's shelter up in Tampa. When Jack mentioned this fundraiser, well..." He shrugged. "Seemed like fate."

They followed him aboard, Kaitlyn's breath catching at how spacious the deck was. Tess immediately started calculating table arrangements while Leah pulled out her ever-present notebook.

"The sunset will be perfect from this angle," Will said, framing shots with his hands. "We can set up the presentation screen here, catch that golden hour light..."

"And the dining area below deck," Captain Mike continued, leading them down. "Plenty of room for your silent auction displays."

Gretchen touched Kaitlyn's arm as the others explored. "Can you picture it? All those people coming together to support Paradise Harbor House? You should be proud of what you've done."

"What we've all done, Mom," Kaitlyn corrected softly. "I couldn't have done any of this alone."

Chelsea appeared with more coffee from the boat's galley. "Jack's showing Leah the upper deck. I think he's trying to convince her it's the perfect spot for a private date."

"Subtle, he is not." Tess laughed, then grew thoughtful. "Though speaking of not subtle... Jamie's bringing extra staff tonight. Said something about wanting everything to be perfect."

"For the fundraiser?" Gretchen's tone was innocent. "Or for you?"

"Very funny," Tess responded as she walked away to explore more of the boat.

"This is really happening," Kaitlyn said softly, leaning on the rail beside Will. "All our work, all our hopes..."

"It's going to be amazing," he assured her, his hand finding hers. "Just like you."

Kaitlyn touched his arm, her voice thick with emotion. "I can't thank you enough for everything you've done. Not just for the fundraiser, but for me personally. My life has been upside down for so long, but now..." She paused, searching for the right words. "Now I feel like the spinning has finally stopped. Like I've found solid ground."

"And you think I had something to do with that?" he teased gently, though his eyes were serious.

She met his gaze, the blue of his eyes matching the water below. "You've had everything to do with it."

Their eyes locked, and for a moment, everything felt perfect. But even in this peaceful moment, thoughts of her father and Sarah tugged at the edges of her mind. The uncertainty of their future relationship cast a shadow she tried to push away, not wanting it to dim this precious moment with Will.

As if reading her thoughts, Will touched her cheek. "Kaitlyn, don't worry about Sarah. I know in my heart that you two will find your way to each other."

"How did you know I was thinking about that?" she asked, wonder in her voice.

He smiled, his thumb brushing her cheekbone. "I'd like to think I know you pretty well by now. The more time we spend together, the more certain I become of that."

Kaitlyn leaned into his touch, marveling at how he could read her silent moments, how he seemed to know instinctively when her thoughts turned dark and exactly how to ease her fears.

In all her carefully curated social media life, she'd never imagined finding something this real, this true. Nothing could be more perfect than being known, being understood, being loved exactly as she was.

"Looks like someone changed her mind," Chelsea yelled to everyone.

From the dock, Elena appeared with more volunteers carrying supplies. "I couldn't stay away, I'm too excited. Besides, I've got extra stuff to drop off. Ready to start marking setup locations?"

Kaitlyn waved to Elena. "Absolutely!"

"The bar setup will go here." Captain Mike indicated a polished wooden counter. "And we've got built-in coolers underneath for your champagne service."

"Perfect for the sunset toast," Tess noted, already envisioning the flow of service. "Jamie's staff will have easy access."

Leah was making notes in her ever-present notebook. "Jack, what time are your publishing contacts arriving? We should reserve the best viewing spots for major donors."

"Six sharp," he replied. "Though knowing Regina, she'll be here at five forty-five. She's particularly interested in the literacy program."

Will had his camera out, documenting the space. "Kaitlyn, come see this angle. When the sun hits here, it'll create the perfect backdrop for the presentation."

Chelsea watched her niece move confidently through the space, directing, planning, solving small problems before they could become large ones. "She's really found her calling, hasn't she?" she murmured to Gretchen.

"She has," Gretchen agreed softly. "Though I never would have predicted this a year ago."

"Life's funny that way," Captain Mike commented, overhearing them. "Sometimes the best journeys are the ones we never planned."

"Speaking of journeys," Elena called from below deck, "we need to figure out the traffic flow for the silent auction. We don't want bottlenecks when people are trying to place bids."

They spent the next hour mapping out every detail—where

the musicians would be positioned, how to arrange the seating to maximize the sunset view, the best spots for Will to capture candid moments of guests enjoying themselves.

"We should mark the spots for the family photos," Kaitlyn said, moving toward the display area they'd designated. "The lighting needs to be just right—we want people to feel the stories, not just see them."

"Like Melanie's interview," Gretchen added. "The way you captured her strength, her hope."

Will nodded, already adjusting his camera settings. "We'll set up soft lighting here, keep it intimate. When people see these images, they should understand that Paradise Harbor House isn't just a place—it's a community."

"Speaking of community," Captain Mike called from the bridge, "wait until you see what happens when we drop anchor in that perfect sunset spot. The way the light plays on the water… it's like nature designed it for moments like this."

Tess leaned against the rail, the breeze playing with her hair. "Jamie mentioned something about timing the dessert service just as the sun touches the horizon. Said it adds a touch of magic to everything."

"Pure romance, that one," Chelsea teased, but her eyes were kind.

Captain Mike appeared with more coffee and what looked suspiciously like fresh Cuban pastries. "Courtesy of your friend Jamie," he explained. "Said something about practicing the dessert presentation."

"Quality control," Tess said solemnly, reaching for one. "Very important."

Tess felt her cheeks warm as everyone's attention turned to her. The pastry in her hand suddenly seemed very interesting.

"Just friends, huh?" Chelsea's tone was too innocent. "Is that why he's been testing dessert recipes on you all week?"

"He tests them on everyone," Tess protested, but even she

could hear the weak defense in her voice. "It's…professional courtesy."

"Oh, of course," Leah agreed, straight-faced. "Very professional. Like those private sunset guitar sessions at Max's?"

Tess shot her sister a look that promised revenge. "Those are just…he's just getting back into playing. Nothing more."

"Mmhmm." Chelsea wasn't even trying to hide her smile now. "And I suppose him rearranging his entire staff schedule to be free for the fundraiser is just professional dedication?"

"You all are impossible," Tess muttered, but she couldn't quite suppress her own smile. The truth was, she and Jamie were… something. Something delicate and new, still finding its shape.

"Leave her alone." Gretchen surprisingly came to her rescue. Then ruined it by adding, "Though I have to say, his key lime pie has gotten even better lately. Amazing what happiness does for a chef's cooking."

"I hate all of you," Tess declared, but she was laughing now. Because they weren't wrong—Jamie had been different lately. Lighter. More like the person everyone said he'd been before losing Emma. And if she had something to do with that…well, maybe that was its own kind of magic.

"You know what would be perfect for the fundraiser?" Kaitlyn chimed in, her eyes dancing with mischief. "If Jamie played guitar during dessert. You know, something romantic…"

"Don't you dare," Tess warned, pointing her half-eaten pastry at her niece. "He's just getting comfortable performing again."

"Actually," Will said thoughtfully, lowering his camera, "that would make for amazing footage. The restaurant owner who supports Paradise Harbor House, sharing his music…"

"See? Perfect!" Chelsea agreed. "And Tess could—"

"Could what?" Tess challenged. "Stand there awkwardly while you all pretend not to stare?"

"Well, you could always join him," Leah suggested innocently. "I seem to remember you used to sing in high school."

"That was thirty years ago!" Tess felt her face flame again. "And if anyone mentions this to Jamie, I swear I'll tell Jack about that poetry journal Leah's been hiding in her desk."

"What poetry journal?" Jack called from above deck.

"Nothing!" Leah shouted back, her own cheeks reddening.

"Actually," Tess said, trying to regain some dignity, "Jamie's friend's band is handling the music. He wants to focus on the food service, make sure everything runs perfectly."

"Oh, I bet that's why he wants to focus on the food," Chelsea drawled. "That way he can focus on you, Tess."

"I walked right into that one, didn't I?" Tess groaned, but she couldn't help smiling. The truth was the thought of Jamie watching her instead of performing did make her pulse quicken a bit.

"Face it, sis," Leah said, "you're not fooling anyone. Especially not with that look on your face right now."

"What look? There's no look!" But Tess could feel herself blushing again.

"That one," Kaitlyn pointed out helpfully. "The same one he gets when you walk into Max's."

"Can we please focus on the fundraiser?" Tess begged. "You know, the actual reason we're all here?"

"Oh, we're focused," Chelsea assured her. "On all the important details. Including how our sister somehow managed to capture the heart of Key West's most eligible restaurateur."

"I hate every single one of you," Tess declared, but her smile gave her away. "Captain Mike, any chance we could throw a few of these people overboard?"

They laughed and enjoyed the remainder of the pastries and coffee and then thanked Captain Mike. Everything was falling into place. The fundraiser was only hours away, and no one was more excited than Kaitlyn.

CHAPTER 23

The sunset cruise fundraiser for Paradise Harbor House was about to begin. Golden hues over the Key West marina meant soon the sky would be a mix of colors by the time all the guests arrived.

There wasn't anything more beautiful than when the sky was a perfect watercolor blend of pinks, oranges, and soft blues. The wind had died down from earlier in the afternoon and the gentle ocean breeze was perfect for taking a boat out on the water.

A long table draped in linen stood at the entrance, where volunteers handed out handcrafted lanyards—each adorned with small sea-glass pendants made by a local artisan. The lanyards doubled as guest passes for the event and would be a perfect keepsake memory of the event.

"Here you go," Leah said with a bright smile, handing lanyards to an older couple. "Enjoy the evening!"

Guests began making their way up the wooden plank leading onto the *Sea Breeze*, a beautiful, spacious vessel with a sturdy double-deck design. The aroma of expertly prepared dishes from Jamie's restaurant filled the air as he oversaw the catering, ensuring a memorable dining experience for everyone on board.

Tess stood near the entrance, watching as guests climbed aboard. As each one approached, they admired the soft string lights illuminating the deck, the crisp white tablecloths draped over the buffet station, and the bartenders mixing drinks with practiced ease. Servers wove through the mingling crowd, already making their rounds, carrying silver trays laden with appetizers.

Elena was deep in conversation with a well-dressed couple near the bar, while Gretchen helped direct a few late arrivals. Kaitlyn, wearing a deep blue sundress, stood beside Will as he captured footage of the guests boarding.

"Looks good, doesn't it?" Will murmured, adjusting his camera lens.

"It looks perfect," Kaitlyn replied, scanning the scene. "Now we just have to hope people open their wallets for the silent auction."

Tess turned as Jamie approached, his chef's coat pristine despite the humid evening. "So, how's the crowd looking?" he asked.

"Like they have money to spend," Tess said with a smirk.

Jamie chuckled. "Good. That's the idea, right?"

As more guests filled the deck, a waiter passed by, offering trays of seafood-stuffed mushrooms, bruschetta topped with heirloom tomatoes, and miniature crab cakes. The scent of grilled fish and fresh tropical fruit from the buffet drifted through the air, making stomachs rumble in anticipation.

Leah stepped beside Kaitlyn, nudging her lightly. "You nervous?"

"Terrified."

Leah laughed. "You'll be fine. Just focus on the cause. That's what this is all about."

A few minutes later, Elena took to the small stage near the center of the deck, microphone in hand. The music softened as she tapped the mic, drawing the attention of the crowd.

"Good evening, everyone. Thank you so much for joining us tonight on this beautiful Key West evening," she began, her voice warm and welcoming. "Tonight isn't just about enjoying good food and great company. It's about making a difference. It's about supporting the families who come to Paradise Harbor House in search of hope, stability, and a second chance."

A hush fell over the crowd as Elena continued, speaking from the heart about the shelter's mission. She gestured toward Will, who nodded before clicking a button on his tablet, sending the interview footage up onto a screen set up above the bar.

The video played, showing the history of Paradise Harbor House with clips of interviews from not only people who have lived at the shelter, but people who have benefited from the good work of the organization over the years.

When it came to Melanie's interview, her words resonated with the guests. Faces in the crowd softened, some dabbing at their eyes as Melanie spoke of how Paradise Harbor House had saved her and Hailee from living in their car.

As the video ended, Elena stepped forward again. "That's why we're here. And that's why we need your support tonight. Below this deck, you'll find all the various silent auction items. If you have any questions, there will be people down there to help you. Please enjoy the party and thank you all again for coming to support Paradise Harbor House."

A round of applause followed, and soon, the event moved into full swing. Guests laughed and mingled, enjoying the ocean breeze and the picturesque view of the setting sun over the Gulf. The bartenders kept drinks flowing—glasses of white wine, tropical cocktails, and fresh citrus-infused water.

The polished teak deck gleamed under the string lights as Leah made her way toward the stern, the gentle sway of the boat beneath her feet matching the rhythm of the waves. Salt-laden air mingled with the sweet scent of tropical flowers arranged in crystalline vases along the railings.

She spotted Jack at the stern, his profile outlined against a sky that had deepened from coral to indigo, the first stars beginning to peek through the darkening canvas above.

"This is quite an event you all have put together," he said, offering her a fresh glass of wine. The crystal caught the light, sending tiny rainbows dancing across the polished deck.

"Thanks." She accepted the glass and moved to stand beside him at the railing, the metal cool and smooth beneath her palm. "Though I can't take much credit. This was all Kaitlyn and Elena's vision."

"Don't sell yourself short." His voice was soft but firm, barely carrying over the melodic strings of the live band and the gentle lapping of waves against the hull. "I've seen how hard you've worked these past few weeks."

Leah took a sip of wine, enjoying the cool breeze that played with loose strands of her hair. "I suppose I have been burning the candle at both ends lately."

"Which is why," Jack said, turning to face her fully, "I was thinking maybe you'd let me take you away for a weekend. Nothing fancy—just a quick trip up to Marco Island. I know this great little place right on the beach."

Leah's pulse quickened. She wasn't sure whether he was moving too fast, but the idea of their first real getaway together scared her. "Jack…"

"Before you overthink it," he said with that knowing smile she'd grown so fond of, "it's just a suggestion. No pressure. But I thought it might be nice to have some time, just us, away from work and responsibilities." He paused, his expression growing more serious. "I care about you, Leah. A lot. And I'd like the chance to show you that without having to share you with the rest of Key West for a couple of days."

"I'd like that," she said softly. "Let me think about it, okay?"

"Absolutely," he said, as he placed a hand on her arm.

She leaned into his touch, savoring the moment until a burst of laughter from nearby reminded her they weren't alone.

The subtle rock of the boat beneath her feet kept Kaitlyn aware of their position on the water as she wove through the crowd. The string lights overhead cast honeyed shadows across the faces of contented guests, while tea lights in mercury glass holders flickered on each table like captured stars. She paused near the buffet, where the aroma of grilled mahi-mahi drizzled with mango-lime sauce mingled with the sweetness of caramelized plantains and the bright scent of fresh herbs.

"Getting good footage?" she asked, sensing Will's approach before she saw him, the familiar scent of his cologne carrying on the breeze.

"The best." He lowered his camera, giving her a warm smile that crinkled the corners of his eyes. "Elena's speech really moved people. And when Melanie came on screen…" He shook his head. "I saw at least three people writing checks right after."

Pride swelled in her chest. "I still can't believe we pulled this off."

"I can." Will's voice was soft but certain. "You're kind of unstoppable when you set your mind to something."

She turned to face him, struck by the sincerity in his expression. The string lights overhead cast a gentle glow across his features, and for a moment, she forgot about the fundraiser, the guests, everything except the way he was looking at her.

"Will…"

"The silent auction's going great too," he said quickly, as if catching himself. "I got some great shots of people bidding. The marketing team's going to love this for next year's promotional materials."

Kaitlyn nodded, trying to ignore the flutter in her stomach.

"Good thinking. We should probably check on the auction tables again."

"Lead the way." He gestured forward with his camera, falling into step beside her as they headed below deck.

Tess made her way to the dessert station, where crystalline serving dishes displayed Jamie's creations like jewels in a case. The air was rich with the scent of vanilla, caramelized sugar, and fresh-baked pastries.

She spotted him directing his staff, his chef's coat, sleeves rolled up to reveal tanned forearms as he arranged delicate chocolate decorations on a tray of key lime tarts.

"The food is amazing," she said, breathing in the mouthwatering aromas. "Everyone's raving about it."

His eyes crinkled at the corners as he smiled, tiny laugh lines deepening in a way that made her heart flutter. "Well, I had good motivation to bring my A-game tonight."

"Oh?" She raised an eyebrow, steadying herself against a nearby table as the boat gently rocked. "And what motivation would that be?"

"You know what motivation." He wiped his hands on his apron before removing it. "When the fundraiser is over, I'd like to take you to dinner."

"I'd like that. I think your food is incredible."

Jamie shook his head. "No, not at my restaurant. I thought maybe we could go somewhere away from Key West. I know a really great place in Key Largo."

Tess tried to remain calm, but her heart raced. "Of course. I'm always looking for new places to go for dinner."

"Good." He stepped closer, his voice dropping lower. "Because I was hoping maybe we could have a talk, maybe get to know each other better. I don't know if it matters to you or not, but I thought you should know that I haven't asked a woman out on a date since my wife died."

Her heart fluttered. "Jamie…"

"I'm not trying to get serious here but I'm feeling things for you that I haven't felt for years. I think it's important that I not ignore those feelings," he continued, reaching for her hand. He laughed and looked down at the deck floor. "Am I making a fool of myself?"

Tess shook her head. "No, not at all. I'm glad you asked me, and I'm especially happy that when you finally felt ready to move forward, you thought of me."

He smiled and nodded. "Thanks, Tess. Thanks for putting a guy at ease. I should check on the kitchen crew," he murmured, though he made no move to pull away.

"Of course," she agreed, equally reluctant to break the moment.

Finally, he straightened, but before turning away, he took her hand in his. "Save me a dance later? Once service is done?"

"You bet."

As Jamie made his way back to the kitchen, Tess leaned against the railing, letting the ocean breeze cool her flushed cheeks. She closed her eyes, feeling the gentle sway of the boat beneath her feet, and feeling an imbalance that had nothing to do with the boat.

The music wove through the evening air like silk, and somewhere in the distance, a seabird called a goodnight to the setting sun. This fundraiser wasn't just raising money for Paradise Harbor House tonight—it was marking the beginning of something new, something precious, something that felt remarkably like home, for everyone.

CHAPTER 24

The morning after the fundraiser, Paradise Harbor House buzzed with a quiet energy.

The event had been a success—guests had donated generously, the silent auction had exceeded expectations, and more than one local business had pledged continued support.

The lingering warmth of the previous night still hung in the air, but Kaitlyn felt something else settling over her: a choice she could no longer ignore.

She stood in the kitchen, staring at the coffee in her mug but not drinking it. Leah and Tess were already out running errands, Gretchen was meeting Chelsea before their trip back to Captiva, and Will had gone to get footage of the sunrise over the marina. The shelter was quieter than usual, but she didn't mind. It gave her space to think.

"Elena's looking for you," one of the volunteers said as they passed by. "She's in her office."

Kaitlyn inhaled deeply. She knew what this was about.

She found Elena at her desk, a notebook open, jotting down a list of follow-up calls from the fundraiser. She glanced up as Kaitlyn entered. "Ah, just the person I needed to see."

Kaitlyn smiled, taking a seat across from her. "That sounds dangerous."

Elena chuckled. "I promise I won't make you fill out spreadsheets again." Then, she set her pen down and folded her hands. "But I do have a proposition for you."

Kaitlyn knew it was coming, but it still made her stomach flip. "Okay. I'm listening."

Elena leaned forward slightly. "I want you to stay, Kaitlyn. Not just as a volunteer, but as part of our team. I want you to consider working here at Paradise Harbor full-time."

Kaitlyn opened her mouth, but nothing came out right away.

"The job wouldn't be glamorous," Elena continued, filling the silence. "You already know the pay isn't great. But what you did last night—coordinating everything, connecting with donors, managing volunteers—you're good at it. And it's not just about logistics. You make people feel like they belong here."

Kaitlyn let out a slow breath. "I—I don't know what to say."

"Say whatever's in your heart," Elena said simply.

Kaitlyn looked down at her hands, then back up at the woman who had become a mentor in such a short time. "I love this place. I love the people. But this wasn't part of the plan."

Elena smiled knowingly. "Plans change. That's life."

Kaitlyn exhaled a soft laugh, shaking her head. "I went to school for business. I spent years thinking I'd end up in marketing, or corporate management, or—" She hesitated. "Something with a salary that actually makes sense."

"I get it," Elena said. "But what if those things don't fulfill you the way this does?"

Kaitlyn bit her lip, glancing out the window at the courtyard. A few children ran past, their laughter echoing, while Melanie sat on a bench talking to another mother who had arrived the week before.

She thought about the video Will had filmed. About how

proud she'd felt watching the fundraiser unfold. About the way her heart had expanded, seeing these women regain hope.

Then she thought about the moment her mother had looked at her last night, not with skepticism or doubt, but with pride.

She turned back to Elena. "Can I have a little time to think about it?"

Elena nodded. "Of course. But whatever you decide, know this—Paradise Harbor House will always have a place for you."

Kaitlyn followed after Will, who had gone to the marina to take photos for a local artist. She found him leaning against the railing, camera slung over his shoulder.

"You disappear after big decisions, don't you?" he asked without turning around.

Kaitlyn smirked, stepping beside him. "Who says I made a decision?"

He turned his head slightly, raising an eyebrow. "Well, did you?"

She sighed, resting her arms on the railing. "Elena offered me a job. Full-time, but you knew that already, didn't you?"

Will nodded. "She told me she was going to offer you a permanent job. What did you tell her?"

Kaitlyn shrugged, "I couldn't say yes, not without thinking more about it.

"And?" he asked.

"And I don't know what to do."

He was quiet for a moment, then said, "I do."

Kaitlyn turned to him. "What?"

"You've already made your decision. You just haven't admitted it to yourself yet."

Kaitlyn frowned. "That's a little presumptuous."

Will chuckled. "Maybe. But I've been watching you. I saw you last night, running that fundraiser like it was second nature. I see the way you talk to the women at the shelter, how much you care."

He shifted slightly, studying her. "I also know you're scared. Because choosing this means letting go of whatever idea you had for your future before now."

Kaitlyn let out a sharp breath. "Yeah. It does, even though I'm not really sure what I had planned. Was not planning anything at all really my plan?"

He laughed. "I guess it's possible, but that only happens when you don't know what to do…when you don't know yourself. I don't think you're the same woman you were when you arrived in Key West. That woman is gone. You've grown so much in such a short time, but I think that's what happens when you're where you're supposed to be."

"But what about my mother and…"

"Kaitlyn, you're not the first person to realize their dream wasn't actually *their* dream," Will said. "Sometimes we chase things because we think we should. But then we find something that actually makes us feel alive."

Kaitlyn stared out at the water, letting his words sink in.

"Whatever you decide," he added, "just make sure it's what *you* want. Not what's expected of you. Not what makes sense on paper. What *you* want."

She turned to him, her expression unreadable. "And what about you? What do *you* want?"

Will's mouth quirked into a soft smile. "That's an easy one. I want to stay in Key West. And I'd really like it if you stayed too. But, you need to stay because you want to, not because I want you to."

Kaitlyn's heart did a little flip, but she ignored it for now. Instead, she just nodded, watching as a sailboat drifted toward the horizon.

"I'll let you know when I figure it out," she said.

Will grinned. "I'll be here."

"Seriously, Jeffrey? Once again you've decided not to put your daughters' feelings first."

"Let's not fight about this, Gretchen. It can't be helped. Joanna has a lot of things planned for the summer. We've got a few colleges lined up to visit and…"

Gretchen interrupted him, "What am I supposed to tell Kaitlyn? You keep pushing her away like this and she'll give up wanting anything to do with you."

"What about all those years when you made it impossible for me to see Kaitlyn? Why won't you take some responsibility for this mess? It wasn't all me," he insisted.

"I've explained things to Kaitlyn and have apologized for them, but that was in the past. We're now given another opportunity to set things right for these two young women. They deserve that."

There was silence on Jeffrey's end of the line with an occasional sound of a woman's voice in the background. She assumed it was Joanna.

"How has Sarah reacted to this change of plans?" Gretchen asked.

"She's not happy about it, but it's not her call. She's only sixteen years old and isn't mature enough to make decisions about this. She's going to have to trust that we know what's best for her."

Gretchen chuckled. "Good luck with that because as far as I can see, you haven't a clue what's best for anyone, especially your daughters."

Angry, Gretchen ended the call and threw her cellphone on the sofa. She put her face in her hands and tried not to cry.

An hour later, Kaitlyn found her mother sitting on the small porch of the bungalow, deep in conversation with Ernest.

"I'm starting to worry about you, Mom. Talking to a rooster?"

Gretchen laughed. "I'm not the only one. The other day I heard Tess talking to him too. He's quite the charmer for a bird."

Kaitlyn sat on the steps, her legs curled up beneath her. The evening air was thick with the smell of jasmine from the vine that climbed the porch trellis, and somewhere in the distance, she could hear the gentle strum of guitar music drifting from one of the nearby bars.

"Are you okay, honey? Something on your mind?" Gretchen asked, studying her daughter's face with the kind of attention only mothers seem capable of.

Kaitlyn glanced at her mother, then exhaled. "Elena offered me a job."

Gretchen didn't look surprised. "Are you going to take it?"

"I don't know," Kaitlyn admitted, picking at a loose thread on her sundress. "I love it here. I love what we're doing. But it's not what I planned for my life."

Gretchen swirled her wine thoughtfully. "Life rarely goes according to plan. Trust me, I know." She paused, looking out at the deepening twilight. "But, I'm curious, did you have a plan after college?"

Kaitlyn gave a small laugh. "Not really. I don't know. For a minute I considered traveling to England or Spain or Italy. You know, just see what there is to see. After that, I'd come back home and look for a job in marketing or finance or something… grown-up. I wasn't thinking of settling down in one place so soon."

She drew her knees up to her chest. "I mean, if I work at Paradise Harbor House, it's a real commitment. I didn't want to get so attached to anyone. If I work there, that will be impossible.

I can't walk away whenever I feel like it. People depend on me to be there for them. It's an important job, and…"

The more she heard herself talk, the more Kaitlyn understood how much she loved helping families get on their feet. She thought about Melanie and Hailee, about the new mother who'd arrived last week with nothing but a backpack and hope in her eyes.

"You know," Gretchen said softly, "when you were little, you used to organize these elaborate 'helping parties' in our neighborhood. Remember those?"

Kaitlyn smiled at the memory. "Mrs. Rodriguez's garden after that awful storm."

"And the Thompsons' garage sale for their son's medical bills," Gretchen added. "You were always gathering people together, finding ways to make things better." She set her wine glass down and leaned forward. "Maybe this isn't so far from who you've always been."

Kaitlyn felt tears prick at her eyes. "But what if I'm not good enough? What if I can't actually help these women the way they need?"

"Oh, honey." Gretchen moved to sit beside her daughter on the steps. "You already are. I saw you last night at the fundraiser. I saw how you talked to those donors, how you made them understand why Paradise Harbor House matters. But more than that, I've seen how you are with the women and children there. You don't just help them—you see them. You make them feel worthy of being seen."

Her mother turned to her fully. "The question isn't whether this fits the plan you made months or years ago. The question is —does this make you happy? Does it make you feel like you're making a difference?"

Kaitlyn swallowed the lump in her throat. "Yeah. It does."

Gretchen smiled, the porch light catching the moisture in her own eyes. "Then maybe that's all that matters."

They sat in silence for a moment, listening to Ernest scratch at the ground nearby, before Kaitlyn murmured, "Would you be disappointed if I stayed?"

Gretchen reached for her hand, squeezing it gently. "Honey, I will never be disappointed in you following your heart." She wrapped an arm around Kaitlyn's shoulders. "Besides, Key West isn't so far from Captiva. And something tells me you won't be alone here."

Kaitlyn thought of Will, of Tess and Leah, of Elena and all the people at Paradise Harbor House. She thought of the way this place had started to feel like home when she wasn't looking.

"Honey, I hate to add one more thing to your plate, but I've just gotten off the phone with your father. Apparently, they're not coming to Key West after all."

"What? Why not?"

"He said something about visiting colleges this summer and it would be too much for them to come down here right now."

Kaitlyn hung her head and stared at the floor. "So, I won't get to see Dad."

It was the first time she'd openly voiced her disappointment in not seeing her father and it was painful. It was the kind of pain she'd stuffed down deep inside, not allowing her feelings to surface. She suddenly felt like a little girl again. The sadness enveloped her, and she let the tears fall.

"I'm so sorry, baby," Gretchen said, wrapping her arms around Kaitlyn.

Kaitlyn let out a slow breath, leaning into her mother's embrace.

"Why doesn't he love me?"

The small tears turned into deep sobbing and Gretchen's heart broke into a million pieces. She and Jeffrey had made such a mess of things that it all had come to bear in this moment between her and her child.

Kaitlyn had shown herself to be such a strong and capable

woman, that Gretchen let herself forget that her daughter was still a child, one who was broken and lost.

Kaitlyn had gravitated to a position at Paradise Harbor House because of an empathy that had long developed from personal experience. Gretchen finally saw her daughter with a mother's eyes, and a woman's heart, and she vowed to make things right.

They stayed in that position for several minutes before Kaitlyn pulled back and wiped her eyes.

"Dad doesn't know what he's missing, not seeing me."

Gretchen smiled and pushed hair from her daughter's face, now wet with sweat and tears. "No, he doesn't."

CHAPTER 25

Chelsea sat at the kitchen table, laptop open to check her email. Ernest strutted past the window, pausing to eye the scene with his usual literary scrutiny, as if sensing the drama about to unfold.

Gretchen filled her suitcase with a few souvenirs from her stay in Key West as she continued packing for her trip back to Captiva. She sorted through the clothes she'd brought to Key West, when her phone rang.

The name on the screen made Gretchen's heart stop: Jeffrey.

"Jeffrey?" Her voice came out steadier than she felt. Chelsea's head snapped up at the name.

"Gretchen." His voice was tight with panic. "Sarah's gone. She left a note—she's driving to Key West to meet Kaitlyn."

"What do you mean she's gone?" Gretchen gripped the phone tighter, sinking into a kitchen chair. "How could you let this happen?"

"Let this happen? She snuck out, Gretchen! She left a note and took off in her car."

"This is exactly what I warned you about!" Gretchen's voice rose. "When she first asked to come meet Kaitlyn, I told you how much it meant to both Sarah and Kaitlyn. But no—your wife decided it wasn't a good idea, and you, as usual, went along with whatever she wanted!"

"Don't bring Joanna into this—"

"Why not? She's the one who convinced you to say no. Sarah's sixteen, Jeffrey. Did you really think she'd just accept being told she couldn't meet her own sister? After everything that's happened? After all these years of lies?"

Chelsea moved closer, her face tight with concern. She could hear Jeffrey's agitated voice through the phone.

"She's not answering our calls. I have to assume she is somewhere between here and Key West." His voice cracked slightly. "Can we please focus on finding her instead of arguing about whose fault this is?"

Gretchen sighed. She had so much to say to him, but he was right. The most important thing right now was making sure Sarah was safe.

"When did she leave?"

"Must have been early this morning. We just found the note. Joanna's hysterical, and I'm leaving for Key West now. Sarah's driving her blue Toyota Corolla." He rattled off the license plate number. "Gretchen, she's only sixteen. She's never driven this far alone."

After hanging up, Gretchen looked at Chelsea, her hands shaking. "Sarah ran away early this morning. Jeffrey said she left a note that she was coming here to see Kaitlyn."

"Does she even have her address? Does she know where Kaitlyn is?"

"I have to assume the only thing she knows is Paradise Harbor House from all the things Kaitlyn puts online. Other than that, I have no idea."

"We need to tell everyone. You're probably right, she'd most likely go there, but just in case, we should make people aware of the situation," Chelsea said, already grabbing her purse. "Let's go to Max's first. Tess and Leah need to know what's happening."

The bar was quiet this time of day, with only a few regular customers eating lunch. Several regulars nodded when they arrived. The mystery novelist who always sat in the corner looked up from her notebook as they burst in.

Connie's friend Rick the retired fisherman who'd helped them source seafood for the fundraiser, set down his coffee. They'd all been part of last night's success at Paradise Harbor, and now they could sense something was wrong.

"What happened?" Leah asked the moment she saw their faces, abandoning the glasses she was sorting. "I thought you two were heading back to Captiva."

"Sarah's run away," Gretchen burst out. "She's driving here. Jeffrey just called—she left a note saying she's coming to meet Kaitlyn."

"Oh my, does Kaitlyn know?" Tess asked.

"Not yet. I'm going over to Paradise Harbor House to tell her, but I'm worried," Gretchen said.

"She's sixteen," Leah said, her voice rising. "Driving alone from Fort Lauderdale? All because Jeffrey wouldn't stand up to Joanna?" She braced her hands on the bar. "First he abandons Kaitlyn, and now he can't even handle this right?"

"I might as well tell you. Jeffrey is on his way too. I haven't seen him in years," she added, her heart racing. "That man will be the death of me. He had the nerve to act like none of this is his fault," Gretchen said.

"Well, isn't that just like him," Leah muttered. "Finally showing up when everything's falling apart."

"This isn't the time," Chelsea cut in, but the regulars were already murmuring, piecing together the family drama they'd glimpsed over the past months. "I know you'd like to wring his neck, but we need to focus on the girls. Before this day is over, there will be two young women dealing with something beyond their years. We all need to keep a level head."

Connie appeared from the back, taking in the scene. Tess's pale face, Leah's white-knuckled grip on the bar. "Go," she said to Tess and Leah. "This is family."

"No," Chelsea insisted. "We need people in different locations. You two stay here—Sarah might come looking for Kaitlyn on Fleming Street first. Gretchen and I will go tell Kaitlyn."

"I'll alert the other businesses," Connie said, already pulling out her phone. "Everyone knows Kaitlyn from the fundraiser. We'll keep an eye out for Sarah's car. Give me the plate number and details and I'll let Jamie and Jack know."

Mike stood up. "I'll walk down to the marina, let the charter captains know. She might head there looking for her sister."

The mystery novelist closed her notebook. "I'll post something in the neighborhood watch group. Quietly," she added at Chelsea's worried look. "Just asking people to watch for the car."

"Jamie's doing deliveries today," Tess said suddenly. "I'll call him, have him watch the roads coming into town." She caught Chelsea's knowing look. "He knows every delivery driver and restaurant worker in the Keys. Word will spread fast."

As they left Max's, they could hear Connie already making calls, her voice carrying the authority of someone used to handling crises. The mystery novelist was typing rapidly on her phone, while Mike headed toward the marina, moving with surprising speed for his age.

Gretchen took comfort in the way the community quickly came together to help. It was the same feeling she had about Captiva Island. Locals banding together to deal with whatever life threw in their path. Knowing this made leaving Key West easier. To have people watching out for Kaitlyn gave her a sense of peace.

At Paradise Harbor House, they found Kaitlyn reviewing paperwork with Elena while Will and a little boy played catch. The normality of the scene—Kaitlyn in her element, discussing shelter business—made what they had to say even harder.

One look at Gretchen's face told Kaitlyn something was wrong. "What happened?" She stood, her heart racing.

"Sarah's coming here," Gretchen said, still breathless. "She ran away from home. Left a note for Jeffrey and Joanna. She's driving to Key West, alone. I guess she didn't like her parents keeping the two of you apart."

Kaitlyn felt the room spin slightly. Will was instantly at her side, steadying her.

"She's sixteen," Kaitlyn managed. "She's driving by herself? What were they thinking telling her she couldn't come? Dad just let Joanna make that decision? I knew she wanted to meet me, but I didn't realize how much. We should have seen this coming."

Elena stepped forward, already in crisis management mode. "Has Sarah's father contacted the police?"

Gretchen shook her head. "I don't think so. Honestly, I didn't think to ask him."

"I'll contact the Key West police. They'll need to know. Will, can you reach out to your contacts at the local news stations? Just in case we need them."

"Your father's on his way too," Gretchen added, pacing now. "She's not answering anyone's calls."

Through the window, they could see Carla gathering her children from the playground, sensing the tension in the air.

Other residents moved quietly through the house. Kaitlyn assumed their own experiences with family crises made them particularly attuned to the weight of the moment.

"I'll call Jack," Will said softly to Kaitlyn. "He knows everyone at the local papers. We can put out alerts without causing panic."

"I think Connie was going to do that,"

"Wait!" Kaitlyn yelled. "Someone needs to get me her cellphone number. I can text her mine. I bet she'll talk to me."

"That's a great idea," Gretchen said. "Let me call Jeffrey back and get it."

Gretchen walked to the corner of the room to call Jeffrey.

Kaitlyn sank into a chair, Will's hand steady on her shoulder. Frustration over the choices the adults in her life had made on their behalf had come to this. *Sarah was driving toward her, alone on the highway, because of what? Because her father had been a selfish and weak man.*

Kaitlyn felt sick to her stomach.

"She's out there somewhere," Kaitlyn whispered. "My little sister. Just…driving toward a stranger because she needs to know the truth so badly, and no one is being straight with her."

"She's driving toward family," Chelsea corrected gently. "And we're going to make sure she arrives safely. As a matter of fact, I'm going to call The Gardens Hotel like I was planning before. You'll need a quiet place out of the way to talk, and they're going to need a place to stay."

"Thanks, Aunt Chelsea," Kaitlyn said.

Elena was already coordinating with local authorities, her calm efficiency a counterpoint to the emotional storm brewing. "They'll keep an eye out for her car without making her feel hunted. It's not the first time I've had to call them for something similar."

"Jack's on it," Will reported, hanging up his phone. "He's spreading the word through his network. Someone will spot her."

Gretchen hung up the phone and forwarded Jeffrey's text to her. "Here's Sarah's cellphone number."

Kaitlyn looked at the number and then Will. She took a deep breath. "Wish me luck."

He hugged her and whispered, "You're going to be a fantastic older sister. Sarah is a lucky young woman."

Kaitlyn could feel tears building, but she fought to keep them at bay; instead, as she pulled away from Will, her shoulders back, she stood tall as she walked to the corner of the room for privacy.

Gretchen's heart broke for what her daughter was going through but she was incredibly proud of how she was taking control of the situation.

Looking at Kaitlyn, she saw not just her daughter but a woman who'd found her strength, her purpose. Who was about to face one of the biggest moments of her life.

Through the windows of Paradise Harbor House, Gretchen imagined the Key West community mobilizing on her family's behalf. Word spreading from business to business, eyes watching the roads, a network of people who'd come to care about Kaitlyn now extending their protection to her sister.

All they could do now was wait, and hope Sarah made it safely to the family she'd never known, but who would welcome her with open arms.

CHAPTER 26

Chelsea left the group and quickly walked to The Gardens Hotel, the historic mansion's white trim gleaming against its rich red brick patio.

The wrought iron gates stood open, welcoming her into what felt like a different era of Key West. As she walked up the shell-stone path, the lush tropical gardens embraced her, providing a peaceful respite from the day's tension.

The former estate of Peggy Mills seemed perfect for what they needed—discreet, elegant, and above all, private. The mahogany doors opened into the cool interior, where the original wooden floors still told stories of Key West's past.

Robert, the manager, greeted her. "Hello, what brings you to The Gardens today?"

"Hello, Robert, I'm Chelsea Thompson. I called earlier about needing two rooms for family members coming into town within the next couple of hours."

Chelsea followed him to the front desk, her voice low. "We need two rooms, preferably near each other."

"Of course. How long will your guests be staying?"

"Let's say two nights to start. We may need to adjust." Chelsea glanced around the elegant lobby, with its perfect blend of tropical sophistication and old-world charm. "One room needs to be ready within the hour. The other guest won't arrive until later tonight."

"The Garden Suite would be perfect for your guests," Robert suggested, "It's private, opens onto its own section of the garden."

The Gardens Hotel's reputation for handling high-profile guests with grace made it ideal for their situation. The four-poster beds, antique furnishings, and private verandas would provide both comfort and seclusion, but what mattered most was the privacy Kaitlyn and Sarah needed.

"Perfect." She handed over her credit card. "And Robert? My niece will be meeting someone here. They'll need access to one of the private garden areas. I'm assuming family will follow."

"The hidden garden behind the pool would be ideal," he said, processing the payment. "It's peaceful there, especially in the evening. The orchid collection provides a natural privacy screen. We have a wine bar as well, and I'll provide you with details on how to access that."

Chelsea smiled, thinking that Sarah and Kaitlyn wouldn't need the wine bar, but if Jeffrey and Gretchen talked, her sister most definitely would want access.

Chelsea felt some of her tension ease. The tinkling of the fountains, the subtle fragrance of jasmine, and the property's old-world grace created exactly the atmosphere Sarah and Kaitlyn would need for some time together.

"Thank you." She accepted the key cards. "One more thing—if Jeffrey Miller arrives asking for his daughter, please direct him to me first. I'll be at the Paradise Harbor House."

Robert's expression remained professionally neutral, but his eyes showed understanding. He'd undoubtedly handled similar family situations before in this historic property that had seen its share of Key West drama since its construction in the 1870s.

"Of course, Mrs. Thompson. I understand."

As Chelsea headed back to Paradise Harbor House, she paused in the garden, watching a pair of white butterflies dance among the orchids. The Gardens Hotel had survived hurricanes, the Great Depression, and decades of change in Key West. Surely it could handle a little family drama.

Kaitlyn took a deep breath and dialed, and Sarah answered right away.

"Hello?".

"Sarah? It's Kaitlyn. Are you okay? Dad called and said you're driving here. Everyone is worried about you. I've wanted us to talk but not this way."

"Kaitlyn!" Sarah paused, her breath audible over the line. "I…I wasn't sure you'd want to talk to me. I thought about sending you a message through the Paradise Harbor House website, but I worried the email would go to the wrong person. I'm glad you called."

"I don't want you to talk and drive, and whatever you do, don't text and drive. Do you have enough gas?"

"Yes, I stopped earlier to get gas. You're on speaker. Is my father…our father mad? He's upset because we're supposed to look at a few colleges this summer, but I wanted to see you first. We had a big fight, my mother was the worst. She doesn't understand how important this is to me. We've already lost years; I don't want to lose anymore."

"I'm here now," Kaitlyn reassured her. "How far away are you?"

"I just passed Key Largo. I think I'm a couple of hours away."

"Okay, you should call your mother and let her know that you're safe and where you are. Tell her you talked to me and we'll look out for you. Dad is on his way here too. He'll be here a few hours after you get here. We're getting you reservations at a hotel but come to Paradise Harbor House first. That's where I am so I'll wait for you here.

Sarah sighed. "Okay, I will. It's just— it's been so hard with them. But I'll call."

"I know it's tough," Kaitlyn empathized, imagining the whirlwind of emotions her sister must be experiencing. Her gaze drifted to the vision board on Elena's wall, covered in photos of families finding their way back to each other. "But right now, let's focus on you getting here safely. I'll meet you at Paradise Harbor House. We're getting you a room at The Gardens Hotel. It's quiet, and it'll give us the space to talk everything through."

"That sounds really nice." Sarah's voice brightened slightly. "I just want to connect with you, Kaitlyn. I want to know everything about you. Do you feel that way too?"

Kaitlyn didn't hesitate. "I do. You don't have to worry about that. We've missed out on so much but that's all over now. You just get here safely and we'll talk about everything," Kaitlyn assured her, brushing away tears.

"And I'm here to help you through this, every step of the way. Just keep driving safely, and remember to pull over to a parking lot if you need to talk or text, okay?"

"I will," Sarah promised, a hopeful tone threading through her words. "Thank you for calling, Kaitlyn. It means a lot."

"I'll see you soon," Kaitlyn responded, her voice thick with emotion. "Drive safely, Sarah. We're all waiting for you."

"See you soon," Sarah replied, a note of determination in her voice.

As Kaitlyn ended the call, the weight of their first conversation settled around her.

She turned to look at Will, who was the first to move, crossing the room to wrap her in a gentle embrace.

"She sounds scared," Kaitlyn whispered against his chest. "But brave too."

"Like someone else I know," Will murmured.

Elena was already in motion, her practical nature taking charge. "Chelsea, you said you'd made arrangements at The Gardens Hotel?"

Chelsea nodded. "The Garden Suite. It's private, away from the main areas. Perfect for a family reunion that needs space to unfold."

"I should call Tess and Leah," Gretchen said, pulling out her phone. "Let them know Sarah's okay and on her way."

"Already texted them," Will said.

Kaitlyn sank onto the sofa, the adrenaline leaving her system. "She sounds so young," she said softly. "I mean, I knew she was sixteen, but hearing her voice…"

"She's the same age you were when Jeffrey left," Gretchen remarked, then immediately regretted it. "I'm sorry. That wasn't helpful."

But Kaitlyn shook her head. "No, you're right. I remember how it felt—wanting answers, needing to understand. At least Sarah's brave enough to go looking for them."

Chelsea sat beside her niece. "What do you need from us? When she arrives?"

"Space," Kaitlyn said immediately. "Just…space for us to figure this out ourselves. No pressure, no expectations." She looked at her mother. "Can you handle that?"

Gretchen straightened her shoulders. "I can try. But I want you both to know I'm here if you need me."

"I told her to come here first. We can drive over to the hotel, but I want you all to meet her too. I know none of you are related, but you all still feel like additional family for her."

"That's how we see it, too," Leah added. "All of us can be her unofficial aunts."

Tess nodded. "I agree. Making her feel loved will go a long way in helping her adjust to the new normal."

"Have you contacted Jeffrey to tell him where he should leave his car?" Elena asked.

Chelsea looked at Gretchen. "I suggest you send him a text and tell him to drive to the hotel. Let him know we've made reservations for him and Sarah."

Gretchen nodded. "Of course, although I expect he'll be thinking Sarah will meet him there."

Chelsea smiled. "That's the point. Sarah and Kaitlyn will be at Paradise Harbor House and Jeffrey will be there. He can wait until they're good and ready to see him."

Through the windows, the Key West evening was settling in, strings of lights beginning to twinkle along Duval Street. Somewhere between here and Key Largo, a sixteen-year-old girl was driving toward them, carrying the weight of family secrets and the hope of connection.

As Kaitlyn gathered her things, Elena touched her arm. "Remember what we tell our families here: healing happens at its own pace. Don't rush it."

Kaitlyn hugged her mentor, drawing strength from Elena's steady presence. "Thank you. For everything."

Kaitlyn thought of Sarah, somewhere on the Overseas Highway, driving toward a future neither of them could predict.

Kaitlyn watched a light blue Toyota Corolla pull slowly into view. Her heart seemed to stop for a moment, then race forward. Will squeezed her hand once before stepping back, giving the family space.

Sarah parked carefully, almost precisely, reminding Kaitlyn of her own meticulous nature. Through the windshield, she could see her sister take a deep breath before opening the car door. The girl who stepped out made Kaitlyn's breath catch—it was like looking at an old photo of herself at sixteen.

Sarah shared her petite build, the same honey-blonde hair, though Sarah wore hers longer, falling past her shoulders in gentle waves. But it was her eyes that struck Kaitlyn the most—the same hazel that she saw every morning in the mirror, now looking back at her with a mix of uncertainty.

Gretchen made a small sound beside her, something between a gasp and a sob. Sarah glanced their way, her fingers twisting the hem of her blue sundress—another gesture Kaitlyn recognized from her own nervous habits.

"Hi," Sarah said softly, taking a tentative step forward. Her voice was steadier than the slight tremor in her hands would suggest.

"Hi," Kaitlyn replied, moving down the steps. She stopped a few feet from her sister, close enough to see the light dusting of freckles across Sarah's nose—just like her own. "You made it."

Sarah nodded, her eyes filling with tears.

Kaitlyn closed the distance between them, pulling her sister into a tight hug. Sarah's arms wrapped around her immediately.

"My sister," Kaitlyn whispered.

CHAPTER 27

*A*t Paradise Harbor House everyone gathered, keenly aware of the delicate dynamics about to unfold with Sarah's arrival.

Will checked his phone for updates and waited for Kaitlyn to introduce her sister to him.

Kaitlyn took Sarah's hand and pulled her inside. "Everyone, this is my sister, Sarah."

Before anyone else could step forward, Kaitlyn gently took Sarah's hand, guiding her attention to a woman who had been waiting with a mix of apprehension and hope. "Sarah, there's someone very important I want you to meet first. This is my mother, Gretchen. She's visiting but lives on Captiva Island."

Gretchen stepped forward, her expression composed but her eyes revealing the depth of her emotions. "Hello, Sarah. I'm so happy to finally meet you."

The weight of their shared history hung in the air, but Gretchen's greeting was warm, setting a tone of reconciliation and understanding.

After a brief, poignant pause, Kaitlyn introduced Tess, Leah and Chelsea. "These are my aunts, Tess and Leah. They live here in Key West. Aunt Chelsea lives on Captiva Island near my mom. They've been really looking forward to meeting you."

Tess and Leah approached with open smiles, their demeanor welcoming. "It's a pleasure to finally meet you, Sarah," Tess said, her voice soothing.

Leah added, "We hope you'll feel at home here with us."

Chelsea didn't waste any time being Chelsea. "I'm a hugger. Do you mind if I give you a hug?"

Sarah laughed. "Nope. I'd love a hug."

"One hug coming up!" Chelsea said as she leaned in and squeezed Sarah.

Elena was next, her introduction brief but heartfelt. "I'm Elena, I run Paradise Harbor House, welcome."

Lastly, Kaitlyn turned to Will, who had been a quiet pillar of strength throughout the evening. "And this is Will, my boyfriend. He's been an incredible support to us all here."

Will extended his hand, his greeting warm and sincere. "Nice to meet you, Sarah. Kaitlyn has told me so much about you."

With the introductions complete, the evening slowly shifted from tentative greetings to more relaxed interactions. The initial awkwardness gave way as conversations began to flow, stories were shared, and laughter started to fill the room.

"Dad should be here any minute, right?" Sarah asked.

Will looked at his watch. "I'd say within the hour. Maybe you two should kill a little time and have something to eat, then head over to the hotel."

Kaitlyn nodded. "Good idea. You must be hungry. Let's get a burger next door. There's a great little place we can sit for a bit."

Chelsea handed Sarah's room key to Kaitlyn. "I left Jeffrey's at the front desk."

"It was nice to meet you all. I hope I see you again before I go back home."

Everyone waved and agreed to get together soon.

Kaitlyn was about to leave when she turned and ran back to

Gretchen. She wrapped her arms around her mother, and whispered, "Thank you for being my mom."

In her suite at The Gardens Hotel, Sarah sat cross-legged on one of the four-poster beds while Kaitlyn settled into a nearby armchair. The elegant room felt like a sanctuary, removed from the drama unfolding around them. Through the French doors, the garden's fountain provided a gentle backdrop to their conversation.

"So," Sarah began, her fingers playing with the edge of a pillow, "what kind of music do you like?" The question came out in a rush, as if she'd been storing it up for months.

Kaitlyn smiled. "A bit of everything, really. But I'm pretty obsessed with Taylor Swift."

"Me too!" Sarah's face lit up. "Dad always complains when I play 'Anti-Hero' too loud, but Joanna's worse—she says Taylor Swift is just feeding teenage angst."

"Mom used to say the same thing." Kaitlyn laughed. "What about movies? What's your favorite?"

"Promise not to laugh?" Sarah waited for Kaitlyn's nod. "I'm kind of obsessed with all the Marvel movies. I've seen them like a million times."

"Seriously? I dragged my college roommate to every single premiere!" Kaitlyn leaned forward. "Who's your favorite character?"

"Wanda. Definitely Wanda." Sarah hesitated, then added more quietly, "Maybe because she lost her family too, you know?"

The weight of that settled between them for a moment before Sarah brightened again. "What was senior year like? I'm kind of nervous about it."

"Honestly? It was both better and worse than I expected," Kaitlyn answered. "The workload's intense, especially with college applications, but it's also when I really figured out who my true friends were."

Sarah's phone buzzed, making them both jump. "It's Dad," she said, glancing at the screen. "He's in Marathon."

Kaitlyn felt her stomach tighten. Marathon meant he was getting closer. "We still have time," she assured her sister. "Tell me more about school. What's your favorite subject?"

"English. I love creative writing." Sarah tucked her hair behind her ear—the same nervous gesture Kaitlyn often made. "What about college? Was it scary, living away from home?"

"College was…an adjustment," Kaitlyn admitted. "But in a good way. You figure out who you are when nobody has any preconceptions about you."

Sarah pulled her knees up to her chest, wrapping her arms around them. "Did you date much in college?"

"A few guys, nothing serious, at least not in college. Recently though, things have become pretty serious with Will." Kaitlyn couldn't help smiling at the mention of his name.

"He seems really nice," Sarah said, then blushed slightly. "I mean, from what I could see. The way he looks at you…" She trailed off, playing with the edge of her sundress. "I kind of have a boyfriend. His name's Alex. But we've never even kissed."

Kaitlyn shifted to sit on the bed beside her sister. "Tell me about Alex."

"He's in my English class. We write notes to each other—actual paper notes, not texts. Everyone thinks it's weird but…" Sarah's blush deepened. "It's romantic, you know? He writes poetry sometimes. Really bad poetry, but still."

"That is romantic," Kaitlyn agreed. "So why haven't you kissed yet?"

"We're both kind of shy. Plus, his parents are super strict about dating. We mostly just hang out at school or with groups of friends." Sarah glanced at her sister. "When did you have your first kiss?"

"Junior year. Tommy Matthews behind the bleachers after a football game." Kaitlyn laughed at the memory. "It was terrible. We both had braces."

"Really?" Sarah giggled. "That makes me feel better. Everyone acts like they're experts at it, but I get so nervous just thinking about it."

"Trust me, nobody's an expert at sixteen, no matter what they say." Kaitlyn bumped her sister's shoulder gently. "The right moment will happen when it happens. Don't let anyone pressure you."

Sarah's phone buzzed again. This time it was a text from Joanna. She ignored it.

"You should at least let her know you're safe," Kaitlyn suggested softly.

"I will. Just...not yet." Sarah turned to face her sister more fully. "What about Will? How did you meet him?"

"He was filming at Paradise Harbor House. I thought he was going to be this pushy documentary guy, but..." Kaitlyn smiled, remembering. "He saw me. The real me, not just what I was trying to project."

"Like Alex," Sarah said thoughtfully. "He doesn't care that I'm not all confident like the other girls. He likes that I'm quiet sometimes. I think it's because he's shy too."

Their shared moment was interrupted by Kaitlyn's phone chiming. A text from Chelsea: *Jeffrey just passed the Seven Mile Bridge.*

"He's getting closer," Sarah said quietly, reading the tension in her sister's face.

"Yeah." Kaitlyn reached for her sister's hand. "But we're in this together now. Whatever happens next, we face it as sisters."

Sarah squeezed her hand. "Promise?"

"Promise." Kaitlyn looked at their joined hands, so similar in size and shape. "You know what's weird? All those years I wished for a sister, and here you were."

"I used to practice telling people I had a sister," Sarah admitted. "In my head, I mean. I'd imagined introducing you to my friends, having someone to talk to about…everything."

"Well, now you do. And I have some pretty amazing aunts too. Aunt Chelsea already loves you—she arranged all this. And Aunt Tess and Aunt Leah are going to spoil you rotten."

Sarah's eyes filled with tears. "I've wanted this for so long. To just…belong somewhere. With someone who understands."

Kaitlyn pulled her sister into another hug, feeling the weight of their shared loss and their new beginning all at once. "Come on, let's go explore the gardens. This place is beautiful and you should get some photos."

Sarah followed Kaitlyn to the courtyard and then they walked through the gardens, enjoying the tranquility of the hotel grounds.

As the Key West evening was settling in, somewhere on the Overseas Highway, their father was getting closer. But in this moment, in this beautiful room at The Gardens Hotel, two sisters were building a bridge across the years that had separated them.

CHAPTER 28

"I'm going over there," Gretchen announced.

"What?" Chelsea asked.

"I'm not letting my daughter deal with Jeffrey on her own. That's not happening."

"Okay, calm down. I hear what you're saying, but didn't Kaitlyn say that she wanted time with Sarah alone? You running over there while those two girls are having a private conversation is not what she'd want."

"Yes, I understand that, Chelsea. But Jeffrey is going to show up any minute. Do you honestly think he's going to honor Kaitlyn's wishes for time alone with Sarah?"

"Gretchen's right. He's going to come barreling in there and make a big scene because his daughter defied him. Jeffrey hasn't made the best choices so far. What would make you think he's going to do the right thing now?" Leah offered.

Chelsea thought for a minute and then nodded. "Fine, but if you're going over there so are we."

Tess stopped sipping her coffee mid-sip and looked up. "Huh?"

"You heard me," Chelsea insisted. "Jeffrey Miller might think he can do and say whatever he wants, but it's been years since he's had to deal with any of us. Perhaps it's time we remind him who we are."

Still confused, Tess asked, "Who are we?"

"We're the Lawrence sisters. He'll have to get through us to get to them."

Gretchen laughed. At first, it was a small chuckle, but the determined look on Chelsea's face struck her as so comical she couldn't hold back the full belly laugh that was bursting to get out.

Tess and Leah joined in and soon the four sisters were laughing so hard, Elena came running into the room.

"What's so funny?" she asked.

Gretchen wiped tears from her cheeks. "All I can say, Elena, is that if you ever need a strong opinionated woman in your corner, call my sister, Chelsea. You won't find any better in this world."

Chelsea took Gretchen's hand. "Come on. Let's go take care of our girls."

The women marched down Duval Street as if they were going to war. When they entered The Gardens Hotel, their determination dampened with the elegant surroundings.

"This place is gorgeous," Tess whispered to Leah. "Why haven't we ever been here before?"

"Because we were busy failing at several business startups, now shh," Leah whispered back.

Robert looked up from the front desk, immediately recognizing the situation from their expressions.

"Mrs. Thompson," he greeted Chelsea. "Your nieces are in the garden area. Shall I show you the way?"

"Please," Chelsea said. "And Robert? When Mr. Miller arrives—"

"I'll alert you immediately," he assured her.

They found Kaitlyn and Sarah sitting together on a bench near the fountain, their matching profiles highlighted by the setting sun. Both girls looked up at their approach, and Kaitlyn's eyes immediately found her mother's.

"Dad's close, isn't he?"

"I'm guessing about fifteen minutes out," Gretchen confirmed. "We thought you might want some backup."

Sarah's fingers twisted in her lap. "Is Joanna with him?"

"No, honey," Gretchen said gently. "Just your father."

"We can leave if you want privacy," Tess offered, but Kaitlyn shook her head.

"Stay. Please." She reached for Sarah's hand. "My mom and aunts are pretty amazing at handling difficult situations. We could use the support."

Before Sarah could respond, Robert appeared in the garden entrance. "Mr. Miller has arrived," he announced quietly. "He's in the lobby."

The sisters exchanged glances and arranged themselves casually but strategically around the garden space. Chelsea near the entrance, Tess and Leah flanking the outer edges, Gretchen close enough to intervene but far enough to give the girls space.

Jeffrey's voice carried ahead of him, Robert following closely behind. "Where are they? Sarah? Kaitlyn?"

He appeared in the garden entrance, stopping abruptly at the sight before him. His daughters sat together, their similarity unmistakable, their united front clear. His former sisters-in-law surrounded them like a protective barrier, and Gretchen stood nearby making her presence known.

Robert slowly slipped away to return inside.

"Sarah," he said, his voice losing its edge. "Thank goodness you're all right. You can't just run away like that. Your mother and I were worried sick."

"Don't," Sarah said quietly. "Don't make this about Mom. This is about Kaitlyn and me, and the years we didn't get to spend together."

Jeffrey took a step forward, but Chelsea's subtle shift blocked his path.

"Sarah, get your things. We're going home," he insisted.

"No," Sarah said, gripping Kaitlyn's hand tighter. "I'm not leaving. Not until Kaitlyn and I have some time together."

"This isn't up for discussion. You're sixteen years old."

"Old enough to know when I'm being lied to," Sarah interrupted, her voice stronger now. "Old enough to know that when you were deciding what was best for me, you missed the mark by a long shot."

Jeffrey's gaze shifted to Kaitlyn, who had remained silent, her shoulder pressed protectively against her sister's. "Kaitlyn, surely you understand—"

"What I understand," Kaitlyn said quietly, "is that Sarah was brave enough to do what none of the adults did. She chose truth over comfort. She chose family over fear. She chose to confront the mistakes in an effort to change her future."

"It's not that simple," Jeffrey protested.

"Actually, it is." Gretchen stepped forward. "These girls deserve to know each other. They deserve the chance to be sisters. Your wife's discomfort doesn't trump that."

"Gretchen, you have no right."

"I have every right," Gretchen cut him off. "Kaitlyn and I have already talked about my involvement in all this. By sticking my head in the sand because I was ashamed of my situation, I let her down. The worst part for me is that I felt ashamed over something I had no control over. I don't want to rehash what happened in our marriage. What I want now is for us to do right by these girls. They've already missed out on so much because of us, let's not deny them this time together."

Leah moved closer to the girls. "Sarah's things are already in her suite. Kaitlyn can stay with Sarah for the night. The room next door is ready for you, Jeffrey. Why don't we all take a breath and start fresh in the morning?"

"I'm not leaving my daughter alone."

"She won't be alone," Tess said firmly. "She'll be with her sister, and your room is right next door to hers."

"And our house is only a couple of blocks away," Leah added.

Sarah stood, pulling Kaitlyn up with her. "Dad, please. Just... let us have this time. I'm safe. I'm where I want to be. Can't that be enough?"

Something in Sarah's voice seemed to reach Jeffrey. He looked at his daughters—really looked at them—standing together, their matching features set in identical expressions of determination.

"One night," he said finally. "We'll talk in the morning."

"Thank you," Sarah whispered.

As Chelsea led Jeffrey away to check in, Kaitlyn wrapped an arm around her sister's shoulders. The Lawrence sisters exchanged glances of relief and victory, while Gretchen watched Kaitlyn with a mixture of pride and protective concern.

"Come on," Leah said softly to Sarah. "We'll help you unpack."

Kaitlyn nodded to Sarah. "Go on, I'll be along in a minute."

Jeffrey stopped and turned to look at Kaitlyn.

"You look good," he said awkwardly. "The fundraiser at Paradise Harbor House…I saw the posts online. You've done well for yourself."

"Don't." Kaitlyn's voice was flat. "Don't pretend you've been watching from afar, caring about my life. You don't get to do that now."

"Kaitlyn, I know I've made mistakes."

"Mistakes?" She laughed, but there was no humor in it. "A mistake is forgetting a birthday. A mistake is missing a school play. You chose to leave. You chose another family. You chose to keep Sarah a secret from me, and me a secret from her. Those aren't mistakes, Dad. Those are choices."

Kaitlyn tried to remain calm as she confronted him. "I realize that Mom made it difficult for you to see me. I don't know all the specifics on that, but I do know that at some point you gave up on me. Your love for me wasn't strong enough for you to fight to see me."

"Kaitlyn, please understand—"

"Stop! Stop trying to explain because no amount of explanation will repair what's been broken between us." She touched her chest. "My heart was broken over and over again because of you. The reason I needed to have this talk with you is to let you know that I'll make mistakes in my life as I grow. That happens to everyone. But I'm not going to make my choices as a broken person. I'm not going to hold back loving or caring for people because you chose to keep your love from me. I won't allow you to dominate my life that way. I'm going to choose to love, to be there for people who need my love…my empathy and compassion. I just wanted you to know that."

Gretchen watched her daughter with tears in her eyes, and Chelsea smiled at Kaitlyn's strength and poise.

"I'd like to make things right," Jeffrey said quietly. "With both of you."

"Maybe you should have thought about that before telling Sarah she couldn't come meet me." Kaitlyn's voice cracked slightly. "Before letting Joanna decide whether your daughters could know each other. You're still doing it—choosing what's comfortable over what's right."

The silence that followed was heavy with years of unspoken hurt. Jeffrey opened his mouth to respond, but Chelsea stepped in.

"I think that's enough for tonight," she said firmly. "Everyone's tired. We can talk more tomorrow."

Jeffrey conceded, his eyes still on Kaitlyn, who refused to

meet his gaze. "We'll talk more in the morning. Maybe we can have breakfast together?"

"Let's talk in the morning, Jeffrey," Gretchen responded.

As Chelsea led Jeffrey away to check in, Kaitlyn let out a shaky breath. Gretchen ran to her and pulled her into a hug.

"You did great, honey."

Kaitlyn hugged her mother and then pulled away. "Thanks, Mom, I think so too."

Kaitlyn turned and went to join Sarah as Gretchen stayed in the courtyard, waiting for her chance to talk to Jeffrey alone.

After the girls retired to their suite, Gretchen found Jeffrey standing alone in the hotel's side garden, staring at the fountain.

"They look so much alike," he said without turning around.

"They're both struggling with trusting you…trusting us," Gretchen said, keeping her distance. "And I don't blame them."

Jeffrey turned to face her. The years had added silver to his temples, lines around his eyes, but his tendency to look away when confronted hadn't changed. "I know I've made mistakes."

"Stop." Gretchen's voice was firm but controlled. "I'm not here to rehash our past. I'm here about your daughters' futures. Both of them."

"Joanna—"

"I don't care about Joanna's feelings right now," Gretchen cut him off. "This isn't about her. This is about two girls who deserve better than what we've given them. Sarah is your daughter with Joanna, and so I had no control over what has been said to her all these years, but Kaitlyn is our daughter, and I'm going to make sure she never gets hurt like this again."

She stepped closer, making sure she had his full attention. "I want to be very clear about something, Jeffrey. If you're going to be in Kaitlyn's life again, if you're going to try to build something with both your daughters, you need to be all in. No more choosing what's comfortable. No more letting Joanna dictate the terms."

"It's not that simple," he said.

"Actually, it is. You saw Kaitlyn tonight. Really saw her. She's built a life here, found her purpose. She's strong, but that strength came from surviving your absence." Gretchen's voice caught slightly. "I won't watch you hurt her again."

Jeffrey was quiet for a long moment. "How do I fix this?"

"You start by listening to them. Both of them. And then you do what's right for your daughters, not what's easy for you or your wife." Gretchen turned to leave, then paused. "They deserve that much, Jeffrey. They deserve everything we should have given them years ago."

She left him standing there, the fountain's whisper a quiet witness to words that needed to be said, to changes that needed to be made, to healing that needed to begin.

Before Jeffrey could retreat to his room, Chelsea stepped out from the shadows of the veranda.

"My turn," she said, her voice carrying the kind of authority that had made her successful in the art world. "You don't get to just walk away."

Jeffrey sighed. "Chelsea—"

"No, you listen to me, Jeffrey Miller. That girl in there? The one you abandoned? She's extraordinary. No thanks to you. And that other girl, who was brave enough to drive here alone because she needed her sister? She's extraordinary too. Again, no thanks to you."

She moved closer, her presence commanding despite her small stature. "You've got two daughters who somehow turned out remarkable despite your best efforts to keep them apart. And now you have a choice to make."

"I'm trying."

"Try harder," Chelsea snapped. "Because let me make something very clear. There are four Lawrence sisters watching you. Four women who have helped raise Kaitlyn, who love her, who would do anything to protect her. And now that includes protecting Sarah too."

Jeffrey started to speak but Chelsea held up her hand.

"I'm not finished. You think Gretchen was tough? You think I'm being hard on you? You haven't seen anything yet. You hurt either of those girls again, you let that wife of yours come between them, and you'll have all four of us to deal with. And trust me, Jeffrey, you don't want that."

She straightened her shoulders, every inch the successful artist, teacher and part gallery owner who could reduce artists to tears with a single critique. "Those girls deserve better than what they've gotten from you. It's time to step up. Be the father they deserve or stay out of their lives completely. There's no middle ground anymore."

Without waiting for his response, Chelsea turned and walked away, her heels clicking sharply on the stone path, leaving Jeffrey to consider just how many formidable women were now involved in his daughters' lives.

CHAPTER 29

*T*ess, Leah, and Gretchen spent the night at Tess and Leah's home, promising to return early the next morning for breakfast. True to their word, everyone gathered in the garden courtyard for breakfast, rather than in the dining room.

As soon as they settled at the table, Sarah began describing her evening with Kaitlyn. Her words tumbled out excitedly, interspersed with bites of fresh fruit and pastries.

"We stayed up so late! Kaitlyn showed me all these pictures from Paradise Harbor House, and we made lists of our favorite movies—we like all the same ones! And she told me about college, and I told her about my friends back home, and—" Sarah paused to take a breath, her face glowing with happiness.

"Did either of you sleep at all?" Chelsea asked, amused by Sarah's enthusiasm.

"Maybe two hours?" Kaitlyn admitted, hiding a yawn behind her coffee cup. "There was just so much to talk about. We thought about renting a movie, but by the time we did, we could barely keep our eyes open."

Gretchen loved seeing the two girls having so much fun together, her heart full at their easy connection. Despite their age difference, despite the years apart, they'd fallen into a natural rhythm of sisterhood.

"We should do something fun today," Tess suggested, reaching for another croissant. "The weather's perfect for the beach."

"Can we?" Sarah turned to Kaitlyn, her eyes bright. "I packed my swimsuit just in case, and I've never been to a Key West beach."

"Smathers Beach would be perfect," Leah said. "It's not too crowded."

Jeffrey appeared in the dining room doorway, looking slightly uncertain about joining them. Before he could speak, Sarah waved him over.

"Dad! We're going to the beach. You should come!"

He glanced around the table at the women, and at his daughters sitting close together, their matching features animated with excitement. "I actually have some work to catch up on," he said carefully. "Seems like more of a girls' day. Maybe we could all have dinner together later?"

Kaitlyn's expression remained neutral, but Sarah's face fell slightly. "Are you sure? It could be fun…"

"Let him work, honey," Chelsea said smoothly. "We've got plenty of sunscreen and beach umbrellas to share between us."

"And snacks," Tess added quickly, seeing Sarah's disappointment. "We'll stop by Harbor Lights and get Jamie to pack us a proper beach picnic."

"Jamie makes the best key lime pie," Leah told Sarah. "And he always gives Tess extra slices."

"Because she makes googly eyes at him," Chelsea teased, making Sarah giggle.

Jeffrey shifted awkwardly. "Well, I'll let you all enjoy your day. Sarah, your mother would like you to call her when you get a chance."

"I will," Sarah promised, but her attention was already back on her sister. "Kaitlyn, can we get one of those big floaty things? I saw them in a shop window on Duval Street."

"You mean a pool noodle?" Kaitlyn laughed. "For the ocean?"

"Is that weird?" Sarah asked, suddenly self-conscious.

"No, it's perfect," Kaitlyn assured her. "We'll get two. And maybe those ridiculous straw hats Aunt Chelsea pretends not to love."

"I do not love those hats," Chelsea protested. "I merely appreciate their practical application."

"You have three of them," Gretchen pointed out.

"In different shades!" Chelsea defended, making everyone laugh.

Jeffrey nodded a quiet goodbye and slipped away as the women continued planning their beach day.

No one seemed to notice his departure except Gretchen, who caught the flash of regret in his eyes. But she turned her attention back to Kaitlyn and Sarah, watching as they finished their breakfast in a bubble of shared excitement.

"We should probably change," Kaitlyn said, eyeing Sarah's sundress. "Beach clothes and lots of sunscreen. The Keys sun is no joke."

"I've got extra sunscreen in my bag," Leah offered. "The good kind that doesn't feel sticky."

"And I've got beach umbrellas in my car," Chelsea added. "Don't give me that look, Gretchen. Of course I keep beach umbrellas in my car. I live on Captiva."

Sarah looked around the table at these women who had so quickly included her in their circle, who treated her like she'd always been part of their family.

"Thank you," she said suddenly, her voice small but sincere. "I mean it. You all have been so kind to me."

"Oh honey," Gretchen reached over to squeeze her hand, "you're family. This is what family does."

"Besides," Tess added with a grin, "any excuse for a beach day is a good excuse. Now, who's riding with who? Because I'm not squeezing into the backseat of Chelsea's car again."

"That was one time," Chelsea protested. "And it was an emergency ice cream run."

As they gathered their things and headed out into the Key West morning, Sarah fell into step beside Kaitlyn. "Is it always like this with them?"

"Pretty much," Kaitlyn smiled. "My Aunt Chelsea is crazy fun, and Tess and Leah too. I think my mom is the most subdued of the four of them. They can be loud, loving, and slightly chaotic. You'll get used to it. "

Sarah laughed. "I'm looking forward to it."

An hour later, they'd claimed their spot on Smathers Beach, Chelsea's umbrellas creating a colorful canopy of shade.

Sarah and Kaitlyn sat on beach towels, matching pool noodles propped beside them, while their aunts arranged an impressive spread of snacks and drinks from Jamie's kitchen.

"He really did give us extra pie," Sarah observed, watching Tess unpack the containers.

"Of course he did." Leah smirked. "The man's completely smitten with our sister."

"I can hear you," Tess called out, but she was smiling.

Sarah leaned closer to Kaitlyn. "Are they dating?"

"It's complicated," Kaitlyn whispered back. "I think they will. Eventually."

Gretchen watched Kaitlyn and Sarah's heads bent together, sharing secrets like they'd done it all their lives. The sight made her throat tighten with emotion.

"They're going to be fine," Chelsea said softly, settling into her beach chair beside her sister. "Look at them—it's like they've never been apart."

The morning passed in a blur of sunshine and laughter. Sarah proved to be a natural in the water, while Kaitlyn preferred to stay in the shallows. Their voices carried back to shore as they tested the buoyancy of their pool noodles, debating the physics of floating while trying to dunk each other.

"Gretchen!" Sarah yelled, grinning. "Can you take our picture? Kaitlyn's teaching me how to bodysurf!"

"More like teaching you how to eat sand." Kaitlyn laughed, splashing her sister.

The day unfolded around them, filled with small moments of connection. Tess taught Sarah how to find the best shells along the tideline. Leah shared her collection of beach reads, delighted to find another mystery fan in the family.

Chelsea sketched the girls in her notebook while they weren't looking, capturing their easy affection in quick, sure strokes, and cellphone cameras captured every moment.

Around noon, they gathered under the umbrellas for Jamie's feast. Sarah sat cross-legged on her towel, salt water drying in her hair, as she devoured a sandwich.

"So," she asked between bites, "does everyone in Key West know everybody else? Because three different people have stopped by to say hi."

"That's just Key West," Kaitlyn explained. "Especially since the fundraiser. The whole town kind of adopted me."

"And now they're adopting you too," Tess added, passing Sarah a cold drink. "That's what happens here. People look out for each other."

"It's different from Fort Lauderdale," Sarah said thoughtfully. "Everything there is so…I don't know, unconnected? Here it feels like one large family."

"Speaking of family," Gretchen interrupted, checking her phone, "your father texted. He's made dinner reservations at Latitudes for seven o'clock."

"Latitudes?" Leah whistled. "Someone's trying to impress."

Sarah turned to Kaitlyn. "Is that good?"

"It's on Sunset Key," Kaitlyn explained. "Very fancy. We'll have to change out of beach clothes."

"Way out of beach clothes," Tess confirmed. "But the sunset view is worth it."

"I didn't pack anything fancy," Sarah worried, but Chelsea waved off her concern.

"That's what aunts are for. We'll find you something perfect. Besides, Kaitlyn needs a new dress too."

"I do?"

"Trust me," Chelsea said with authority. "You both do. Consider it your first official sister shopping trip."

Sarah's face lit up. "Really? Can we?"

"After lunch," Gretchen said firmly. "Eat first, then shopping."

As they finished their meal, more locals stopped to chat. The mystery novelist from Max's brought them fresh coconut water. Rick the fisherman passed by with his granddaughter, who was about Sarah's age. Even Jack paused on his morning walk to say hello.

"See what I mean?" Kaitlyn nudged her sister. "Key West family."

Sarah watched another group of locals wave as they passed. "It's nice," she said softly. "Belonging somewhere."

Kaitlyn squeezed her hand. "You belong here too now. With all of us. You'll have to come down often for a visit."

Sarah smiled. "I'd love that.

After lunch, they packed up their beach gear and headed to Duval Street. Chelsea led the way, steering them past the tourist shops toward the boutiques she trusted. Sarah's eyes grew wide at the window displays.

"I usually just shop at the mall," she admitted, following Kaitlyn into a store filled with flowing sundresses and elegant resort wear.

"Welcome to Chelsea's version of education," Leah teased. "Fashion first, everything else second."

"I heard that," Chelsea called from a rack of dresses. "And I'll have you know that proper attire is very educational. Sarah, honey, what's your favorite color?"

"Blue," Sarah and Kaitlyn said simultaneously, then looked at each other and laughed.

"Of course it is," Gretchen smiled. "You're definitely sisters."

Chelsea emerged with an armful of dresses. "Try these. Both of you. Latitudes at sunset calls for something special."

The next hour passed in a whirl of fabric and laughter. Sarah discovered she loved the way silk felt against her skin. The sisters took turns modeling outfits, their natural similarity making them look like before-and-after photos in different styles of the same color.

"What about this one?" Sarah twirled in a pale blue dress that floated around her knees.

"Perfect," Kaitlyn declared. "You look beautiful."

"You both do," Gretchen said softly, watching them admire each other in the mirror.

A text from Jeffrey buzzed on Gretchen's phone: *Boat to Sunset Key leaves at 6:30. Don't be late.*

"Speaking of time," Chelsea checked her watch, "we should head back to get ready. Sarah, have you ever been on a boat?"

"Just once, on a school trip," Sarah said, carefully handling her new dress as they left the store. "Is it scary?"

"Not at all," Kaitlyn assured her. "The water's usually calm this time of day. And the sunset will be amazing."

They walked back toward The Gardens Hotel, the sisters in the middle of their protective aunt formation, carrying shopping bags and chatting about dinner plans. Sarah's happiness was infectious, her excitement about their evening plans making everyone smile.

"I can't wait to tell Alex about all this," Sarah said, then blushed when everyone turned to look at her. "He's...um...sort of my boyfriend."

"Sort of?" Tess raised an eyebrow.

"Oh, this we need to hear about." Leah grinned.

"Later," Gretchen intervened, seeing Sarah's pink cheeks. "Let's get you both ready for dinner first."

Back at The Gardens Hotel, their suite transformed into a whirlwind of pre-dinner preparation. Chelsea took charge of hair and makeup, while Tess steamed the wrinkles from their new dresses.

"Do you really think I need lipstick?" Sarah asked, watching Kaitlyn sort through her makeup bag.

"Trust me," Kaitlyn said, "I know what I'm doing.

"Just a little," Kaitlyn promised, selecting a soft pink shade. "Nothing too dramatic. You're sixteen, not heading to a nightclub."

Leah sat on one of the beds, going through her phone. "Jack's going to meet us at the dock," she reported to Kaitlyn. "And Jamie's joining us too, apparently."

"Really?" Tess's voice carried from the bathroom, trying to sound casual.

"Yes, really." Gretchen smiled.

"I sent Will a text and asked him to come too," Kaitlyn added.

"This is going to be awesome," Sarah said as she smoothed her blue dress nervously. Looking at Gretchen she asked,

"Do you think my mom will be mad about all this? The shopping and everything?"

"Let me handle Joanna," Gretchen said firmly. "You just enjoy being with your sister."

"Done!" Kaitlyn announced, stepping back to admire her work. "Take a look."

Sarah turned to the mirror and gasped softly. Kaitlyn had enhanced her natural beauty without making her look overdone. Her honey-blonde hair fell in soft waves, and her makeup was subtle but perfect.

"You look beautiful," Kaitlyn said, standing beside Sarah in front of the mirror, their reflection showed their undeniable connection—same height, same delicate features, same sparkle in their hazel eyes.

"We look like sisters," Sarah whispered, joy evident in her voice.

"You are sisters," Chelsea said, dabbing at her eyes while trying not to smudge her own makeup. "Now, let's get going before I completely ruin my mascara."

They gathered in the hotel lobby, a parade of colorful dresses and excited chatter. Will and Jamie were already waiting, both looking sharp in button-down shirts and dress pants.

"Wow," Will said softly when he saw Kaitlyn. His genuine admiration made her blush.

"You clean up nice," Tess told Jamie, who couldn't seem to take his eyes off her coral dress.

Jeffrey appeared from the hotel entrance, looking somewhat formal in a suit. "We should get walking down to the docks. The water taxi's waiting."

As they walked toward the dock, Sarah fell into step beside Kaitlyn. "This is so exciting, and the day has been perfect."

Kaitlyn smiled. "It has and tonight will be just as much fun."

Indeed, they made quite a group: the Lawrence sisters leading the way, Will and Jamie flanking the girls, and Jeffrey bringing up the rear. The evening air was perfect, carrying the salt-tinged breeze that made Key West evenings magical.

At the dock, Sarah's eyes widened at the sight of the boat. "The adventure continues."

"Wait until you see the restaurant," Tess said, accepting Jamie's help onto the boat. "The view is spectacular."

Jack met them at the dock. "Looks like the gang's all here," he announced, taking Leah's hand. "Let me help you."

"Thanks, Jack. I pictured myself falling flat on my face."

They settled into their seats, the sisters naturally together, as the boat pulled away from the dock. Sarah gripped Kaitlyn's hand as they picked up speed, but her nervous expression quickly turned to delight as they skimmed across the water toward Sunset Key.

"This is amazing!" she exclaimed, the wind catching her hair. "The water's so beautiful!"

Kaitlyn watched her sister's joy, feeling a surge of protectiveness and love. In just twenty-four hours, Sarah had carved out a permanent place in her heart, filling a void she hadn't even known existed.

As they approached Sunset Key, the restaurant came into view, its lights twinkling against the darkening sky.

The hostess led them to a prime table on the terrace overlooking the water, where the sunset would soon paint the sky in brilliant colors.

"This is fancy," Sarah whispered to Kaitlyn as they settled into their seats. Crystal glasses, and white linens gleamed against the wooden tables.

"Just wait until you taste the food," Jamie said, pulling out Tess's chair. "They have an amazing chef here."

Jeffrey cleared his throat. "I took the liberty of pre-ordering some appetizers. I remember Kaitlyn always loved crab cakes."

"You remembered that?" Kaitlyn asked, surprise evident in her voice.

"I remember a lot of things," Jeffrey said quietly.

An awkward silence fell, broken by Chelsea asking Sarah about her favorite foods. Soon, the table was alive with conversation again.

Will told stories about filming in Key West that made Sarah laugh, while Jamie and Tess discussed the menu in the kind of detail only restaurant people would appreciate, and Jack, amiable as he always was, only had eyes for Leah.

"Look," Sarah touched Kaitlyn's arm, pointing toward the horizon. The sun was beginning its descent, turning the sky into a canvas of orange and pink.

"Make a wish," Gretchen said softly. "That's what we used to do when you were little, remember, Kaitlyn?"

"I remember." Kaitlyn smiled, watching her sister close her eyes briefly.

"What did you wish for?" Leah asked Sarah.

"Can't tell." Sarah grinned. "But I think it might already be coming true."

The evening unfolded around them, filled with good food and better company. Jeffrey tried to include both his daughters in conversation, asking Sarah about school and Kaitlyn about Paradise Harbor House and her future.

Though there was still tension, it felt less sharp than before. His efforts didn't go unnoticed and seemed to bridge the gap just a little, knitting together the fabric of a family long separated by circumstance and secrecy.

As the dinner plates were cleared and dessert was brought out, the evening air buzzed with the sounds of the ocean and the quiet chatter of contentment.

Jack, ever the romantic, raised a glass. "To new beginnings," he toasted, his voice carrying over the table.

Everyone raised their glasses in agreement, the simple act

sealing their collective commitment to mending and growing together.

And as the stars began to twinkle in the night sky, Kaitlyn leaned back, a contented sigh escaping.

Tonight wasn't just about rekindled family ties; it was a celebration of hope, of the possibilities that lay in the everyday moments, and of a future where the past no longer held them back but pushed them forward.

CHAPTER 30

Chelsea, Tess, Leah and Gretchen stood on the veranda of The Gardens Hotel, watching the scene in the courtyard unfold. They'd already said their goodbyes to Sarah and Jeffrey and left Kaitlyn alone to have her last moments with her sister.

Sarah loaded the last of her things into the trunk of her car, the cool morning air filled with the salty tang of the sea. Kaitlyn stood beside her, wrapped in a light sweater against the morning chill.

"I can't believe you're leaving already," she said, her voice thick with emotion. "I'm glad you came but it wasn't long enough."

Sarah leaned against her car, her eyes tracing the lines of the palm leaves above. "I know, but Dad wants to make sure I get back before we miss the college visits," she replied, trying to mask the tremble in her voice.

Jeffrey, standing a few feet away, pretended to be busy with his phone but Kaitlyn could tell he was listening.

"Hey." Kaitlyn touched Sarah's arm, drawing her back from her thoughts. "This isn't goodbye, okay? It's just…see you later."

Sarah nodded, a small smile breaking through. "See you later," she echoed. She glanced over at Jeffrey, who now approached, his expression softening.

"You have my number now," Kaitlyn continued, pulling Sarah into a tight hug. "Anytime, for anything, all right?"

"All right," Sarah managed, her voice muffled against Kaitlyn's shoulder. As they pulled apart, Sarah wiped away a stray tear, her resolve firming. "I'm going to hold you to that. You're going to get tired of me."

Kaitlyn shook her head. "Never."

Jeffrey cleared his throat, stepping closer. "Ready to hit the road?" he asked, though his voice betrayed his reluctance to leave the newfound peace. "I'll follow behind your car."

Sarah nodded, taking a deep breath of the sea air one last time before sliding into her car.

Jeffrey looked at Kaitlyn. "Is it okay with you if I give you a hug?"

Kaitlyn managed a slight smile and nodded. "Sure."

Her father held her tight as she breathed in the scent of his cologne. "Daddy," she whispered.

Responding to her, he squeezed tighter, and said, "Don't be a stranger."

She pulled away, looked down at her feet and nodded, wiping a tear from her cheek. She knew it was all he could manage and for now, it would have to be enough.

He looked at Gretchen and nodded, then got into his car.

Kaitlyn waved from the driveway watching as Sarah pulled out onto the street, Jeffrey's car following closely behind.

As the cars turned the corner and disappeared from view, Kaitlyn felt a pang in her chest. The goodbye was harder than she'd anticipated, but the promise of new beginnings lingered in the air, like the warmth of the rising sun.

Gretchen's hand was on her shoulder and her aunts stood beside her.

"How are you doing, honey?" Gretchen asked.

Kaitlyn nodded. "I'm okay. At least I will be."

One by one the aunts wrapped their arms around Kaitlyn. "You did great," Leah said.

"You were amazing, sweetie," Tess said.

"Thanks, everyone. I couldn't have done any of this without your support. I love you all so much."

"Group hug!" Chelsea announced. "And then, I hate to say it, but I've got to get packing and get on the road back to Captiva." She looked at Gretchen. "What about you? When are you heading back?"

Gretchen looked at Kaitlyn. "I'm not sure. I was thinking today, but it's up to Kaitlyn. What do you have on your plate today?"

Kaitlyn shrugged and then smiled. "I guess it's time I go find Elena and accept her job offer."

"YES!" Leah and Tess yelled at the same time and then did a fist bump.

Gretchen and Kaitlyn laughed. "Why don't you go do that while Chelsea and I pack."

"Sounds good," Chelsea said. "I've just got to see Robert to check Jeffrey and Sarah out of their rooms. Wait a few minutes and I'll walk back with you."

Walking out of the courtyard, Kaitlyn felt the weight of the morning's farewell but also the lightness of hope. This was just the start, she reminded herself. The road ahead was long, and their story was just beginning.

"Well," Chelsea announced, hefting her bag, "Captiva awaits."

"Are you sure you won't stay one more day?" Tess asked, though they'd been through this already.

"Can't. I've got a new exhibit opening this weekend." Chelsea turned to Kaitlyn. "But you, my precious niece, better come visit soon. Both of you," she added meaningfully.

"Both of us?" Kaitlyn raised an eyebrow.

"You and Sarah, of course. Tess and Leah can manage without you for a weekend."

Gretchen picked up her own bag. "I should get going too. It's a long drive."

The goodbye hugs were lengthy and slightly tearful, with promises of phone calls and visits. Chelsea whispered something in Kaitlyn's ear that made her laugh, while Gretchen held her daughter just a little longer than necessary.

"I'm so proud of you," Gretchen murmured.

After final waves and one last round of hugs, they watched Chelsea and Gretchen drive away. Tess wiped a tear, trying to be subtle about it.

"Don't you start," Leah warned, her own eyes suspiciously bright. "We've got work tonight, and I'd like to keep my mascara in place."

At Paradise Harbor House, Elena welcomed Kaitlyn's decision with a warm hug and a stack of paperwork. As they went through the details of her new position, Kaitlyn felt the rightness of her choice settling into her bones.

"Will's already talking about a documentary series," Elena mentioned, eyes twinkling. "Something about the transformative power of community."

"Of course he is." Kaitlyn laughed, just as Will appeared in the doorway, camera in hand.

"I heard my name," he said, grinning. "All good things, I hope?"

Kaitlyn smiled. "It's not possible for me to say anything bad about you."

He looked at Elena. "Mind if I steal your employee for a few? I promise to bring her back soon."

Elena laughed. "You have my permission."

"Where are we headed?" Kaitlyn asked as they made their way toward the dock.

"I realized something this morning. Do you know that you haven't tried my favorite conch fritters since you've been in Key West? I thought it was about time I introduced you to Conch Republic."

"They're the best, huh?"

"You bet. Come on, let's order some and I dare you to disagree with me."

The hostess directed them to a table right next to the dock. A large catamaran filled with people pulled up alongside them. Will ordered the conch fritters and two beers. He lifted his glass in the air. "Here's to new adventures."

She smiled. "New adventures."

They sipped their beer and then Will reached across the table and took her hand. "So," he said, "are you ready for this new chapter?"

Kaitlyn squeezed his hand. "More than ready."

"Well, I'm thrilled you'll be staying. It means I get to see a lot more of you in the coming months."

"Only months?" she asked.

"Well, I wanted to say years but I thought that might scare you."

She shook her head. "After everything I've been through, it would take a lot more than that to scare me."

His face turned serious. "Years, then."

Lost in his eyes, she was startled when the waitress brought the conch fritters.

Will waited for Kaitlyn to take the first bite. He watched her expression closely. "Well?"

Kaitlyn nodded as she chewed and then gave a thumbs up. "The best."

His laughter made the people around them look. "Ha! What did I tell you?"

They enjoyed lunch together and then he walked her back to Paradise Harbor House.

"Can I see you tonight?" he asked.

"Yes, I'd like that."

The afternoon flew by and she smiled, realizing that the minute Will left, all she could think about was when she'd see him again.

Later that evening, Kaitlyn found her aunts getting ready for work. Ernest strutted past, pausing to eye Tess suspiciously.

"He knows that look," Leah groaned. "*I* know that look. Tess, whatever you're thinking—"

"Hear me out," Tess sat forward eagerly. "What if we combined our bartending skills with your business sense? We could start a mobile cocktail service—"

"No."

"But think about it! We'd call it 'Sisters & Spirits'—"

"Absolutely not."

"Or maybe 'Tipsy Tutors'? We could teach cocktail classes—"

"Tess."

"Fine." Tess slumped back in her chair, but her eyes still sparkled with possibilities. "But you have to admit, the name is catchy."

Kaitlyn couldn't help laughing. Some things never changed—and maybe that was exactly as it should be.

"What?" Tess asked innocently. "We're good at making drinks now. It's not like the coffee cart disaster."

"Or the wind chimes fiasco," Leah added.

"Or the chicken tour debacle," Kaitlyn chimed in.

They all burst out laughing, and Ernest clucked his literary disapproval.

"Okay, okay," Tess conceded. "But maybe just a small business plan? For fun?"

Leah threw her hands up in mock surrender as she walked out the door. "I'm going to work before you convince me to invest in a floating tiki bar."

Tess's eyes lit up. "Now that's an idea—"

"I'm leaving, Tess!"

As Kaitlyn headed out to meet Will, she could hear her aunts' continued banter as they walked down the street, Tess's creative schemes met with Leah's practical objections.

The familiar rhythm of their sisterly sparring was its own kind of music—the soundtrack of home. But as much as Kaitlyn loved living with them she knew in time she'd need to find her own place.

Above them, the Key West sky grew dark. The stars twinkled their approval, and somewhere in the distance, Ernest began composing his literary criticism of whatever venture Tess would dream up next.

He returned to his nesting spot while the women left the small, yellow bungalow to begin their night.

Some things changed, some stayed the same, and some—like the love of family, found and forged—only grew stronger with time.

THE END

Thank you for reading Key West Promises.
I hope you enjoyed this story. For more information on my other series, please check out the following pages.

ALSO BY ANNIE CABOT

THE PERIWINKLE SHORES SERIES
Book One: CHRISTMAS ON THE CAPE
Book Two: THE SEA GLASS GIRLS
Book Three: ON CLIFF ROAD

THE CAPTIVA ISLAND SERIES
Book One: KEY LIME GARDEN INN
Book Two: A CAPTIVA WEDDING
Book Three: CAPTIVA MEMORIES
Book Four: CAPTIVA CHRISTMAS
Book Five: CAPTIVA NIGHTS
Book Six: CAPTIVA HEARTS
Book Seven: CAPTIVA EVER AFTER
Book Eight: CAPTIVA HIDEAWAY
Book Nine: RETURN TO CAPTIVA
Book Ten: CAPTIVA CABANA
Book Eleven: CAPTIVA COTTAGE
Book Twelve: CAPTIVA MOONLIGHT
Book Thirteen: CAPTIVA BOOK CLUB
Book Fourteen: SLEIGH. BELLS ON CAPTIVA

For a free copy of the prequel to the Captiva Island Series - Captiva Sunset- please sign up for my newsletter here: https://dl.bookfunnel.com/1k2zenybuw

ABOUT THE AUTHOR

Annie Cabot is the author of contemporary women's fiction and family sagas. Annie writes about friendships and family relationships, that bring inspiration and hope to others.

With a focus on women's fiction, Annie feels that she writes best when she writes from experience. "Every woman's journey is a relatable story. I want to capture those stories, let others know they are not alone, and bring a bit of joy to my readers."

Annie Cabot is the pen name for the writer Patricia Pauletti. A lover of all things happily ever after, it was only a matter of time before she began to write what was in her heart, and so, the pen name Annie Cabot was born.

When she's not writing, Annie and her husband like to travel. Winters always involve time away on Captiva Island, Florida where she continues to get inspiration for her novels.

ACKNOWLEDGMENTS

With each book I continue to be grateful to the people who support my work. I couldn't do what I do without this team. Thank you all so much.

Cover Design: Marianne Nowicki
Premade Ebook Cover Shop
https://www.premadeebookcovershop.com/

Editor: Lisa Lee of Lisa Lee Proofreading and Editing
https://www.facebook.com/EditorLisaLee/
Beta Readers:
John Battaglino
Nancy Burgess
Michele Connolly
Anne Marie Page Cooke